Murder

Makes it Mine

Christina Strong

Murder Makes it Mine
(A Masters & McLain Mystery #1)
Copyright © 2017 by Christina Strong

Christina Strong may be contacted by mail c/o Steeplechase Publishing (address next page), through her Facebook page (please like!), CStrongAuthor on Twitter or at http://www.MastersandMcLain.com

Reviews for Christina's work:

"After the last page, I felt as though I said good-bye to old chums, the definite sign of a good book. I lingered over the closing door rather than rushing to shut it behind the last word."
- Crescent Blues Book Views

"[Her] writing bursts with charm and energy."
- Publisher's Weekly

Early Reviews for Murder Makes it Mine:

"I loved this story...the main characters were very likeable...and Rags had me chuckling out loud more than once."
Eva W., a reader from PA

"The banter between Samantha and McClain was priceless. I loved how... friends followed the winding garden path, unearthed the details, and worked together to dig up whodunit. A clever story."
Marshall N., a reader from CA

Steeplechase Publishing
Steeplechase Group, LLC
Post Office Box One
Violet Hill, Arkansas 72584
www.Steeplechase.Group

ISBN-13: 978-0-9631563-3-4
Large Print - 18 pt Arial
First Edition: November 2017
10 9 8 7 6 5 4 3 2 1

Christina Strong has 16 published works under different pen names which are currently in the process of being re-released (except Married in Black). Her newest venture is the mystery series of Masters and McLain books. We invite you to join the adventures beginning with *Murder Makes it Mine.*

As **Christina Cordaire—**
Regencies:

Heart's Deception   *Daring Illusion*
Love's Triumph   *Beloved Stranger*
Pride's Folly

Historical Romances:
Forgiving Hearts (a Best Seller)
Loving Honor
Winter Longing
Spring Enchantment
        – Haunting Heart's Series [ghost]
Loving a Lowly Stranger

Time travel:
A Ring for Remembrance (a novella) in Jennifer Blake's Quilting Circle

As **Christina Kingston**—
Ride for the Roses
The Night the Stars Fell
Ride the Winter Wind
Ride the Wind Home
Married in Black (Book Club release)

As Christina Strong—
Murder Makes it Mine
      (Masters & McLain book #1)

Steeplechase will be re-issuing many of Christina Strong's books in large print.

Murder Makes it Mine is available in the following formats:
e-book (Amazon): ASIN: B076WX5DV3
Regular print paperback:
      ISBN: 978-0-9631563-1-0
Large print (18-point) paperback:
      ISBN: 978-0-9631563-3-4
Hardback: ISBN: 978-0-9631563-6-5
LP Hardback:ISBN: 978-0-9631563-2-7
Audiobook pending.

Thank you for reading this book and supporting Steeplechase Publishing.

Chapter One

"Murdered!" Samantha clenched the phone's receiver with a hand that had suddenly frozen. "What are you talking about?"

"I'm talking about the body they just found!" Samantha could hear the hysteria in Laura's voice.

"Now calm down, Laurie and tell me what you're talking about."

Her usually placid neighbor babbled, "A stranger. Dead. A dead man here. Right here!"

"Honey, take a deep breath." Samantha took her own advice, then asked, "Just how do you know about this? And how do you know he was murdered? The man could have died of natural causes, couldn't he?"

"Then who took his identification and

sanded off all his finger prints and cut his nails to where he bled? Just tell me that."

"Removed his fingerprints?" Samantha shuddered. "Are you sure. Did you see his hands?"

Irritation steadied Laura. "Of course I didn't see, Samantha. What a perfectly dreadful thought."

Samantha's tone changed to one people use with difficult children. "Then how do you know someone removed his fingerprints?"

"Because," Laura told her as if *she* was the child, "I heard Colonel McLain tell the police officers."

Samantha frowned mightily. Though she hadn't met their new neighbor yet, she'd been briefed by her friends and was beginning to form a firm dislike of him. She couldn't help herself. That independently wealthy military retiree seemed to have put his nose into everything! Supposedly he had his own Learjet, too, and he'd had no trouble paying for the Stoddard place next door without taking out a mortgage.

Samantha gave herself a mental shake. Her thoughts were beginning to sound like sour grapes, and she knew herself well enough to know she wasn't jealous. She just resented anyone who came along so blithely to take the place of her dear, departed friends Mimi and Ben Stoddard. The wound of losing them was still too fresh. It was for all of them who had known the Stoddards. She just wished that she could behave better about this man who was somehow, in her mind, trespassing on their memory.

Finally she asked, "What has *he* got to do with it?"

"Oh. He was the one who found the body. On his morning run, you know."

"Actually, I don't know. I don't know what the man does." Samantha didn't even try to keep the acid out of her voice.

"Well, he does. Run every morning, I mean, and there was this dead man right there over on the next street. He'd been dragged part-way under that huge purple Formosa azalea on the corner that keeps you from being able to see if another car is coming. You know."

Samantha did know the Formosa. It was magnificent. Fully five feet high and ten feet across if it was an inch. She hoped it hadn't been injured. Azaleas were so brittle.

With an effort she dragged her mind back to the dead body. Trying to be sensible she said, "If he's a stranger, I imagine he was visiting someone. Surely his host will come forward and tell the police who he is, don't you think?"

"Well, I guess that could happen, but . . ."

"We'll just have to wait and see, won't we." Shaken as she was by her own dreadful attitude as well as the murder, she was trying to get off the subject so she didn't make it a question. "Come over for a cup of coffee, Laurie. I just made a fresh pot."

"Oh, yes. I'd love to. Be right there. Bye."

The phone went dead and Samantha just stood looking at it in her hand. Then she said softly, "Murder." A shiver ran down her spine. "How awful." It took her a full minute to remember to hang up the phone.

***

The next morning, Samantha walked her Yorkshire terrier as usual. The rhythm of life went on, after all, she told herself, no matter what awful things had happened.

Their walks were never very long. They were tailored to the small size of her charge. When they got back to the edge of her property she said to the little dog, "Since we're out here, Rags, we might as well see what progress the peonies have made."

She looked over the low brick wall that separated her property from the two estates that sprawled on the river. Her best friend Laura Fulton's peonies were already knee high. Samantha had to repress a spurt of envy even as she admired the deep green plants. She sighed. They'd probably bloom before hers were even ankle high.

All the Riverhaven gardeners watched the Fulton estate to gauge what would soon appear in their own gardens. Laurie's property being on the river gave it a microclimate that was warmer than Samantha's, thanks to the temperature of the river's water. Her own garden here behind Laurie's wall was a good hundred yards from it. She glanced over her own back wall at the neat garden of the Chamberlains's who lived directly behind her and saw no sign of their peonies, either.

Walking over the lush grass and listening to the birdsong that filled the bright spring air around the feeders lifted her spirits. She was almost her usual self again. The rush of horror she'd felt when Laura Fulton had called to tell her about the murder was past. The news had carried it briefly that evening, but nothing more had been mentioned since. The police simply stated that they had no clues as to the murdered man's identity.

They didn't report that the murderer had filed off the poor man's fingerprints, just that his identification had been stolen. Samantha's nose wrinkled as she recalled the word 'filed' but that was the word Laura had repeated when she'd come for coffee. She'd said it was the way the police had expressed it.

Nothing more had been on the news report except the usual 'and that the investigation is on-going', and that was that.

She reached her peony bed only to find that the peonies were little more than the short ruby-hued shoots they'd been when she'd checked them last week. Samantha frowned; she'd really expected more growth.

The Virginia climate was famous here in the Tidewater area where the Gulf Stream flowed north and warmed their shores as it passed. It promised early spring and tantalized you with buds and shoots and clear, sunny, sandal-wearing days. Then, when you'd taken half your summer clothes out of the attic storage to stick in your closet, it *snowed and ruined your garden.*

She sighed again and rounded the corner of the house and paused to enjoy the tulip tree blooming pink and white in the side yard. Andrew's tree. It had been the inspiration for the article she'd written on *'Trees That Flower in the Spring.'* The lovely little tree was the last thing she and Andrew had planted together. He'd chosen it as a surprise for her because she loved pink. They'd thought they would have the rest of their lives together to watch it grow.

Years ago Andrew had bought a lot in Riverhaven because long ago the whole area had belonged to her family. He'd teased her that he'd requested Norfolk for the final duty station of his naval career so that he could bring her home. He'd been so pleased to have surprised her with the lot in Riverhaven and had said it was the least he could do after dragging her all over the world.

Planning the house had been heavenly. They'd even made it wheelchair friendly. "Because," Andrew'd said, "we're going to grow old right here, holding hands from our wheelchairs."

Looking away from the tree to blink back sudden tears, Samantha noticed a plant stake askew in the flower bed against the low brick wall that separated her property from what had been the Stoddards's. Stepping carefully and with easy familiarity where she knew no tender plant lurked just under the rich loam, she worked her way back to where, in a few more months, her delphiniums would soar regally skyward. She could already see them in her mind's eye.

Placing a hand on the top of the four-foot wall to steady herself, she leaned down and reset the stake, taking great care to place it exactly as it had been. An instant later she shot bolt upright, as a firm, dirt-smeared masculine hand gripped her own.

Rags began barking fiercely.

A deep grunt came from the Stoddards's side of the wall, and a perfectly strange man reared up, scowling. Almost nose to nose they stared at each other.

Samantha was the first to recover. Yanking her hand out from under the stranger's, she stepped back away from the wall—right into the delphinium stake.

She heard the sharp crack as it broke off. "Damn," she said distinctly.

The man on the other side of the wall frowned. "Good morning to you, too. Where the hell's the traditional plate of cookies?"

Samantha took refuge in her Southern manners. "Oh, I do apologize! I was thinking about having to replace a support stake for one of my delphiniums without damaging its crown. The stake broke off as I stepped back, you see." She smiled suddenly, a warm, sunny smile that should have disarmed him.

It didn't.

He pushed his old khaki fishing hat back on his head. "Why do you want to stake 'em, anyway, when they're here in the shelter of this wall? It's just an old habit."

"Why?" She tilted her head, thinking.

"That's a good question. The new strains of Delphiniums do have stronger stalks. I suppose I stake them because everyone I know always has."

He gave a disgusted snort. "I suppose if they all jumped off a bridge you'd be right behind 'em?" He started to turn away.

Her laughter brought him back around. "That's exactly what my mother used to say." She frowned slightly. "Come to think of it, *I* always said it to my children, too." She cocked her head, considering. "What dreadful creatures of habit we are."

On the other side of the wall, the stranger was considering, too. He gave Samantha his undivided attention. The woman had caught his interest. She could laugh at herself. Rare, he mused. Far cry from the female Chamberlain neighbor whose house backed up to hers. Now there was an old dreadnought if he'd ever seen one. This one was different, for sure. He looked her over critically. Had a little meat on her bones, but not chubby. Not like the lanky dreadnought. That one was as flat as a pancake—all angles and topped with a face like a hatchet.

Of course, he didn't consider himself

any judge of women. Not the decent sort, anyway. Over twenty years in the Corps taught a Marine a lot, but *that* certainly wasn't part of Basic. He was afraid that this was a nice little woman.

Blast it! He felt his hopes for peace draining away. If there was one thing he didn't need, it was an attractive woman for a neighbor. Long ago he'd discovered that the attractive ones were usually looking for a husband. Give him a sloppy, comfortable woman every time. *They* weren't looking around for a permanent escort . . . or a meal ticket.

He was sick and tired of being chased by everything in skirts. Born rich and grown handsome, he'd been pursued by females for as long as he could remember. His choice of a career in uniform hadn't seemed to have diminished his desirability in the eyes of the opposite sex, either. He'd been avidly hunted by 'em from the cradle.

Now that he was retired, he had absolutely no intention of getting involved. He'd paid his dues in a stormy and unsatisfactory marriage when he was young, and he wasn't about to subscribe again!

Damn the woman! Why did this neighbor have to be a pretty little thing, with her soft halo of light brown hair and her wide blue eyes? He gave another snort of disgust, this one was aimed at himself. He shook his head. The pretty ones were by far the worst.

Maybe he'd luck out and she'd be married. Worth being rude to find out. "You walk that dog every day, or does your husband do it sometimes?" Pretty safe question he figured.

Samantha's brows drew together. This stranger was getting personal and they hadn't even introduced themselves yet. "I am a widow," she informed him in her frostiest voice. If there was one thing she could do without, it was some strange man who clearly thought he was God's gift to women asking her personal questions.

Wishing he'd evaporate, and knowing he wouldn't, she didn't even try to smile pleasantly as she offered her hand. "I'm Samantha Masters, how do you do?"

He wiped his own hand down his khakis and took hers. "Colonel John Francis McLain, USMC!" Then, with a reluctance that bordered on pain, he added "Retired."

"Welcome to the neighborhood, Colonel." With a reluctance that equaled his, she added, "You must let me know if there is anything I can do to help you."

So here it came. McLain fought to keep a grimace from his face. It was the old familiar pattern. He'd had it all his life. Cookies. Dinner invitations. The works. How the devil was he to get his book written if he had to fight an evasive action against attack from this quarter? Why the deuce couldn't women just leave him the blazes alone?

Samantha turned to go and picked her way carefully out of the flower bed, thinking, *There! I've done my duty to the new arrival. The ancient and sacred law of Virginia Hospitality has been upheld.* She firmly ignored the calm inner voice that gently chastened her for not actually providing food—or even wanting to.

She set off briskly for the house, hoping to get away from her new neighbor before he could make any request of her. *Now I just hope that he leaves me alone!*

On his side of the fence, McLain guessed things were looking up, she wasn't hanging around. Then to his disgust she stopped and turned back again, saying, "I wasn't aware anyone new had moved into the Stoddards's place. Forgive me for being such a poor neighbor." She spoke the required words over her shoulder, then was ashamed that she'd deliberately neglected to infuse them with the warmth of true hospitality. Turning to face him, she asked, "Has your phone been hooked up yet?"

"Tomorrow or the next day."

"If you should need one before then . . ." She let her words trail off as she turned away again. With a casual wave of her hand, Samantha turned her back on him and walked briskly to the house. Colonel John McLain certainly looked old enough to be able to finish the sentence for himself.

Chapter Two

Promptly at two the next afternoon, Laura Fulton, Samantha's best friend, pulled her Mercedes into Samantha's driveway. Samantha grabbed her big wicker purse and her dog's leash from the entry hall table and dashed out to the car. "Thank you for doing this, Laurie. It's nice to have an able assistant to drive when one's handling a wild beast."

Though picking up Rags from the groomer where she'd taken him early that morning was Samantha's own errand, Laura had said that she preferred to drive. She'd flatly refused to just ride along to hold Samantha's 'wild beast of a Yorkshire terrier.' Now, Samantha couldn't resist teasing.

Laura fixed her with a level gaze and

instructed her darkly, "Put your seat belt on, Samantha, and keep it firmly in mind that just one set of tiny little tooth marks in my nice leather upholstery and our friendship is at an end."

"I didn't ask you to drive, you know. I only wanted your company. We could've taken my Buick."

"Ha! Then *I'd* have been stuck holding the wild beast. Tiny tooth marks on my very own personal anatomy count, too, I'll have you know."

Samantha chuckled. Laura always pretended she didn't like Rags, and he pretended to take advantage of her. They were like old friends who kept up seemingly disagreeable banter to cover the depth of affection they felt for each other. Samantha got a big kick out of watching the two of them.

They were silent past the Yacht and Country Club and as Laura pulled out onto Hampton Boulevard. As they crossed the bridge and swept past what used to be— and always would be to long-time Norfolk residents—the old Marine Hospital at its foot, Laura said, "Our new neighbor is a retired Marine Colonel, Samantha. Have you met him yet?"

"I sort of ran into him at the back wall."

"What did you think of him?"

"Laura."   Samantha's voice held a warning note. "Don't go getting any ideas. I do not—repeat not—want a man in my life."

"Not even to escort you to the Symphony?"

"Why?" Samantha shot her a glance. "Are you and Bob getting tired of having me tag along?"

"Of course not. It's just that it would give you a different arm to cling to when we cross those blessed uneven bricks around Scope Arena when the underground parking's full and we're parked out on the street. And you've always said . . ." Belatedly, Laura realized that the light at Powhatan was red. She slammed on the brakes. Cars swerved around both sides of them as two University students ran the light.

"Careful," Samantha warned as the signal was about to turn green. Laura was the dreamy artist in their group of friends, and was sometimes a little disconnected. A trusting soul, she actually drove forward when her light turned green. Unfortunately, the kids from Old Dominion University—often late by virtue of not being able to find anyplace to park—were a little cavalier when it came to obeying traffic signals.

Samantha felt strongly that defensive driving was a must in Norfolk traffic. Between the rushes to and from the Naval Station Norfolk at one end of Hampton Boulevard and the shipyards and downtown Norfolk at the other, traffic was a nightmare. Laura, however, never worried about such things. She solved the problem her own way. She simply didn't drive then.

Laura got through the intersection and past the University safely, and it was clear sailing the rest of the way. There was a space right by the door of the *Pet Palace* and Laura slipped her Mercedes into it.

Rags must have recognized the sound of her engine.

It was more than obvious he was ready to go home and then some by the time Samantha put her hand on the door of the groomer's. She could hear his occasional inquiring bark. The minute she entered, Rags went wild. Yipping and flinging himself against the bright chrome bars of his cage, he let the world know he'd been ready to go home long before now. There was no mistaking his 'where have you been and what kept you' attitude.

Samantha paid the groomer in the silence imposed on them by the incredible volume of sound from his tiny pair of lungs. Suzette, as she styled herself— she worked primarily with French poodles, after all—freed the indignant Rags from his captivity and handed him to Samantha with a flourish. Into the instant silence she said, "As usual, no bow. Sorry."

Samantha laughed. "It's all right, Susie. I don't like bows on boys anyway."

"Good thing since he won't tolerate one." She gave Rags a last pat. "See you in two weeks." Susie waved gaily and turned back to the dignified gray poodle standing patiently on the grooming table.

As the door closed behind them, Samantha murmured to the Yorkie, who was frantically clawing the front of her linen suit in his effort to lick the skin off her chin, "Susie's a saint, you little brat. She'd have to be to put up with you." She twisted her head aside to see the handle on the car door.

Laura eyed Rags warily and told Samantha, "If you say one nauseating thing to that mutt, you walk home." And to the dog, "Hello, Rags." She made her tone resigned and unwelcoming.

"Weerf!" Rags was in no way deceived. His stump of a tail beat a greeting.

Samantha settled him in her lap and smoothed her hand over his back before beginning to scratch gently behind his ears. "Since you won't let me buy you gas, Laurie, how about some lunch?"

"What'll we do with Rags? We're certainly not leaving him in my car, I can tell you."

Samantha grinned. "I've brought my largest purse."

"You're on!"

Rags took one look at Samantha removing her wallet, handkerchief and cosmetics from her woven wicker handbag and started growling. He was still percolating, as Laura called his low, continuous growl, when she slid her Mercedes into the last parking space behind the restaurant. "How in the world are we going to manage this if he keeps that up?"

"Hush, Rags. Be quiet." Samantha was stuffing him into her large wicker contraption. She'd already taken out the money to pay for lunch and shoved it into the pocket of her linen blazer along with her handkerchief and lipstick. "Don't worry. He'll stop."

True to Samantha's word, the Yorkshire settled down in the bottom of the oversized purse the minute they entered the restaurant. He was sniffing audibly, trying to separate and identify the wave of cooking smells that inundated them. Fortunately, his sniff was lost in the sounds of cutlery and conversation from the busy crowd of diners. Only the two women accompanying him were aware of the bright glitter of his black button eyes through the spaces between the wickerwork of Samantha's purse.

The feisty Yorkshire had stopped sniffing by the time the hostess led the three of them to a table. As a result, she didn't suspect a thing.

"Well," Laura muttered, "Will wonders never cease?"

Samantha just laughed at her.

They'd barely given their server

their drink orders when suddenly Laura stiffened. "Oh, dear."

"What is it?"

"There. Over against the window."

"Why, it's Alison." Samantha's voice held a note of delighted surprise. "I thought she was working down in Chesapeake. Wasn't she selling condominiums over there for Herb Talley?"

"Yes, she was. She is. That's why I'm surprised to see her all the way up here on Twenty-first Street." There was an edge to Laura's usually pleasant voice. "There are plenty of good places to eat lunch in the Greenbrier area."

Samantha raised an eyebrow at her friend's testiness. Looking toward Alison's table, she studied the young man sitting with Laura's niece. Slender to the point of being wiry, he had a narrow face that was a little too intent to be pleasant. It was crowned by a wealth of carefully barbered and combed blond hair. She was too far away to see what color his eyes were, but she could easily tell by its fit that his suit was expensive.

"You don't like the young man she's with," Samantha skipped he preliminaries and stated the obvious, "Why?" She and Laura had been friends forever, and over the years, their style of communicating had evolved to a shortened form.

Laura glowered. "I don't like the fact that she's come this far from her job to have lunch with him. He could at least have met her halfway."

Samantha regarded her friend steadily.

"Oh, all right." Laura gave up. "I think he's trying to talk her out of going back to finish college."

"Alison is far too intelligent to let anybody do that, Laura. You're worrying needlessly."

"I'm not sure anymore." Now a frown marred Laura's usually serene brow. "I hope you're right."

"Oh, Laura." Samantha put her hand on her friend's arm. "Trust me. You really are worrying needlessly."

Laura's soft brown eyes met Samantha's. "Talk to her, will you? She always seems to listen to you."

"Of course I will." She smiled to take the sting out of her next remark. "But I still think you're making mountains out of molehills."

The waitress came just then to take their order. Both women were occupied for a moment, and when they looked up again from their menus, Alison and her companion were getting ready to leave.

As they turned toward the door, Alison saw them. Her face lit up.

Samantha waved a greeting.

Pulling her young man along behind her, Alison charged over. "Aunt Laura! Samantha! Hi! What are you all doing here?" She pecked each of them on the cheek.

"Having lunch, of course." Samantha laughed up at this girl she considered her honorary niece.

"After collecting Rags from the groomer." Laura's somber tone made it sound like they'd made a trip to the guillotine.

"Then Rags is here!" Alison bent down to look for her four-legged favorite. "Rags! Where are you?"

Simultaneously her real and her honorary aunt shushed her. They needn't have bothered. The place was still noisy enough to cover the sharp sound from Samantha's purse.

Alison had heard the single, imperious

yap Rags had given, though. She bent down to greet the little Yorkshire.

Samantha used the distraction to study the intense young man in front of her. There was a faint look of disapproval on his face.

Samantha hoped she wasn't being influenced by Laura's dislike, but she didn't think she was going to warm to him, either. She didn't like the cold expression in his pale blue eyes. It was plain he was bored at being dragged over to meet her. Clearly she held no interest for him. Odd. Alison usually chose nice people for her companions. Of course she and Laura were over thirty, and in the good old U.S. of A., youth lacked the respect for their elders with which other countries treated those older and wiser. She couldn't help thinking that perhaps it was because the countries themselves were older and, one hoped, wise.

Alison was unaware of her escort's disapproval or Samantha's perusal, however. She'd swooped down on the capacious wicker purse. "Oh, what a wonderful purse!" The girl held it to her smooth cheek and crooned, "Nice purse.

Lovely purse. Oh, aren't you the good purse."

The wicker vibrated with the pleased wriggling of the dog it contained. She rocked it a moment more, gave it a kiss and gently placed it back on the floor at Samantha's feet. She told it, "There, there. Be a good purse," and gave it a final pat.

Laura rolled her eyes and muttered, "Oh, Good Lord." Above all things, Laura detested a scene. "Stop that, Alison." She tugged at her niece's short linen skirt. "If you keep that up, they're going to hear you."

Samantha patted Laura's arm. This was a gathering place for young people. Except for a college boy ogling Alison, nobody was noticing them—they were obviously over thirty and therefore invisible. For her part, she was watching Alison's escort. He looked distinctly annoyed. Coloring, he told the girl, "Stop being silly, Alison. You're making a spectacle of yourself."

Alison straightened, cheerfully ignoring his comment, and tugged him a little forward. "Samantha, I'd like you to meet my friend, Randal Hale. He's our latest addition at Greater Tidewater Realty. Randal, this is my honorary Aunt, Samantha Masters."

"How do you do," Samantha tried to speak with her customary warmth and nodded to the young man.

Randal Hale's irritation disappeared the instant he heard Samantha's name. He smiled at her winningly, the voltage so high she blinked. "I'm so glad to meet you, Mrs. Masters. You're that property just before you go into Laura's gate, aren't you?"

"Yes." Now Samantha was amused. She'd never thought of herself as a piece of real estate before. Usually it was, 'Oh, Samantha Masters! You're the one who does the column for *Gardens for Today*,' or, 'Oh, yes. 'Whoever' has told me so much about you!' Now, suddenly, she was the property just outside her best friend's gate. It made an interesting change, she had to admit.

"Someday I like to drop by and talk to you about . . ."

It was Alison's turn to look disapproving. She scowled and yanked his arm. "Come on, Randy, I'll be late getting back to work."

Turning a smiling face toward Samantha, she leaned down and gave her Aunt Laura another quick peck on the cheek. "See you two later." Bending a little lower as she moved away, she hissed, "Be a good purse," waved and was gone.

Laura settled back in her chair with a sigh.

"She's just young and full of life." Samantha offered. "You wouldn't want it any other way."

"She isn't the one who upsets me. Do you realize Randal Hale would have made a play to list your house just now if she hadn't dragged him off?"

"Well, she did, so no harm done." Samantha let her gaze go to where the young couple had exited. "He certainly is an intense young man." She was careful not to add that she didn't like him.

"I don't like him, Samantha." Laura looked mulish.

In spite of the fact that Laura had just voiced her own sentiment, Samantha tried to be fair. "Are you sure you wouldn't feel that way about any young man that Alison was enthusiastic about?"

"You didn't like him either."

Samantha wrestled with that for only a moment. Laughing, she gave in. "True."

"Then don't try to get me to like him, or

I'll make you walk home."

Samantha threw up her hands in surrender. "Please. Not with my heaviest purse!"

Chapter Three

First thing in the morning the next day, Samantha began her new walking program, determined to regain some measure of fitness. Swinging along at a brisk pace, she was soon sorry she hadn't listened to her housekeeper. Jasmine Johnson was right again. She usually was. As Samantha was trying to beat Rags out of the door, Jasmine had scooped him up and said, "Now don't you go out there in those good slacks and that pretty matching sweater. You know perfectly well you're gonna sweat 'em up somethin' terrible!"

And she was. Her mother might have drummed into her that 'horses sweat, gentlemen perspire, and ladies glow,' but there was no denying that she, Samantha Eugenie Swann Masters, was glowing so hard that there were patches of just plain *sweat* under the arms and in the middle of the back of her expensive sweater.

Over her muttering about it, she heard an evenly cadenced tattoo of footsteps, then a hearty, "Good morning!" Her new neighbor, Colonel McLain, breezed by, running easily and not even breathing half as hard as she was. Drat the man!

Well, at least he hadn't stopped. Thank the Lord for small favors.

Churlishly, she didn't answer him. He was almost out of sight around the corner half a block ahead anyhow. Immediately she felt guilty.

"Oh, spit." Sometimes being born a Virginian was a thorough pain in the neck. Maybe if she'd been born elsewhere, or even born here later when conscience had become less of a burden, she might have been able to ignore him without the least twinge of remorse. How nice that would have been. But no, she had to get the guilties.

Probably as punishment, an ache was developing in her right calf. It was an ache that was getting impossible to ignore. Almost immediately, she began limping.

In another minute she was hobbling. She couldn't help it. "Oh, shoot." She paused to rub her calf and discovered a huge knot in the muscle.

"Samantha!" A reedy voice called out to her. "Oh, Samantha, is that you?" A tiny woman with a frantic look on her face hurried across her immaculate lawn toward Samantha. "Oh, I'm *so* glad you're here. The most awful thing has happened. You must come and see!"

Samantha forgot her aching leg and limped to meet Emilee Twiford. "What is it?"

"Come. You'll have to see. You won't believe it unless you see it for yourself. You simply won't believe it." Emilee turned and led the way around the back of her huge house to the spacious backyard. There, havoc met Samantha's gaze. Emilee's garden, the garden she spent all her time on, lavished all her attention on, was a shambles.

In the flower bed, everything that had come up had been lopped off at ground level and shoots and leaves lay strewn about the yard. Even Emilee's prize rose bushes had been hacked back, removing all the fresh, new growth.

Anger flooded Samantha. "How could anyone do such a thing?" Emilee worked so hard on her yard. She didn't have the money to hire anyone to help her. Emilee's income, which had seemed a very generous provision when her husband had been alive to make it, was a mere pittance in today's economy. Emilee was barely scraping by, and she was working herself to the bone to do that.

Because Emilee was trying so hard to make ends meet, all the neighbors conspired to get her to accept their 'leftover' lawn fertilizer and rose food, and shared new plants with her so that she didn't have to spend a cent on her garden and lawn. If Emilee happened to mention wanting a new flower, one of them 'just happened' to have a spare that needed weeding out, and gave it to her. If it was something that had to be ordered from a nursery, to gain the time to do it, they told her they'd be separating said flower clump soon and promised her one.

The conspiracy went beyond Emilee's magnificent garden, too. When it was Emilee's turn to host a meeting of any sort, they were careful to see that it always fell in the spring or summer, so that there'd be no chance that anyone would discover that Emilee did without heating except when it was so cold it endangered the plumbing of her huge house. And the Bridge group always scheduled Emilee's day to coincide with the bake sales the Garden Club put on to finance the landscaping and mowing service for the two entrances to their neighborhood. That way everyone could bring leftovers to Emilee's to keep her from having any expenditures. They couldn't stop her from making iced tea or they would even have done that. If anyone present had ever said they'd prefer a coke the others would have murdered them.

Looking after Emilee had long ago become a neighborhood project. And now some vandal had ruined it all! Samantha could just howl! "Oh, Emilee." Samantha's voice was husky. "I'm so very sorry."

Sympathy was more than the tiny woman could bear. She stopped twisting her hands and put them over her face instead. Quiet sobs shook her frame. "Oh, Samantha. I try so hard. So very hard . . . and now this."

"Let's go in and have a cup of tea." Samantha put an arm around Emilee's frail shoulders and shepherded her into her spacious kitchen. Leading her to a chair at the kitchen table, she asked, "Where do you keep your tea?"

"There in the canister beside the stove." She pointed wearily to the spotless appliance. "I'm so tired, so very tired." She sagged in her chair. "Oh, Samantha, what am I going to do?"

"You're going to have a cup of tea and relax. That's what you're going to do." She limped over, filled the kettle at the sink and placed it on the stove. "Laura and I will alert the Garden Club, and they'll all come over and make the garden lovely again. After all, it's still early spring. Most of the plants will just come up again. And if they don't, all of us have enough to give you some to fill in any blank spots."

Emilee stiffened. "I don't like charity, you know, Samantha."

No, Lord, she doesn't. She likes working herself to death to keep up the illusion that she can manage this great, hulking house and the acre lot it sits on with nothing more than what her long-dead husband provided for her. And she can't. Nobody could. Inflation had changed all that.

Now, all of us just want to keep her from killing herself, and I'm not sure we can do anything to stop her! All of that Samantha said in her head, as she walked around the kitchen with her knotted calf making her tiptoe on that side.

Out loud, she asked quietly, "Emilee, dear, what do you like in your tea?"

"Just sugar, please." Then she relaxed and let Samantha comfort her.

***

Genius! Samantha congratulated herself as she limped homeward. She'd been a positive genius to talk Emilee into looking into the condominiums Alison was selling. Herb Talley and his Greater Tidewater Realty could get top dollar for the expensive corner Emilee owned. The little dear could buy her condo and invest what was left over from the sale of this property. She'd be able to live very comfortably once she'd moved. She'd even be able to afford the gas to drive back to the neighborhood to play Bridge! Yes, and a good many other things, too. Why, invested properly, or in a good annuity, Emilee's money would make it possible for her to take a garden tour of Europe every year or so and still live well.

Samantha felt as if a weight had been lifted from her. Herb Talley would be glad to help. Not only was he a longtime neighbor and friend, he owned one of the most successful real estate firms in the Hampton Roads area and he was always saying that people wanted places near the Norfolk Yacht and Country Club. It was the perfect solution.

If her calf hadn't decided to turn to stone, her walk would have been absolutely vivacious as she left Emilee's. It had, though, and as she approached the giant Formosa azalea that had overgrown its proper place and spilled over onto the asphalt of the street, she limped to the curb and sat down on it with a plop. She refused to let it enter her mind that this was where the poor murdered man had been found.

Kneading the tight muscle in her calf just brought tears to her eyes. *Oh, bother, Father!* Unless she could get the darn knot out, she was going to have a very painful hobble the rest of the way back to the house. How aggravating! Clenching her teeth until the back ones grated, she swiped the sleeve of her sweater across her eyes. Dealing with frustration had never been one of her strong points.

The Colonel chose that moment to trot around the big purple azalea. He was still moving with undiminished energy and still not breathing hard, drat him. Lavender petals swirled to the black asphalt of the street in the wind his passing created.

"What the devil?" He danced lightly to a halt and looked down at her.

Samantha glared up at him.

He took that as a good sign. If she'd been lying in wait for him, she'd look up helplessly, not scowl at him like that. "What's the problem?"

Samantha just rubbed her calf and ignored his growled inquiry. Nothing her mother or aunt had taught her covered the situation. She decided that surely she could be rude if she were in excruciating pain and she was. "I'm fine. Go away."

McLain brightened perceptibly. Surly. Great. She could hardly be trying to impress him if she was surly. Nor hardly be trying to attach him if she was sending him away. Maybe he was going to be safe from this one, after all. He knelt and grabbed her calf.

"Ouch!" She didn't even know this . . . this person and he was holding her leg as if he had a God-given right to touch her! Samantha was outraged.

The Colonel gave her calf a squeeze, firmly holding on to it when she tried to pull it away. Charley horse. She really *had* a knot in her calf. And it was as big as one of her fists. He was feeling better all the time. "Shut up and hold still. I'll have this out in a jiffy."

Samantha could think of a great many things to say in response to such a rude order. She couldn't speak calmly and evenly when she wanted to whimper with the pain his kneading of her calf was causing, however, so she obeyed him and 'shut up.'

'Shut up.' *That* left her seething. No one had ever told her to shut up in her whole life. Never. Insufferable man.

After a minute, the pain decreased. So did the size of the knot. Now she began to resent the fact that she was going to have to be grateful to this overconfident jerk.

"Better?" He knew very well it was. He

could feel the difference.

"Hmmmm," Samantha kept her answer to the minimum.

"You tried to do too much for your first day."

Samantha's gaze shot to his face. How did he know this was the first time she'd walked? He'd just moved in to the Stoddards's last week. How could he know how often she walked? "Why do you think this is my first day out walking?"

His laugh was an insult. "Oh, for Pete's sake. If you'd been out before, you'd have proper gear."

"Proper gear?" She said it frostily, one eyebrow lifted.

"Yeah. Tennis shoes aren't for walking. You need pro walkers." He gestured at her. "And nobody but a nitwit would come out in their good clothes."

"Am I to assume from that remark that you consider me a nitwit?" She gave him her most saccharine smile.

"Look, lady. I'm just trying to play Good Samaritan here. I'm not up for character evaluation."

"Good." She tried to say it repressively, but the relief she felt at his having worked the knot completely out of her calf ruined the effect.

John McLain pulled her to her feet, turned her in the direction of her house and told her, "Go home. And don't come out here again without a decent pair of shoes and some sweats."

She knew she ought to say, "Thank you for your help." It had to be said. To her credit, when she finally got it out, she didn't say it through clenched teeth.

"Yeah." His bright blue gaze held hers. "If I see you out tomorrow morning, I'll start you on a fitness program." With that he loped off.

She supposed she ought to be glad he didn't smack her on the bottom to start her walking towards home. Looking after his effortlessly moving figure, she told him what she thought of his offer to help her get fit. He may be fit as could be, but whether she was or not was her own business.

Scowling, she considered his offer. Decision made, she muttered under her breath, "Fat chance!"

Chapter Four

Bridge on Wednesday was at Tyler Brokenborough's. By mutual agreement the players had decided they wouldn't discuss the murder. There were no new developments, and any talk would have seemed pointless.

Tyler greeted each one of them with air kisses next to their cheeks. All the players were prompt. They didn't dare not to be. Agnes Chamberlain was playing.

While everyone was settling down, one of Samantha's favorite partners, Olivia Charles, pulled her aside to introduce her to a lovely younger lady. "Samantha, I want you to meet my dear cousin." She gave her companion a hug as she said, "This is my evil twin, Janet Wilson."

Samantha looked at the sweet face of

the willowy blonde and laughed. "Evil twin, indeed. You should sue for slander, Janet. Besides, no twin of Olivia's could be less than delightful." Smiling she offered her hand. "It's so nice to meet you."

"How do *you* do, Mrs. Masters." A radiant smile lit the young woman's face. "Olivia has told me so much about you. I'm glad to meet you at last."

"Why, I'm flattered." She glanced at Olivia, and found her frowning a little. Before she could figure out why, they were interrupted.

Agnes Chamberlain was bearing down on them. "Would the three of you stop slathering butter all over each other and get to your places. It's time to play Bridge if you please."

Turning obediently away, Olivia muttered, "*And* if you don't please."

Janet Wilson giggled and followed Olivia. As she walked away, Samantha heard her tease her cousin with a whispered, "Now who's being evil?"

Half an hour later, Samantha put her cards up to her face and yawned behind them. She was paying for her grand experiment with aerobic exercise big time.

Sticking with her walking program was good for her, she knew, but all that fresh air she'd gotten walking early this morning was making her sleepy now. Anyhow, she'd rather blame the exercise than the mystery she'd read until midnight.

Lifting her coffee cup from the corner of the table, she took a healthy swallow, hoping she'd get used to her new exercise regimen before the Bridge Club met again next week. Last hand, she'd almost trumped her partner's ace.

Tuning in to what the others were discussing, she found that, with the subject of the murder forbidden, the table talk centered around the destruction of Emilee Twiford's garden.

"How awful," Tyler said.

"Things like this just don't happen here in Riverhaven." Brenda Talley was indignant. As the wife of one of the area's most prominent realtors, the one who handled most of the transactions in Riverhaven, Brenda took a proprietary interest in everything that happened in the neighborhood.

Understanding glances passed between the others. Then Janet Wilson said, "This *is* dreadful. Do you think there's any chance that it'll happen again?"

Agnes Chamberlain's comment was delivered in a scathing voice. "Well, what do you think *we* can do to stop it?"

There were furtive glances. Even if they'd had a plan that had been worked out by a master strategist to stop the vandal, no one was going to offer it when Agnes thought there was nothing to be done. Disagreeing with one of Agnes's pronouncements, or in this case one of her typically daunting rhetorical questions, simply wasn't done. Not unless the brave soul who did so was prepared to carry her head home under her arm.

"Has anybody notified the police about it?" Olivia Charles looked at Samantha. "Surely you did."

Samantha sighed. "I did, of course, and they came out and wrote a report. They were very sympathetic to Emilee." She glanced toward the vandal's victim, "Weren't they, dear?"

Emilee smiled mournfully and said, "Yes, they certainly were but I don't expect them to do much."

Samantha gazed around her circle of

friends. "Times have changed. I'm afraid the police have bigger fish to fry these days than our garden vandal."

"Oh, dear," their hostess, Tyler Brokenborough, voiced the general worry, "I just pray this is a single occurrence, and that we won't have to worry about having a continuing threat to our yards . . . not to mention our peace of mind."

"Harrrump!" Agnes Chamberlain swept them with a gimlet eye.

Tyler, after one look at Agnes's tightening countenance, flinched visibly and took up her duty as Bridge hostess. For the benefit of all present, she closed the conversation with a quiet but firm, "But let's keep our minds on the cards, shall we?"

Play continued for a while in silence.

"By the way," Brenda Talley's voice rose to carry to all those at the other tables. "I have something interesting to tell you." She led to her partner's ace and went on, "I got a phone call the other day from a young man asking about the Stoddards. He said he had learned the house was sold and remembered that Herb and I were such good friends with them that surely we would have handled the sale and would know where they were. He was devastated to learn they were killed in that automobile accident." She looked around at them. "It took quite some time to calm him, but after I had, I asked him if he'd like to come back here and stay with us for a while."

Everyone watched her, puzzled; Agnes impatiently.

Brenda smiled. "All right, I'll get to the point."

Agnes muttered, "You always do. Eventually."

The Bridge group looked a little surprised that she hadn't said 'It's about time.'

Hesitating just one more second, Brenda told them with high excitement in her voice, "Young Ben Stoddard is coming home!"

Her announcement had the desired effect. The entire room was thrown into a tizzy. Comments flew.

"No!"

"Really?"

"You mean he's still alive?"

"How wonderful! I truly thought he must have met with foul play. He'd always been such a good boy, I couldn't see him just running off and letting his poor parents worry like they did."

"Oh, dear." Emilee's face was stricken. "What a shame he's too late to see his parents."

They all thought of their friends, the Stoddards. Ruled by anxiety for their missing son they could not trace, they had lost their health and, finally, lost heart.

Two months ago, they'd sold a home too filled with memories of their missing boy and left Virginia for a luxurious retirement center in Florida. They'd been killed in an automobile accident on their way down the coast.

The whole group mourned them. Mimi Stoddard had been a regular at Bridge and their very good friend. Ben Stoddard had been attorney for most of them. They'd been such a courageous pair, and pillars of the community. Greatly admired, sorely missed.

Emilee sniffled.

"But Benny's coming home! Oh, I'm so glad." Olivia Charles's warm smile was heartfelt. There were quick tears of joy in her eyes. "How happy Ben senior and Mimi would have been to know that he was safe after all."

Agnes Chamberlain grunted, "Huh. Fat lot of good this does 'em now."

The whole room cringed.

Then Agnes demanded, "What's his excuse for disappearing off the face of the Earth and never letting his poor parents know he was alive?"

Brenda smoothed a hand over her sleek, fashionably blunt-cut hair and answered with relish, preening herself for being the one in the know. "He's been in jail in one of those awful middle-eastern countries." She looked around at the others, her eyes sparkling. "He was carrying a backpack for a friend, and it turned out to have some sort of dope in it. Marijuana, I think."

Agnes said, "Huh. I never before knew the boy was stupid."

Olivia jumped to Ben Stoddard Jr.'s defense, her throaty voice warm with compassion, "Oh please don't say that. I know you don't mean it. You know very well he was never stupid, Agnes. He was very bright and very dear. I was his Sunday school teacher for years, and we were the best of friends. He was always kind and obliging."

"Obliging. Yes, and it was certainly

obliging of him to tote the knapsack with the dope in it for his friend. Look where *that* got him."

"Oh, Agnes." Olivia wanted her to understand. "Benny would have *trusted* the person he carried the knapsack for. He was always quick to believe the best of everybody, always slow to judge."

Agnes had absolutely no intention of understanding. She had that sour look she got when she'd made up her mind to be unpleasant. Under her breath she growled, "More fool he."

Olivia refused to rise to that. Instead she turned away and asked, "When is he coming, Brenda?"

"I wasn't aware any of you knew him so well, Olivia." Brenda looked at her appraisingly. "I thought he'd been sent off to school most of his life."

"That's true, he was so gifted and his parents easily could afford to send him to that special school, but he was home for a large part of most of the summers. And every school vacation, of course." Olivia's face was shining. "When will he be here?"

"Some time next week."

"Oh, good. Please let me know when he gets here. I can't wait to see him!" Olivia was aglow with the thought.

Agnes couldn't resist. "Oh, don't be such sentimental fools. He's not coming home to socialize." She threw her companions an arch look. "He's coming back to collect the fortune the Stoddards left."

Seeing Brenda blanch and the expression on Olivia's lovely face change from fond happiness to approaching outrage, Samantha decided it was time to change the subject. 'The girls' were equal to the occasion, however, and the room was instantly filled with their chattering. They were all anxious to cover Agnes's dreadful remark.

Their charitable effort was wasted on the one they sought to shield. Her imperious voice cut through the general hub-bub. "Would it, I wonder, be in any way possible for you girls to keep your minds on Bridge long enough to finish this hand?"

With guilty looks, and carefully hidden smiles, 'the girls,' keeping their eyes to themselves so nobody would laugh at how easily their friend Agnes bossed them around, hurried back to their places and picked up their cards.

Agnes had spoken.

Chapter Five

Arriving home after Bridge, Samantha plopped her purse and gloves down on the narrow hall table and let out an explosive sigh.

Jasmine Johnson came out of the kitchen, an ancient, tattered dishtowel in one hand, a spray can of furniture wax in the other. "Did you have a rough time at Bridge?" A grin split her handsome, dark face.

"Hmmmm," Samantha admitted. "Agnes Chamberlain was in rare form."

"My, oh, my." Jasmine shook her head. "That lady surely can make herself unpleasant."

"Yes, and she can do it without even trying," Samantha agreed. "Sometimes I wonder why we play bridge with her." She cocked her head. "I guess it's a case of if we don't, who will."

"Just thank your lucky stars you're not her husband." Jasmine shook her head. "That poor man."

Samantha chuckled. "Yes. Everybody in the neighborhood pities poor Art Chamberlain."

"That woman could drive a man to drink, that's for sure."

Samantha laughed. "As if Agnes would let him!"

She riffled the stack of mail Jasmine had left for her. Distracted by a card from her children, she said, "One wonderful thing happened at Bridge, though."

"Oh?" Jasmine sprayed polish on her rag and ran it over the piano.

"Brenda Talley told us that young Ben Stoddard is coming home."

Jasmine stopped dead, the rag and can of polish fell from her hands. Her voice shook as she turned to Samantha with quick tears in her eyes. "Wha—what?"

Samantha startled and was instantly remorseful. Dropping the mail, she went to Jasmine and hugged her. "Oh! I'm so sorry. I'd forgotten how close you were to the boy. I should have remembered and told you the news better."

Samantha could have bitten her tongue for forgetting that Jasmine had worked for the Stoddards every day and even some weekends for dogs' ages. Goodness, she'd practically raised Ben Stoddard Jr. while his parents had worked at amassing their millions. Jasmine and Olivia Charles had both been very close to the boy.

"Benny's coming home." Jasmine sniffed and dabbed her eyes with a corner of her apron. "I've prayed so long, so hard." She managed a watery smile. "I can't wait to see him."

"It won't be long. He'll be here sometime next week. He'll be staying with the Talleys."

"That's wonderful news. Wonderful. We'll have so many things to talk about. Oh, my!" Her laugh was joyous. "So many memories."

Samantha gave her housekeeper another quick hug. They stood and just smiled at each other at the thought of Benny Stoddard coming home.

***

Half an hour later the phone rang.

Samantha, in her bedroom to change, stripped off an earring and answered. "Hello?"

It was Laura. "Hi, Samantha. I just got home from my doctor's appointment. How did Bridge go?"

"We all missed you. Olivia's cousin Janet Wilson played for you."

"Did she mind?"

"No, I think she was glad for a game."

"Maybe I should be absent more often."

"Silly Goose. You know she only gets to play once in a blue moon. Herb keeps her too busy at the office to play regularly." Samantha hadn't heard the chuckle she'd expected with Laura's comment about playing Bridge less often. It troubled her. Her hand tightened on the phone as she asked, "What did your doctor have to say?"

"Praise God, he said that the mole was just a common garden variety. Nothing to worry about."

"Oh." Samantha let her breath go in a sigh of relief. "Good." She could breathe again. She couldn't help letting Laura hear. "I'm so glad you went. Better to go ten times for nothing than to chance missing the one time it's something serious."

Laura laughed, but the sound was strained. "From the way you said that, I can tell that that was yet another of your mother's precepts."

"Yep. But you'll have to admit she was right about that one. I'm so glad it was a false alarm for you, dear. Too many women die because they don't have things they're suspicious about looked at by their doctor." Still she worried that Laura sounded . . . grim. Something was bothering her friend. After a moment, she asked, "What's the matter, Laurie?"

"Hmmmm." Laura's tone changed. She stopped trying to disguise the fact that something was wrong. There was a long pause. Then, "Samantha, have you got time to slip over here for a cup of coffee? Alison's not home yet."

"Sure. Be right there." She replaced the receiver, changed into jeans and a tee-shirt and called to Jasmine. "I'm going over to Mrs. Fulton's, Jasmine. I should be back before you're ready to leave." She thrust her feet into her loafers.

"All right. If you're not, I'll lock up, so you take your door key." To Rags, she said, "You come back here dog, you ain' going nowhere." Rags returned to her with a resentful yap at Samantha. Jasmine scooped him up unceremoniously to keep him from trotting after his mistress.

"Good boy, Rags, stay with Jasmine." Samantha snatched up her keys on her way out. Walking fast, she cut diagonally across her front lawn toward the tall gateway to the Fulton estate. The houses on the river had spacious grounds and qualified for that description, while all the other houses in the neighborhood were, like Samantha's, just exceptionally nice homes on large lots.

As she rushed through Laura's tall iron gates, she wondered what in the world was going on. Never before had Alison's absence—or her presence, for that matter—had anything to do with Laura and her getting together for a cup of coffee. There wasn't anything they kept from Alison, there never had been. Now, suddenly it seemed that there might be something. It worried her.

She hurried up the gravel drive. It was long enough to give her time to notice her surroundings, and truly they were impossible to ignore. Laura's azaleas were in bloom and they were beautiful. Mature plants that had had the best of care, they were a heady riot of color. They swirled around the foundation of Laura's tall Georgian mansion, filled the wide center of the circle the drive made in front of the house, and gaily bloomed here and there in islands dotted around the two acre lawn to lead one's eye out to the wide, calm river.

Samantha loved Laura's yard.

Crunching across the last bit of Laura's gravel drive, Samantha ran up the steps and across the terrace to the side door that led into the kitchen. She never used the front entrance unless Laura was giving some sort of party and they all had decided to be formal. Most Southerners never did. Back doors were for good friends.

Laura threw open the door before Samantha had even touched the knob. "Come on in. I picked up some Prince of Wales and some Earl Grey if you'd rather have tea. If so, which would you like?"

"Earl Grey, please." Samantha watched her friend closely. Laura was tense as she had sounded on the phone. It certainly didn't take a close examination to see that.

Samantha frowned. Laura had said that her visit to the doctor had been fine, so what was the matter? As the scent of bergamot wafted from the teapot, she asked, "Laura, tell me what Alison not being home yet has to do with anything."

Laura's expression was troubled as she turned from the stove to face her friend. "Oh, Samantha, the vandal struck again last night, and I don't want her to be upset about it."

"What did he do this time? Nobody at Bridge mentioned anything."

"They don't know. I haven't told anyone." She turned miserable eyes to Samantha. "It was my greenhouse."

"Oh, no! Not your orchids."

"Yes." She bit her lip. "When you finish your tea, I'll take you out to see."

Samantha was amazed that Laura wasn't more upset. She had the best collection of orchids in the area and she spent a ton of money on it, not to mention hours and hours of time. Her greenhouse was always heated, the light regulated just so, the circulation of air perfect and her gardener, Mr. Pritchard, an expert on orchids. Her orchids were—next to her niece—her pride and joy.

"Laura, tea can wait." Samantha's voice showed her concern. "Let's go see your greenhouse."

"Great." Relieved, Laura headed for the door.

Samantha followed her friend. They walked across the front of Laura's property, crossed the gravel drive, and turned to their left just inside the entrance gate.

The greenhouse nestled in the corner against the wall that separated Laura's property from that which had been the Stoddards's. Long and low, it was built of the same mellow brick as the mansion and wall, and the bottom half of it was partially sunk into the ground so that the greenhouse was hidden behind the wall if one looked in from the street. A short flight of steps led down to its door.

Moss grew emerald green velvet on the lower bricks. It made the steps slippery. Fortunately there were only a few. Then the door opened inward for easy access to the interior.

Overhead, the glass of the roof was painted white to make the light that entered the greenhouse gentle in its profusion.

Sections of the roof were free-moving panels that could be elevated to let out heat or to invite fresh air in. Inside, there were waist high tables in orderly rows, each of them eighteen inches deep and each filled with Laura's own special mixture of fir bark, coco husk chips, charcoal and perlite.

Nothing was too good for her orchids. Laura looked after them as if they were her children. Samantha mused that perhaps they were in a way.

Laura and Bob had not been blessed with children of their own, so at first Laura had chosen to lavish attention on her plants instead of to give in to her heartache over her lack. Heaven knew her garden and greenhouse rewarded this devotion by becoming the envy of most of the city's serious gardeners.

Then fate had intervened and given Alison to Laura. Alison was Laura's husband Bob's orphaned niece. The love between the two of them was obvious. From the moment Alison, a frightened, grieving ten-year-old, had arrived, Samantha's heart had been certain there was no longer any need to worry about her friend.

Now, as they approached the greenhouse, Samantha was relieved to see that Laura's greenhouse glass, except for a dusting of green pollen from the oaks in the yard, was perfect. The white paint that defused the light was without a break anywhere. The glass that formed the roof showed no damage, only the slight traces of scratches from twigs that had blown across it in storms.

Samantha said, "Thank heaven the glass is intact."

"Yes."   Laura was holding herself tightly under control. "It could have been a lot worse." She opened the door and descended the three inside steps to the brick floor of the partially sunken structure. There, just beyond the foot of the steps, the vandal's work was clearly in evidence.

Terracotta shards of smashed pots littered the floor of the greenhouse. Leaves from orchid plants were strewn among them. A pile of uprooted Cymbidiums was heaped in the doorway. Bags of Laura's special potting soil had been cut open. Their contents had been spilled around the entire greenhouse. Into the large pile of potting soil mounded around the delicate, pale Cymbidiums, tools were stuck at odd angles.

It looked as if maliciously mischievous children had been at work.

Or a madman.

Chapter Six

Samantha was having trouble getting to sleep. After praying the Lord's Prayer and mentioning the short list of people and things she thought needed His attention most, she was still awake. The memory of what she had seen in Laura's greenhouse kept her tossing and turning.

The wanton destruction of Laura's orchids and the pile of special orchid growing medium with the gardening tools viciously stabbed into it had put her nerves on edge. Now, she lay and chided herself for magnifying every noise into something harmful—if not to her person, then at least to her garden.

As she tossed and turned, she mulled the vandalism over in her mind, but could come up with no suspects. That was what was so utterly awful about vandals. They left the whole community wondering who could do such a thing and drawing all sorts of conclusions—most of which would have to be incorrect.

Certainly it made neighbors suspicious of one another's children. And *all* the children couldn't be guilty. That was what made it so unfair—that inescapable placing of suspicion on the innocent.

She sighed. The same was true of thieves, of course. Or any sneak, for that matter. The unwarranted suspicion their crimes placed upon the innocent was unforgivable. She seethed at the injustice of it. Finally, she mentally threw up her hands. "Oh, stop it, Samantha!"

Rags startled up out of his sleep on the foot of her bed and whined his displeasure at having his dreams interrupted. "Sorry, Rags," she told him. Rags yapped once, then dropped his head again. His round black eyes watched her for a moment more, then he closed them again with a sigh.

Samantha punched her pillow into an uncomfortable lump, plopped her head on it in a determined manner, and finally fell into a fitful sleep. She dreamed of Cymbidiums attacking her with garden tools.

She didn't dream for long.

"Rrrrr. Grrrr. Yap, yap, yap!" Rags left the bed like a rocket. He stood in front of the French doors in the end wall of the bedroom, quivering from ears to tail with the urge to do battle. Samantha bolted upright. "Rags! What is it? What's the matter?"

Rags wasn't paying her the least attention. He was throwing himself against the French doors that led out to the side yard, scratching madly at their bottoms and sniffing at the crack where they met the floor as if he would drag whatever it was that he was so excited about into the room by the sheer power of his inhalation.

Samantha felt the hair rise on the back of her neck. Fear trickled from there down her spine to her knees and turned them to jelly. Someone was out there in her yard. The vandal! "Oh, Dear God!" she breathed as a prayer. It was the madman that had savaged Laura's orchids, she knew it.

For the first time in her life, Samantha understood the phrase 'her blood ran cold.'

The French doors, long her favorite feature of her spacious bedroom, instantly lost that status. Suddenly they seemed too frail a barrier to withstand whatever was outside them in the dark. Desperately, Samantha wished Rags would stop clawing at the organdy sheers that covered them. She was absurdly grateful even for their non-existent protection.

Moving as stealthily as if she were being observed and must avoid detection, she reached up beside the head of her bed and jabbed at the switch that turned on the floodlights mounted at the four corners of her house. Light flared outside. The draperies at her windows glowed to translucent life.

With all her heart, Samantha blessed her dear departed husband Andrew for his foresight in installing the double-headed fixtures on each corner of the house. They swept the entire yard outside with their bright glare. Andrew had done it for her safety when he realized he was no longer going to be there to look after her. This was the first time she'd ever touched the switch that activated those lights. The relief that washed over her as it worked left her weak.

Where had she put the revolver that Andrew had insisted she learn to use? She slipped from her bed and scrabbled through her lingerie drawer.

Oh, why had she thought she didn't approve of handguns? Now that her safety, indeed, her very life, could depend on the one her husband had gotten for her, she found her disapproval fast disappearing.

Even if she called the police this instant, it would take them twenty minutes to arrive. What good would that do when the intruder was just outside her door right this minute? She could be dead ten times over before the police got here!

Her mind was spinning as she stared at the gathered white semi-sheers covering her French doors. Never would she use a gun to defend her yard, of course. Nor, for that matter would she shoot to defend anything in the way of mere property. She'd come to that realization long ago, when she'd given serious thought to the matter of carjacking and decided that if she got carjacked, she'd just sensibly give up her vehicle.

This wasn't about a car, though. This

was about her personal, cherished, very own self, and that was an entirely different matter. She wasn't about to give *that* up. Not without a fight.

Suddenly the night silence was broken! The ringing of the phone sounded sharply in the quiet of her room. Samantha dived for it. Clumsy in her haste, she dropped the receiver. "Oh! Hello! Hello?"

"What's with all the lights?"

"Yowl, yap, yap, Grrrr. Rrrrr!" Rags was still at the French doors, but now his head was cocked and his growl less ferocious.

"I turned on the outside s-spots because my dog s-says that somebody's out there." She hated having stuttered, hated the way her voice sounded. There was no helping it. She had no breath to put under it. She couldn't seem to get any. Irritated, she continued firmly in the thread of voice that her fright had left her. "I hope the lights will scare them off."

"Yeah."

"Who is this?"

"McLain. I'm on my way."

"You don't . . ." But she was talking to a dead line. ". . . have to come," she finished weakly. She dropped the receiver into its cradle, stared at it a moment, then started for the door nearest McLain's, pitifully grateful that he *was* coming.

Rags sent a last defiant "Yap!" toward the French doors and ran after her, his toenails clicking on the spaces of hardwood floor between the area rugs. Samantha scooped him up into her arms. "Oh, Rags, I'm so glad I have you!" She hugged his tiny body to her, taking comfort from his brave little presence.

Throwing his head back, the tiny terrier licked her chin. Samantha was so distraught she didn't even turn her face out of his reach.

McLain was there before Samantha's hand touched the door knob. He pushed into the kitchen the instant she unlocked the door, slipped around it like a shadow and closed it instantly. "Nothing. Nobody's there," he reported.

Samantha closed her eyes in relief.

"Tough about that pretty tree in your side yard, though."

"Oh!" Samantha was distressed. The pretty tree in the side yard was her tulip tree—the last thing she and Andrew had planted together.

"Yeah. Somebody's broken a lot of the branches off it."

Samantha wanted to cry.

Rags caught her mood, whined once, then did that thing that Laura Fulton called percolating.

McLain scowled down at him, then told Samantha, "Look. I'll go get some of my old field gear and camp out there on your patio if it will make you feel safer."

Samantha could feel another wave of relief wash over her. Gratitude to this man, however, was not an obligation she cared to be under. She straightened her shoulders and looked him in the eye. "Thank you, but that won't be necessary. I'm fine."

He raked her with an assessing look. "Yeah. Sure you are." He was gone before she could answer.

It would be wonderful to have a guardian on the patio, and she knew she *was* grateful to the Colonel, but there was another side of her—definitely the largest side—that just couldn't let her admit it.

So, "Oh, great," Samantha said aloud. "Great, Rags. Now I'm going to have to explain a man sleeping in my yard!"

Now that her heart wasn't pounding so hard that it shook the fierce little dog she held in her arms, she clasped him tight one more time and told him in a forlorn voice, "I wish they hadn't hurt the tulip tree."

Rags licked her chin again in an effort to offer comfort, but Samantha put him down and asked him with forced brightness, "Would you like some hot chocolate?"

"Yip!"

Samantha smiled. Chocolate was awful for dogs, she knew. Four ounces of solid chocolate could kill a puppy. But Rags loved it, so whenever she made hot chocolate, she'd fix him his own saucerful, extra light on the chocolate and heavy on the milk. He thought he was in heaven.

She was setting his saucer on the floor when something scratched the kitchen door. It opened immediately, and a scowling McLain walked in. "Great Scott, woman. Why the hell isn't this door locked? Don't you have sense enough to lock your damn doors?"

Charm, Samantha decided, was not one of this man's strong points. In fact, she was beginning to suspect that profanity might be. "I thought you would be returning. I've made you some hot chocolate."

"Chocolate?"   He said it as if she'd offered him a cup of drain cleaner.

"It's good. Try it. You'll like it." She held a mug out to him. "Trust me."

He sat at the kitchen table staring down at the chocolate. "Hope it tastes better than that stuff we used to get in our rations."

Samantha chuckled. "From what I've heard, it would have to, wouldn't it?"

Nodding, he let her have that one. With cautious reluctance, he sipped the steaming brew. His eyebrows shot up. "Hey, not bad." The eyebrows returned to scowl-ready position. "Now tell me what's going on."

Samantha explained about the garden vandal. ". . . and he seems to be picking on women who are alone."

McLain shifted back in his chair. When she said 'women alone,' a wary look came over his face. "Hmmm." His eyes narrowed thoughtfully, but the wariness lingered in their depths. "That's interesting."

Samantha wondered what ailed the man. She gave a mental shrug. No matter, she had to thank him for his efforts on her behalf whether he looked strange or not. "I want to thank you for coming to my rescue, Colonel McLain."

He looked decidedly uncomfortable.

"I mean," Samantha went on, "it was nice of you to come over to check things out." What *was* his problem?

He rose and took his cup to the sink. "Yeah, well. It was no trouble."

This time Samantha's eyebrows shot up. "It was trouble for you to offer to camp out in my yard and trouble for you to go get your things to do so." She tried to smile at him, even though at this point she wished he'd just go mind his own blasted business. "Especially when you could sleep in a nice warm bed."

Her last sentence galvanized him like a shot. "Listen." He reached the door in a single stride and threw her a harried look. "I need to go set up, okay? Thanks for the hot chocolate."

He left, Samantha thought, like a scalded cat. "Now what in the world was the matter with *him*?" she asked Rags.

Rags cocked his head and blinked.

Samantha picked up her cup and added it to the Colonel's in the sink. She twisted the faucet with more force than usual.

While the water was running it hit her. Oh dear! Of course! He thought she was coming on to him. His behavior was obviously motivated by the same thing that made married men, in the second sentence of their conversation with a single woman, mention that they had a wife. It was fear. Fear. Pure unadulterated masculine fear. The Colonel was scared to death that she was after him!

She stood thinking that over for a minute. What could have transpired to make the poor man all but run from her? Then she recalled her statement that he could be sleeping in a warm bed and her eyes went wide with shocked realization. Hot blood flooded her cheeks. Dear Lord! He'd thought she'd meant *her* bed!

For an instant, she was outraged. Then the humor of the situation hit her. She burst into peals of laughter.

McLain roared from the terrace, "You all right in there?"

"Yes." Samantha actually giggled. Oh, if he only knew! "Everything's fine."

With that, she switched off the kitchen light and, followed closely by Rags, went, chuckling, to bed.

The little Yorkshire scratched at the bed-skirt to be lifted onto the high four-poster, and waited for her to pick him up and join him. Usually he waited until she was asleep so he could sneak up by jumping first onto the bench at the foot of her bed, then to the bed itself.

For once, Samantha didn't scold him to go to his own well-cushioned, beribboned basket. After all, the courageous little darling was upset, she told herself.

***

The next morning, Samantha awakened and stretched like a contented cat. With a Marine Colonel on guard outside all night, she'd slept like a rock.

Pulling on her robe, she padded barefoot to the window that overlooked the patio. The Colonel and his sleeping bag had disappeared, thank heaven. She got a big picture of herself trying to explain to her neighbors the presence of a sleeping Marine on her terrace.

That problem behind her, she had but one in view. That was the Colonel. Now that she knew what his trouble was. Thinking about it brought a smug smile. She knew what she had to do. Surely it wouldn't count against her if she happened to enjoy her planned solution.

After all, didn't simple Christian kindness dictate that she relieve the Colonel's mind? Didn't that same Christian charity demand that she dispose of the problem? To leave the poor man frightened to death that she was on the hunt for him was hardly kind. She knew in her heart of hearts that it was her duty to put his mind at ease. It was the right thing to do.

Was it *her* fault that she simply didn't have time just now to put the poor man out of his misery?

Chapter Seven

The next afternoon, when Samantha picked up the phone there was determination in every line of her body, and a terrible smile on her face.

Having seen McLain flinch when she waved at him this morning on her way to the grocery store would have irked her immensely if she hadn't a plan in mind.

Besides, Benny Stoddard was expected home any day now. She didn't want to have to worry about loose ends right now, and the dear Colonel's irrational fear of her was definitely a loose end. It was time to clear things up.

"Colonel McLain's residence." The masculine voice on the other end of the phone line was smooth as velvet—a far cry from McLain's rasp—and it took Samantha by surprise.

"Oh. Ah . . . I'd like to speak to Colonel McLain, please. This is Samantha Masters."

"One moment, please."

There was a lengthy pause, then, "Yo!"

Samantha ignored McLain's lack of telephone manners and got right to the point. "This is Samantha Masters. I should like to invite you over for coffee, dinner or dessert, Colonel McLain. You may choose the date and the time, *and* the occasion. I am perfectly free for the rest of this week and well into the next."

There was an explosion of breath on the other end of the wire. "You don't leave a guy much of a loophole, do you, Mrs. Masters?"

"Not in this case, Colonel. I have a definite need to talk to you, and, as I have a pretty good idea that you've an aversion to being invited to the home of an attractive widow," Samantha ignored his snort and went on, "I don't intend to give you an excuse to say that you are otherwise engaged."

"Well, I'll be damned!"

"Very most probably. The subject,

however, is not your eternal reward. The subject is when and for what you are coming to my house."

"Mrs. Masters, I don't really know what to say."

"Well that makes a nice change, doesn't it?" Samantha said with malicious sweetness.

She was determined to straighten out this man's thinking, even if doing so *did* put his mind at ease. If she had to *drag* him to neutral ground, she was willing to do that, too. With that in mind, she said, "Perhaps you'd prefer to go to a restaurant?"

"Oh, to hell with it. I don't know what the devil you're up to, but I have a feeling I'd just as well give in and get it over with."

Samantha let out the breath she'd been holding. "You'll feel so much better if you do," she assured him in the voice she used to soothe naughty children.

Chuckling he said, "All right. When do you want me?"

"As I said, the choice is yours." She was relaxed, now. "If you care to get it over with quickly, you can run over right now for a cup of coffee."

"Chocolate."

"I thought you didn't like chocolate."

"You changed my mind."

"All right, chocolate."

"Ten minutes."

"Very well."

Samantha hung up and wiped her hands down the side of her jeans. Heavens! She must have been nervous, her palms were damp.

Well, the beginning of the job was done, at any rate. Now, as soon as she put his mind at ease, she'd be all ready to enlist some emergency muscle power for her vandal-trapping plans. Colonel John Francis McLain, with his Marine training and his ugly attitude would suit her purpose exactly.

That thought put her more in charity with her intention to relieve his mind. Evidently, she admitted, she wasn't a very good Christian to enjoy the poor man's discomfort as much as she so obviously did.

"I'm sorry, Lord," she whispered as she took down the chocolate pot. Striving hard to mean that sincerely, Samantha went about preparing the beverage McLain had requested.

***

"Colonel McLain," Samantha began firmly as soon as she had him settled at the table in the breakfast nook. "Though I have never made it a habit to discuss my personal feelings with any but those of my most intimate friends," she paused as she poured him a cup of chocolate. Was he squirming? She hoped so. She went on, "I feel it necessary to do so now, with you."

"Now, see here, Mrs. Masters, I never . . ."

"Please, Colonel. Do not interrupt." She gave him her sternest school teacher look and commanded, "Put your mind at ease. You are not, nor will you ever be, someone I could consider an intimate friend."

She enjoyed watching his face. She was finding it difficult not to smirk. It was so easy to see relief warring with outrage at her last remark.

Smiling instead, she settled to the job at hand. "To start at the beginning, I was happily teaching at Northside Junior High when my husband came into my life. He was warm and witty and kind, and we found we had a great deal in common. Oh, he was a handsome and dashing and brave young naval officer, too, but I had never thought to marry. There were too many worlds to explore, as they say, to tie myself down.

When I found, however, that life was simply not as enjoyable when Andrew was not around, and realized that the only way I could keep him permanently in my life was to marry him, I consented to be his bride." She shot him a glance. "I didn't want to go through life missing him, you see."

McLain was lost in fierce concentration. He was not only confused, he was more than a little irritated. He'd heard of lots of reasons for marriage, but never using it like a blasted bookmark.

Samantha tried to keep it simple enough for *him* to follow. "I did all the things expected of a wife. But I didn't really like marriage. I found the role I was committed to play not only tedious, but confining. But I did it, and I did it well, because I loved Andrew with all my heart."

She peered at him closely and decided that he wasn't getting the point. "Do you understand, Colonel McLain? I did not like the confining nature of marriage. Did not like having to make every decision about *my* actions in light of how they affected *another* person's life—a husband's, no matter how dear, his career, or even our children.

"Life then was not as it is now. Married women did not have careers, they stayed at home and raised the children and took care of the house. I found, as I'd always suspected, that such a life did not suit me, alas, but I did it, and as I said, I did it very well, because I loved Andrew."

She placed her cup carefully in its saucer and looked at him expectantly as she told him, "And there you have it."

McLain shook his head like a boxer coming off the ropes. He glared at her from under his brows. "There I have *what*?"

"Why, your guarantee of safety, of course." She frowned at him. Glory, the man was dense! Hopelessly dense. "I thought I'd just made it perfectly clear. I disliked being married, therefore I certainly have no designs on you. Indeed, I was so busy running *from* you that it took me a while to realize that you thought I did have."

His face turned beet red. "Why, I never thought . . ."

"Nonsense, Colonel. In spite of the fact

that I gave you absolutely no reason to feel pursued, you showed every pitiful symptom of the hunted American male." Her eyes dared him to deny it. "Now just admit it to yourself and be done with it. There's no need to make *me* feel uncomfortable because *you* insist on entertaining your adolescent fantasy."

"Adolescent fantasy! Now look here, woman. I've been chased by the best, and I . . ."

"Forgive me for the interruption, Colonel McLain, but if you have avoided 'the best' as you have just named the poor benighted females who may have run after you, then why on earth were you so frightened of me?"

"F-frightened!" It was an explosive splutter.

Samantha held up a peremptory hand. "Not another word! We've spent too much time on this tiresome subject as it is. We have something of greater import to discuss, and I for one, intend to begin now."

"You . . ."

"I said now, Colonel!"

***

On his way home from Samantha Masters's, Colonel John McLain was in an expansive mood even if he had spent the whole damned afternoon there. He felt as if a troop-carrying helicopter had been lifted off his shoulders.

Amazing how simple things were when people just came right out and said what they thought, McLain mused as he made his way through Samantha Masters's side yard toward his own wall. Remarkably simple.

Of course, he was a little annoyed that he hadn't been the one to put things right, but then, under the circumstances, that would hardly have been gentlemanly.

Gentlemanly. Huh. There'd been a bad moment when he'd thought Samantha Masters was being less than gentlemanly. She'd come on too much like a drill sergeant for his comfort.

Too bad she hadn't told him before that she hadn't liked the bonds of matrimony. Too bad that she hadn't said that she'd loved her husband and was glad to have her children, but hadn't liked being a stay-at-home housewife.

She'd said that 'She hadn't liked having

her life being no more than an annex of someone else's—hadn't liked merely being 'Andrew's wife' or "David's mother.' Well, hell, he could understand that. Any woman worth her salt would prefer being a person in her own right, free and clear.

It sure had been a strange sort of conversation. And it had sure as blazes been one way. The dratted female hadn't let him get a word in edgewise.

He could be big enough to forgive that, however. It *had* taken a big load off his mind, after all. If she hadn't liked being a wife for somebody she'd loved, he figured, then she certainly wouldn't try to marry him for a meal ticket! He heaved a gusty sigh of relief just as he reached the wall and placed his hand on it to vault over.

Instantly, there was a quickly smothered exclamation of surprise nearby, a rustle of bushes, and the sound of somebody moving rapidly away from him on the other side of the wall. Somebody was trespassing on his property!

"What the devil!" He was over the wall like a shot, and charging through the bushes in hot pursuit of the person he'd heard running away.

Was he about to apprehend the vandal who'd been upsetting the neighborhood? McLain wondered briefly if the culprit was armed. No matter, the bushes would make it difficult for anyone to bring a weapon to bear before McLain would be on him, and then it would be too late. Like any Marine, McLain excelled at hand-to-hand combat.

"Besides, so far the toughest things you've taken on are rose bushes, you jerk!" he muttered as he pushed through his own dense shrubbery in pursuit.

He heard the crunch of gravel briefly as his quarry broke cover and hit the driveway. Bursting from the shrubbery himself, he sprinted down the drive, peering from side to side, searching the clear expanses of lawn for a running figure and the shadows for someone attempting to hide.

He passed the Chamberlain house, then the side of the Clarkes, and reached the street still breathing easily. Turning right, he continued his search at a jog along the front of the Clarkes and the McWilliams. Seeing nobody, he turned down the side of that house toward Samantha's. Still no sign of the person he hunted.

Suddenly the peace of the night was

shattered by ferocious, ear-piercing barking.

McLain gave a start and missed a step, nearly turning his ankle. "Damn dust mop!" What the Masters woman's mutt lacked in size, he sure as hell made up for in volume!

Lights sprang on in the Masters house, and Samantha appeared at the front door. "Who's there? Is something the matter?" She bent and scooped up the yapping dog, unlatched the screen with her free hand, and stepped out onto her porch. "Hush. Hush, Rags," she quieted the snarling animal.

"Good God, Woman! Do you always dash out into the night when there's a ruckus?" McLain's voice was rough with annoyance.

"If I choose to." Samantha informed him coolly. "And I didn't dash, as you so quaintly put it. I merely stepped out to see what all the fuss was about." She enjoyed adding, "And please keep your voice down. You'll wake the neighbors."

"Lady, you're kidding yourself if you think anybody slept through that mutt's yapping." He glared at Rags.

Rags began percolating. The little dog

clearly resented being called a mutt.

Samantha ignored McLain's jibe. "What's going on?"

"On my way home I heard somebody crashing through my bushes."

"Come in." Samantha stepped back and swung the door wide.

McLain scowled. He didn't take kindly to orders from anybody in skirts, but guessed this wasn't the time to say so. Irritably, he brushed past her into the house.

"Some coffee? It's still warm."

"Rather have another cup of chocolate. I'm wired enough without more caffeine."

"I'll bet you are." She led the way to the kitchen and set about fixing more hot chocolate. It didn't seem the time to tell him there was as much caffeine in it as there was in coffee. "Did you get a look at who you were chasing?"

"Not a glimpse. First he was in my shrubbery, then on and off the drive before I could get clear of the blasted greenery. I searched as well as I could running to be sure he didn't get away, but never saw hide nor hair of the bast . . . , er, him."

Samantha smiled a frosty thank-you for his moderating his language and stirred the heated milk into the powder in two mugs. Adding miniature marshmallows to make up for the fact that she was giving him instant chocolate this time, she handed McLain his mug. "You say 'him,' are you sure it was a man?"

"Can't be sure of anything, but I got the impression the body barging through the bushes was a heavy one."

Samantha repressed a shiver. The idea of a large person vandalizing the neighborhood definitely didn't appeal to her.

Until this moment, she'd been sure it was kids with too much time on their hands and too little parental supervision concerning their whereabouts. That certainly wouldn't be a new story—that of bored teens turning to wanton destruction of property. They frequently did such things. It was often their way of working off resentment toward a society that seemed to produce them only to ignore them.

She'd always believed that maybe their misbehavior was a way of getting noticed. Reluctant to think that they realized the extent of the heartbreak and injury they sometimes caused by their actions, she preferred to think them thoughtless rather than malicious.

She placed the blame on their desire to gain a little attention from society in general and their parents in particular. Sadly, nobody seemed to have time for children anymore.

Now, however, that theory didn't fit. It seemed there was something much more sinister going on. She gestured McLain to the cozy breakfast table, and joined him. "What do you think?"

"I think Frank and I are going to mount a watch and catch that bird."

"Frank?"

"Frank Takamoto, my ex-gunnery sergeant. Now he looks after me."

That must have been the man with the velvet voice who'd answered McLain's phone. Mystery solved. "Good idea. I'll help."

"No deal. Women have no business chasing around in the dark after somebody who could turn ugly."

Samantha fought a surge of annoyance. Why was it this man thought everybody should live in the dark ages just because he did? "There are women in combat with our troops all over the world, you know," she said quietly.

"Yeah. And more than one poor sap is probably in an early grave because he stuck his neck out to save some dame in combat boots."

Samantha stared at him. Opened her mouth then closed it. She had to admit that what he said was probably true. She hoped that men would continue to revere and protect women. In fact that was one of the things that disturbed her, too, about women on the battlefield—that women might cause men to take risks they might not take for another man. The good Lord knew that men took horrendous chances to save their buddies in every battle, but she still felt they would go beyond that to save a woman soldier. Even so, she didn't like to hear McLain saying it.

"Colonel McLain, some of our women soldiers acquitted themselves very well," she said firmly.

McLain snorted. "Yeah, and I'd like to remind you that they did a fine job *before* they elbowed themselves into the fighting end of things, too. They were just great at doing the stateside jobs, freeing up men to go out and do the fighting. In my opinion, they should have stuck with that." His chin jutted at her aggressively.

Samantha started to speak, then decided it was pointless. McLain wasn't going to change his opinion about women in combat just because she argued with him. Besides, she wasn't sure he wasn't right. Maybe women weren't made to charge around with eighty pound packs on their backs.

He *was*, however, going to change his mind about her helping catch the person who'd vandalized her tulip tree. It was *her* tulip tree. And she and Andrew had planted it with their very own four hands. Colonel John Francis McLain was going to change his mind about her helping trap the vandal who had injured that precious tree, by golly, or her name wasn't Samantha Eugenie Swann Masters!

Chapter Eight

The next evening, Samantha put her strategy into operation. That afternoon, she'd thrown Rags's ball for him until the little fellow was completely worn out. Then, when at last it was dark and he was deeply asleep, lying stretched out flat on his thick blue cushion with his silky mustache whuffling as he snored, she crept from the house.

She stood with her back against the door for a moment, waiting for her eyes to become accustomed to the dark. She wondered if perhaps her purpose had somehow influenced the night. It certainly seemed a lot darker than it did when she just went walking in the garden at night.

Samantha shivered once in tribute to her feminine fear of the dark and re-tightened the knot of the black silk scarf she'd used to cover her bright light-brown-almost-blonde hair. It seemed a little chillier, too. The temperature must have dropped ten degrees from what it had been before she'd changed into her black slacks and turtleneck, bought for the occasion just this afternoon.

She slithered along in the shadows, searching ahead and around her for any sign of another person in the dark. She nearly jumped out of her skin when she disturbed a sleeping bird and it flew from its nest in a bush at her shoulder.

"Steady, old girl," she whispered to herself as she rounded the corner of her house and wondered how to cross the expanse of lawn without cover. She was just congratulating herself on her very professional use of the word 'cover', and was definitely feeling bolder, when a hand seized her arm in an iron grip.

Her captor's other hand clamped over her mouth to stifle the scream that rose in her throat. She struggled madly, but her assailant pulled her against his chest with an arm like a steel vise and held her there easily.

"Just what the hell do you think you're doing out here?" McLain snarled in her ear.

Samantha relaxed in relief, then stiffened again in anger.

"Please watch your language, Colonel McLain," she snapped at him.

"And will you *puleeeze* keep your voice down!"

"Sorry." This time she whispered.

"Damn well should be. If the vandal was anywhere around here, you've certainly scared him off." His scowl got even fiercer. "Probably for good!"

"Wonderful!" she hissed at him. Somehow her sarcasm lacked its usual force when whispered. Vastly irritated that that was so, she tore her arm free of his grip. "Then we won't have to worry about any more damage to the gardens in the neighborhood." She turned to stomp off.

"Damnit, woman, Where the blazes are you going now?"

Still whispering, she told him, "To someplace where the air is a little less blue." She turned back to put McLain in his place. "It may come as a shock to you, Colonel McLain, but not every woman enjoys being treated to parade ground profanity."

McLain's face broke into a grin. "Okay, okay." He lifted his hands in a gesture of surrender. "I was out of line. I apologize. All right?"

Samantha stared at him a long minute. Oh, dear. He had his face painted with smears of black paint just like a commando. Perhaps she should have done something like that. Would cold cream take it all off, she wondered.

Suddenly, into the silent moment Samantha had created between them, came the unmistakable sound of the latch on the gate to the Chamberlains's beautiful backyard being released.

McLain and she stared at each other. Triumphant messages flashed back and forth between them. Their quarrel was forgotten instantly. The vandal! They had him cornered!

Stealthily McLain began to creep toward the sound. He grabbed Samantha's wrist and pulled her into a crouching position behind some Azaleas. Slowly they parted the bushes and looked into the next yard.

A dark figure, obviously trying to escape

detection, rounded the Chamberlains's screened porch and set off across their front yard. Thirty seconds later, gravel crunched under his shoes and he had disappeared around one of the massive granite pillars that marked the entrance to the Stoddards's . . . no, to *McLain's* driveway. Then after the brief crunch of gravel, soft silence told them their quarry had stepped off the driveway onto its grass verge.

Hurrying, they made their way to the spot at which the man had disappeared. Tiptoeing along behind McLain, Samantha had to admit that she found his wiry bulk a great comfort. Maybe she was even a little glad they'd found the vandal together. She wasn't quite as eager to make a single-handed capture as she'd been in the daylight. Maybe she owed an apology to the crusty Colonel.

Yes. And maybe she'd get it done, too. Just as soon as she saw pigs fly!

She stifled an exclamation as he slammed her against the brick wall that surrounded his place.

"Where's he gone?" McLain breathed into her ear.

"Probably into your tool storage shed." She refrained from adding "Stupid," but just barely. She was overwhelmed by exasperation. Honestly. There wasn't anywhere else the man could have gone!

"What tool storage shed?" McLain whispered. He was clearly at a loss.

"That tool storage shed," Samantha said scathingly, losing most of the effect she was after because she had to whisper it to him. But her gesture lifting one arm dramatically with her wrist leading, then raising her hand to flick her pointing finger forward in an imperious thrust said it all.

McLain looked at her as if he thought she'd lost her mind, then sighted down her rigid arm to where a low mound of earth rose from its Tidewater-flat surroundings. At the same time he realized that he was now the happy owner of an almost underground tool storage shed he heard the soft plop of its door falling closed.

Samantha pushed away from the wall as the dark shape they were tracking hurried off toward the other end of it. Their quarry was making for Laura's!

Samantha moved cautiously in that direction. McLain was close on her heels.

They both saw the man's silhouette briefly as he clambered up and over the wall. Samantha fought through the last of McLain's shrubbery and burst out on to the lawn. She increased her speed as she felt the smooth surface under her feet.

McLain grabbed her by the back of her new black turtleneck and pulled her to an abrupt halt. "Hold on," he hissed. "I don't think he knows we're after him."

"So what! Let's catch him! And stop stretching my new sweater." Samantha slapped at his hand.

"Blast your sweater. We have a good chance to see what he's up to. If I can keep you from charging in like an old fire horse, maybe we can learn whether or not he has an accomplice."

"Oh."

Fortunately for their shaky truce, McLain didn't comment further.

Samantha was smarting. Old fire horse indeed! She tried to make it feel better by balancing the epithet against his suggestion that they might capture the vandal's accomplice as well. She didn't succeed.

With Samantha darting dagger glances

at McLain, they crept toward the wall at the point at which the vandal had climbed it. McLain placed his hands flat on the bricks that capped it and, as an impressed Samantha watched, raised his body to the top of the wall.

Straddling it, he looked down at her and put his finger to his lips. When he started to throw his leg over to drop down the other side, Samantha caught his ankle in a determined grip.

Gently he tried to kick free. Samantha pulled down sharply. McLain glared at her and gestured over the wall. Samantha glared back and shook her head so hard that her black silk scarf slipped down around her neck.

Rolling his eyes skyward, McLain reached down a hand. Firmly grasping her wrists, he gave a heave, and she was sitting on the top of the wall with him.

Samantha gave him a smile that was half thanks and half triumph, and rubbed her wrists.

McLain looked as if he could cheerfully shove her off the six-foot wall.

Together they peered through the darkness. Where on Laura's property was he?

Suddenly, Samantha heard a familiar rattle. Terracotta rang its sandy peal as one flower pot fell against another.

In her excitement, Samantha clutched McLain's camouflaged sleeve.

"Damnit, woman. Don't push me off the wall." His cursing, Samantha noted, lacked its usual zest when whispered.

"Be still," Samantha hissed back at him. "He's in the greenhouse!"

"How do you know that?" Even he hadn't placed the single noise, muffled as it was in the mist that was twisting up through Laura's property from the river.

"It's the only place Laura keeps empty flower pots." She peered down trying to figure out a way to get off the wall.

McLain stopped her squirming with a none-too-gentle hand on her thigh.

Samantha shot him a withering look and pushed his hand off her leg.

McLain slithered soundlessly to the ground, turned and held up his arms to her. She launched herself with some trepidation, and was standing beside him a split second later.

"I don't suppose it would do any good to

tell you to wait here," he said so softly she almost didn't hear him.

"None whatsoever." Even in a whisper, Samantha managed a tone that left no doubt that she was in the game to stay.

"Okay. Is there a light in the greenhouse?"

"Certainly."

"When I throw open the door, switch it on." He moved smoothly toward the greenhouse door.

Samantha hated to interrupt such practiced and perfect stalking, but she had to. She grabbed the back of his jacket and yanked him to a halt.

She got immense satisfaction from the scowl with which he rewarded her action. "Can't," she told him. "The switch is in the house. The only light you can turn on from out here is a bulb with a string hanging in the center of the greenhouse."

"Shit," he said succinctly, keeping his voice low.

"Colonel McLain!" In her indignation, Samantha spoke aloud.

There was a startled exclamation from the man in Laura's greenhouse. Then he was running for the door, knocking flower pots and plants out of his way as he came.

McLain ran to meet him. The vandal didn't have a chance. As he emerged from the glass house, McLain tackled him. The force of his momentum carried the two of them out onto the lawn where they crashed to the ground without McLain relinquishing his grip.

The vandal cried, "Please! Let me go! I'm not doing anyone any harm."

A startled Samantha recognized the man's voice. "Good heavens!" she exclaimed. "Art Chamberlain! What on earth are you doing out here?"

Chapter Nine

McLain paced the end of his enormous living room, and tried not to snort out loud. Seldom recently had he been as thoroughly disgusted as he was at this moment. He glared toward the huge leather couch where Samantha sat comforting their neighbor, and fought to overcome his distaste for the man Chamberlain.

"Really, Mr. Chamberlain, we *do* understand." Samantha patted the man's shoulder reassuringly. "We're just sorry we startled you so."

At that, McLain *did* snort out loud.

Samantha glared at McLain.

"Thank you, Mrs. Masters. I know it's difficult to understand," Mr. Chamberlain shot a mild, reproachful look at the angry ex-Marine, "but Agnes is sometimes rather

. . . opinionated. Drinking is something she just can't tolerate." A blush as delicate as any girl's crept up from his collar. "When I realized that it wasn't worth the fight to try to keep a bottle in the house, I began keeping one in the Stoddards's—I beg your pardon," he flashed a glance at McLain, "in *your* tool shed, Colonel McLain. It being mostly underground, you see, things stay cooler there." He spread his hands in a self-deprecating gesture. "I hate warm scotch." He looked toward his host, wanting him to see that he was only trying to get around a problem. A personal problem.

Samantha glared at McLain again. McLain cleared his throat with a force that threatened to shake the panes in the huge windows that looked out on the river and stubbornly refused to say anything to make this man feel any better. Finally he growled, "Frank," and jerked his head toward one end of the room.

Frank Takamoto—McLain's former gunnery sergeant, now the Colonel's perfect butler—went to the wall at one side of the room. At his touch, a section of the handsome wood paneling slid back.

Behind it was a well-appointed bar. He reached down four highball glasses and inquired Samantha's preference with a lift of the first glass in her direction.

Samantha smiled. "Bourbon and water, please. Light."

Frank nodded, and McLain replied "Scotch," in a tone that plainly said he knew all along that she'd choose wrong.

"Mr. Chamberlain?" Frank's smooth voice was a balm to the man's lacerated nerves after the rasp of his employer's.

With a severe look, Samantha let McLain know she expected him to follow his butler's gracious lead.

The stoop-shouldered man on the couch looked as if Christmas had come. "Scotch, please. May I have ice?" He sounded like a child in a candy store.

"Yes, sir." Frank answered briskly, tonging frozen cubes into the glass. "Will you have soda or water, sir?"

"Oh. Soda please." He looked earnestly at Samantha. "I really prefer it to water, but there is absolutely no way I can keep a soda siphon from being noticed in my neighbors' tool sheds." He smiled nervously at his attempted joke then settled back comfortably with his highball, staring down into it with a beatific smile on his face, at peace with the world.

McLain walked over to plop in the chair nearest his unwelcome guest. "While you were out on your liquor runs, Mr. Chamberlain, did you ever notice anything unusual?"

So that's why you asked him in for a drink! Samantha's eyes were accusing. You weren't making it up to him that you'd knocked him down and frightened him half out of his wits at all!

Mr. Chamberlain blushed and all his pleasure in his drink evaporated. He shot Samantha a glance as if to ask for her support. Clearly he was reluctant to answer McLain's question. Samantha wondered why.

"Nooo," he said slowly. "Nothing out of the ordinary." But he didn't meet McLain's eyes.

Shocked, Samantha knew he was lying. He *had* seen something! Something he didn't want to tell. At least not to tell McLain. She determined to ask her old friend and neighbor that question again, but not now. Not when McLain was there to intimidate him. She was sure he'd seen something, but whatever it was, Art Chamberlain wasn't about to talk about it in front of a stranger.

Anyway, McLain was very foolish if he thought someone new to the area would immediately be taken into its confidence. Especially someone as brash as John Francis McLain—who had the added disadvantage of being from somewhere other than the South.

Samantha smiled and lifted her glass. "Cheers."

"Yeah, cheers." McLain responded, his tone flat.

Mr. Chamberlain emptied his glass more rapidly than he might have, and excused himself. Frank saw him out, and Samantha rose as she heard the door close behind their neighbor.

She turned to her host. "Thank you for the drink, Colonel McLain." Her tone was frosty.

"But you didn't approve of the fact that I didn't fawn all over that wimp. Right?"

Samantha rounded on him. "Well, since you insist on bringing the subject up, no, I *don't* approve of the way you treated poor

Mr. Chamberlain. He was a guest in your home, after all. And he was here at your express invitation. Your treatment of him was nothing short of rag-mannered!" With an effort, she managed to stop there, but her eyes still flashed at him.

"He knows something."

"That's no excuse for you to be surly."

"Hell, was I surly? Hmm. Okay. So I don't like henpecked husbands. So sue me."

Tight-lipped, Samantha turned again to go.

"Glad you could come by."

It was the last straw. She whirled back toward him. "If you'd lived with Agnes Chamberlain for forty years, you'd be hiding *vats* of scotch all over town, so don't act so blamed sanctimonious."

McLain threw his hands up in the traditional gesture of surrender. "Okay, okay!" Then quietly, "I'll walk you home."

"I can walk myself home, thank you!"

"So I'll follow you home." His eyes glinted with amusement, daring her.

Finally, Samantha laughed.

***

First thing the next morning, Samantha

went looking for Art Chamberlain. She was as certain as the Colonel that he'd been holding back last evening at McLain's, she had every intention of finding out just what it was that he'd seen during his night prowls. Cutting through her own back yard, she arrived at the Chamberlain front door with her sneakers damp from the morning dew.

Agnes Chamberlain answered the door, perfectly groomed and smiling just as Samantha knew she would be. Habitually, Agnes rose at six, dusted and vacuumed the entire house, ran the floor polisher over the few floors that were bare, and hoped for a neighbor to drop in to share a cup of coffee for the rest of the morning.

"Come in, come in, Samantha. How wonderful it is to see you!" She was beaming. "Dear me. It's been an age since you last had a minute for coffee with me." As Agnes talked, Samantha pulled off her damp tennis shoes, placed them neatly side-by-side on the mat just inside the front door, then followed her hostess toward her sunny kitchen in her sock feet.

Agnes turned to ask, "Coffee or tea?"

"Coffee, please. Yours is always so good."

Her hostess beamed, accepting the compliment. Everyone knew that Samantha usually drank tea.

They were silent for a moment, then Samantha asked, "Is Mr. Chamberlain busy this morning?" She made her question sound elaborately casual. "Perhaps he'd like to join us."

Agnes turned away from the coffee grinder, the measure full of dark beans in her hand. "You know, it's the oddest thing, Samantha." She turned back to grind the coffee beans. "Arthur woke me at four-thirty this morning and said that he'd had a call from his brother and had to go to Atlanta right away." Agnes said 'Adlana,' of course, as people from the area did. Almost to herself she added, "Funny the phone didn't wake me. I must really have been tired to sleep so deeply." She turned back to the coffee maker and poured in the ground beans.

Samantha didn't find it a bit odd that the ring of the phone hadn't awakened Agnes. She was pretty sure there hadn't been any phone call. Or, that if there had been a call, that Art Chamberlain had made it.

Dutifully, she said, "I hope it's nothing

serious."

"Arthur didn't know. He'll call when he gets there, then we'll know. How's Laura?"

"Fine." There was nothing odd about Agnes's question. Everyone asked Samantha about Laura instead of asking Laura herself. It wasn't as if Laura was standoffish, it was just that she was so busy with her yard and flower beds that no one apart from those at Garden Club got to see her . . . except Samantha.

Samantha always teased Laura that she was only best friends with her because she was her closest neighbor and it took the least time out of Laura's gardening day to get to Samantha's house.

"And how is little Alison? Still happy with her summer job? She surely thinks those places she's selling are heaven on earth."

Samantha smiled. "Yes, she does, and it's a good thing. I can't think of anything more onerous than trying to sell something that you're not enthused about, can you?"

"No, and it would be especially tiresome for that nice child." Alison *was* a nice child. No, Samantha corrected herself, Alison was a nice young lady, now. She was well-liked in the whole neighborhood, she always had been. Samantha was as proud as Laura that Alison was doing so well at her job. Being an honorary aunt in the true Southern tradition didn't make feeling proud of someone difficult at all.

Then Agnes had another thought. Samantha watched as, in typical Agnes fashion she passed from one mood to another. Everybody who knew her was used to the way thoughts seemed to *attack* Agnes Chamberlain. Frankly, Samantha privately thought it just might be the other way around.

"I've been wondering about this vandal. I think it's some kid. Probably belongs to one of the families that we've had move into the neighborhood lately."

Samantha looked startled, and Agnes told her what she meant immediately. "You know—running after the almighty dollar so hard they miss out completely on the lives of their children." She scowled fiercely. "And the poor children are usually terrors as a result."

Samantha made an effort to get her friend to look on the cheery side of her own supposition, though. "Some of them are charming."

"Charming!" Agnes flew off on her next tangent. "With their much-bragged-about MBA's and not the first idea of a single social grace?" Agnes gave a snort that McLain would have envied. "All they seem to me to have is expensive taste in clothes and cars."

Samantha smiled and murmured something incoherent. She was used to Agnes's seemingly harsh judgments. She tolerated them like everybody else in their crowd, because she knew that in spite of her frequently scathing words Agnes had a good heart.

Hadn't Agnes been the first to offer to baby-sit for that young wife whose spouse had been injured in a car wreck last fall? If Samantha remembered correctly, Agnes had spent the entire three weeks the young man had been in the hospital in constant attendance on his family. And unless she was very much mistaken, his children still came over regularly to 'Aunt' Agnes's for cookies!

Difficult or not, Agnes was a good egg.

Pouring their steaming coffee into lovely Limoges cups that had been her great-grandmother's occupied Agnes for a moment. When she came to the kitchen table carrying them, there was no trace of her sour mood. She smiled. "I wanted to tell you how much I enjoyed your column on readying the garden for spring, Samantha. It was excellent! Cream or sugar?"

"Thank you, Agnes, and no thank you." Samantha smiled, not bothering to straighten her 'thank-yous' out. Agnes knew she took her coffee black. Ritual hospitality had dictated the offer of cream and sugar. "My next one's on spring perennials."

"Been doing anything interesting with your other flowers lately?"

"Hmmm. I'm trying for an attar of roses to give to Olivia for her birthday. She loves their scent so, and I have that one red rose that outdoes all the others for sweetness and strength of aroma. I'm hoping to bring it off all right."

"Is it difficult? The process, I mean."

"No, not very. It's just that it's my first try at it. I've never attempted to get oil from rose petals before. It's a lot different from making potpourri, I can tell you."

"I know you'll be successful." Agnes

smiled. "Let me be the first to smell it when you finish."

"If I finish. There's always a chance of an awful mess."

They laughed at that, and Agnes murmured appropriately. They drank the rest of their coffee in between inconsequential comments and friendly silence. When they'd finished their coffee and the visit, Agnes walked Samantha to the door.

As she slipped her damp tennis shoes back on, Samantha wondered just what it was that Arthur Chamberlain had seen while he tippled in the dark of night.

Obviously he'd seen something. Had it been something that had put him in such a quandary that he needed to get away? To have time to think about whether or not he should share his knowledge? She couldn't think of any other reason for his secretive departure. He simply must have seen something. Otherwise why would he have left so unexpectedly?

Thinking back on his behavior at the Dratted Colonel's Samantha hadn't thought he'd seemed fearful. He'd been leery of their new neighbor before, perhaps, but not fearful.

As she walked between houses to get to her own, Samantha felt a little shiver. Whatever it was he'd seen, she sincerely hoped Arthur Chamberlain's info wouldn't get him in trouble.

Chapter Ten

Great heavens!   It was Bridge Club Wednesday again. Samantha wondered where the week had gone. At least it had gone quietly for all its haste in passing.

There had been no more talk of the poor murdered man. The police seemed stymied. No more acts of vandalism either, and the whole Bridge group was in high spirits—even Agnes Chamberlain for a welcome and wonderful change.

"Janet is with us again today. She's subbing for Mary." Anne Stuart, their hostess, announced. "And we must all thank Alison for filling in for Tyler today." She laughed a little and went on, "For which we must also thank Brenda's Herb, who is subbing for Alison at the condos in Greenbrier."

There was general laughter at this, then, after a murmur of appreciative greeting to the substitutes, one of the players asked, "Is Tyler all right?"

"Oh, heavens, yes. She's fine. She just lost a filling. The dentist wanted to get it taken care of before any more damage was done. She sends her apologies." Anne offered a tray of goodies. "I declare, Janet, I don't see why you don't become a regular."

"Oh, thank you, Anne, but I can't. Mr. Talley has too much work for me to do."

Brenda Talley shot the blonde secretary a sharp glance. "Not more than you can handle, I hope." Her voice was more than a little cool.

"Oh, no. The office is just busy." Janet Wilson bent her head over the tray Anne offered, giving all her attention to selecting two pastries and letting her shoulder length hair swing forward to curtain her face.

The girl was hiding from Brenda, Samantha thought. It didn't take a detective to see that there was considerable friction between the two women. Janet was such a beautiful young woman, and Brenda was so terribly possessive of her handsome husband. Samantha guessed it was to be expected. Knowing Herb, she knew it was unwarranted. Not only was he deeply in love with his prickly wife, he was also too busy.

For a while, though, Brenda had even been really upset with Olivia for asking Herb to hire her young cousin. Pity she wasn't more secure in her marriage. Herb had never given his wife cause to doubt him. Never. Brenda was just . . . Brenda.

Alison must have sensed the tension, too, for she watched the two women a moment before saying, "Oh, I almost forgot. Mrs. Charles?"

Olivia Charles turned soft brown eyes her way. "Yes, dear?"

"Aunt Laura wanted me to tell you she'll have those cruise pamphlets you wanted at the house this evening. I'd have brought them, but she hadn't gotten back from town with them yet." She threw up her hands, slapped one against her forehead and said to herself, "Duh, Alison! Right! Obviously, if your aunt had gotten back from the travel agency, you wouldn't be here subbing for her, you dummy!"

The room erupted into laughter. Olivia

jumped up and threw her arms around Alison. "Let her know that I'll be by to pick them up early tomorrow night, please. Tell her, too, that we're so very glad she sent you here to play." Another hug, and she fairly twinkled at the girl. "And also tell her what fun it is to hear such a lovely, grown up young lady sound like a kid just one more time."

They broke away to look into each other's eyes.

Then Alison grabbed and hugged Olivia fiercely. "I love you, Mrs. Charles!"

Olivia laughed with delight. "I love you, too, Alison. We all do."

***

Home that evening, Samantha was resting from her pleasant time at Bridge, when she was alerted by Rags's frantic yapping. An instant later her door chimes sounded, and she answered to find McLain standing impatiently on her doorstep.

He raked her silk-clad form with his eyes. "What in hell do you call that getup?" He pushed past her into the house.

"A caftan." She closed the door behind him. "And won't you please come in?"

Samantha's sarcasm was wasted

on McLain. "Any coffee?" He shot the question over his shoulder as he led the way to her kitchen.

Samantha threw up her hands and followed him, muttering darkly. Rags was close on her heels, percolating. The dog was eyeing McLain's pant legs intently.

Samantha wondered whether or not to warn him. With a faint thrill of malice, she decided not to. Instead, she asked, "Not chocolate?"

"This is business. Coffee." McLain watched her as she began lifting down mugs and filling the pot of the coffee maker. "What did you find out?"

Samantha was decidedly out of sorts. McLain, with his amazing talent for doing so, had put her there by his overbearing manner. Pushing past her into her home had definitely not made any points with her. Calling her lovely caftan a 'get up' hadn't helped his image, either. As a result, she wasn't going to give anything away. "About what?" she asked innocently.

"You know damn well about what. I saw you go to the Chamberlains's this morning. Wha'ja find out?"

"You certainly see a lot from that tower

of yours, Colonel McLain."

"Yeah, well it overlooks most of this end of the neighborhood."

"I must speak to the Garden Club about planting something fast-growing along that wall."

"Never mind the wall. What did Chamberlain know?"

"I have no idea."

"Whadaya mean, you have no idea? You were there half the morning."

"I was there long enough to have a cup of coffee, not half the morning."

"*Will* you get to the point." His comment was a criticism, not a question. Samantha smiled to herself. She could see that McLain was fast losing patience. It felt delicious.

"The point is that *I* was there," she paused for dramatic effect, hoping to drive him to distraction, "but . . ." she checked the coffee with elaborate care, then turned to look at him.

He looked as if he could cheerfully strangle her! She even saw his fingers twitch.

Samantha felt an immense satisfaction. Finally she finished her sentence,

". . . Arthur Chamberlain was not."

"What?" McLain took his hand off the lid to the cookie jar and turned to stare at her. "This is empty," he informed her.

"I know. I only bake cookies when my children are coming."

"Oh."

Samantha relented. She brought out and sliced a piece of her special apricot pound cake for him.

McLain's attitude improved perceptibly. "Thanks." He smiled briefly at her and got right back to his topic, frowning again. "So where was he? Where'd he go?"

When Samantha had finished telling him about Chamberlains's trip to Atlanta, he demanded, "Why'd he go?"

Samantha felt a distinct touch of annoyance. "How should I know? Even his wife doesn't know."

"Then it wasn't a planned trip?"

"No. Mr. Chamberlain told Agnes his brother had called early this morning and that he had to go to him."

"The battle-axe accepted that?"

"Evidently she has no reason to mistrust her husband." It was Samantha's turn to frown. She couldn't believe she'd just let this man call her neighbor a battle-axe. Association with McLain must be dulling her social conscience.

"Huh! Wonder how she'd feel if she knew he ran around town all night getting sloshed."

Samantha lost all patience with McLain. "Taking a sip or two here in your and Laura's backyards does *not* constitute galloping around the entire city getting inebriated!"

"You don't have to get huffy." He waved his fork at her. "This is good."

"I am *not* huffy." She put McLain's mug down in front of him with such force that coffee popped up out of and plopped back down into the mug.

"You coulda fooled me."

"I'm so glad you like the cake." Again it was sarcasm wasted. The man was impervious!

"Temper, Sam."

Samantha felt her molars grate. Smiling with her teeth clenched, she placed her own coffee on the table with infinite gentleness and sat down across from him. "I must tell you, Colonel McLain, that I prefer that people refrain from shortening my name to 'Sam.'"

"Z'at so?"

"Yes, that is so. It's one of my little peculiarities."

He studied her a long moment, his blue eyes glinting with something that might have been humor. "We have to figure what's going on here, Sam."

"Samantha," she corrected. Heavens! It would serve him right if she told him to call her Mrs. Masters!

He ignored her. Frowning, he searched his mind. "There's got to be more to this vandalism than we're figuring. Kids aren't this consistent. You said it's been going on a while. I know that doesn't seem significant to you, but these days kids want more excitement. Trust me. I've seen enough raw recruits to know kids."

Samantha didn't like the idea of doing it, but she had to admit that he was probably right. She herself hadn't had a lot of experience with young people lately, not since her daughter Karen had been in Girl Scouts and she'd had lots of interaction with the girls. Heavens! Was it really that long ago?

The *Virginian-Pilot* certainly supplied her with enough horror stories about carjacking and youth gangs lurking around the malls, but she just didn't believe that the good kids were so far outnumbered. They just went unreported, she was sure. It was a shame, but only bad news sold newspapers, it seemed.

Her neighborhood had always been fortunate. Why it had to suddenly get a spate of bad teens was simply beyond her. Personally, she'd no doubt that it was teenagers, for if it wasn't, then who was it? It certainly wasn't her dear neighbor Art Chamberlain!

She heartily resisted the thought that any grown-up in their right mind would do such senseless damage. Why would they?

Of course, when she'd seen the wreckage in Laura's greenhouse, she'd been uncertain that the vandal was actually *in* his right mind. The damage had seemed a little organized to her. That thought brought a shiver. It *could* be a deranged adult.

McLain interrupted her unwelcome thoughts. "Look, Samantha. We need to find a reason for this. It has to have some sort of pattern."

There was a sharp rap on the door. Samantha jumped, then rose to answer it. She let Alison in from the terrace. "Alison, this is Colonel McLain, our new neighbor," she introduced them. "This is Alison Fulton, Colonel McLain, Laura Fulton's niece."

McLain rose for the introductions. Samantha was inordinately pleased to see that he did, evidently, have a few manners.

After the amenities, Alison grinned apologetically, and said, "Sorry, Aunt Samantha, but Aunt Laura is making her famous chocolate chip cookies and has run out of nuts. She sent me over to see if you had any pecans."

Samantha smiled warmly at the girl, glad to see her taking time to do something with her aunt. Lately, work and her new beau — Randy Hale, the young man Laura disliked so, and if truth be told so did she— had kept her too busy for much time with Laura.

She opened a cabinet and handed Alison a bag of pecan pieces. "Tell Laura she's lucky. These would have been long gone if I'd had time to bake cookies and mail them to the kids."

Alison smiled brightly to acknowledge

Samantha's remark and nodded to McLain. "Nice to meet you, Colonel McLain."

McLain inclined his head and grunted somewhat affably.

"Oh, Alison, dear." Samantha put out a hand to detain her young friend. Aware that Alison knew most of the young people in the neighborhood she asked, "Colonel McLain and I are trying to puzzle out who might be able to shed a little light on our vandalism. Can you think of anyone who might have done such things . . . or seen something unusual? Try as I might, I can think of no one."

"No." Alison colored and seemed a little agitated. "No, I don't have any idea." She bobbed her head apologetically. "Please excuse me. Aunt Laura will have a fit if I don't get right back. You know how she's been about me going out at night since all this started. And her oven's on, too. I'd better get going." Alison backed to the terrace door. "Thank you for the pecans, Samantha. Aunt Laura will be glad you had them. Nice to have met you, Colonel." She turned when her hip hit the French door, pushed it open, and was gone like a shot.

McLain looked after her thoughtfully. "Never had quite that effect on a girl before."

"Alison *is* usually a little more self-possessed," she understated mildly. Allison had certainly been flustered. "Guess she was shocked to see a man at my table."

McLain looked momentarily uncomfortable until Samantha said, "The young always put a romantic interpretation on such things, you know. And she is, of course, unaware of how unpalatable you are."

"Unpalatable! Now see here . . ." Then he saw the expression in her eyes.

"Gotcha!"

"Shi . . ."

Samantha threw out her hand. "Don't you dare use that word in my house, John McLain!"

McLain took refuge in his coffee cup, draining it and holding it out to her for more.

Samantha, who prided herself that she was never one to rub it in, dutifully poured him a second cup.

When the last of his third slice of apricot pound cake had disappeared from McLain's dessert plate, he looked up and asked, "Well, I suppose I have to go home now?"

"It's still well before nine."

"Then we need to get our heads together on this vandalism thing. So whadaya waiting for?"

Samantha resisted saying she'd been waiting for him to finish making a pig of himself. Instead she removed his plate from the table and rinsed the crumbs off it into the disposal side of the sink before slipping the dish into the dishwasher. "I'll get a tablet so we can make a list."

As she moved away, she heard him grumble, "Better bring a pencil, too."

Always with the orders! Obviously, she could count on being bossed around, now that she'd made the acquaintance of this *charming* man who was her new neighbor. Well, Samantha promised herself, she would just see about that!

***

McLain arrived at Samantha's terrace door promptly at seven-thirty the next evening, as they'd finally agreed the night before.

Samantha opened the French door with a distinct feeling of resentment.

She'd meant it when she'd told him she'd rather he came at eight. Drat the man! *He* didn't have to wash dishes.   He had Frank Takamoto, the lucky dog. McLain, not Frank.

"You're looking cheerful this evening." McLain observed with a hint of malice.

"You're just fortunate I had a dishwasher that was almost full."   Samantha was pleased that her annoyance showed in her voice.

"What's an almost full dishwasher got to do with it?"

Samantha gave him an indignant look. "You don't think I'd run it half-empty, do you?"

"No clue, Sam.   Never gave it much thought, somehow."   He cocked an ear toward the machine under discussion. "Sounds like it's doing just fine to me. What's the problem?"

"The problem," Samantha said in a frost-edged tone, "is that it is extremely difficult to finish dinner at an enjoyable pace, clear the table, clean the kitchen, do the dishes and be ready for," she forced herself to refrain from using the words 'an invasion,' "a *guest*," she made the word 'guest' sound anything but welcoming, "by seven-thirty!"

"Oh, stow it, Sam. We have something important to discuss. We don't have time for you to stand there jawing at me over a little half-an-hour." He plopped down at the kitchen table and picked up the pad they'd used for notes the night before.

Samantha pushed the aggravation she felt at his disrespectful speech down into the same place in her mind that she'd already shoved her peevishness at his first use of her detested nickname. She had to clench her teeth to keep it there.

Determinedly, Samantha gave herself over to the interest she felt in what he had to say. She handed him a mug of coffee.

"Hey! I thought I'd been invited for hot chocolate."

"No. You invited *yourself* for chocolate. But you didn't leave me time to prepare it properly, and I'm out of instant."

McLain looked at her in open admiration. "God, Sam. When you put that prissy little mind of yours to it, you can really be a bitch."

"Colonel McLain! I'll thank you to moderate your language in my presence."

"Okay, so you're shy about compliments." He watched with satisfaction the two high spots of color in her cheeks, then decided to stop jerking her chain.

One last yank. He couldn't resist it. "Maybe we can make chocolate later?"

"Perhaps." Samantha said the word with a snap.

McLain looked into Samantha's level, narrowed eyes, and changed the tone of the conversation. He didn't want it to crash before he got it off the ground.

"Look," he told her. "This sketch we did of the places the vandal has done his dirty work shows a definite pattern." He studied her briefly. She'd overcome her irritation and was clearly interested in what he had to say.

Just then, Rags tore in from the living room, went to the terrace door, and pawed the door frame. When he didn't get an instant response, he let out a single sharp bark.

"I believe that mutt of yours wants out."

"Coming, Rags," Samantha said vaguely, her mind still locked on McLain's statement that there was a pattern.

With a pattern, maybe they could . . .

Rags was having a fit. Flinging himself against the door repeatedly he increased the volume of his barks.

"Stop that, Rags! You know better than that. You'll scratch the door."

McLain rose. "Come on. Let's take the mutt for a walk. Maybe fresh air will clear some of the cobwebs for you." Very softly he told Rags, "And maybe we can get *you* run over."

"Yes. Fine." Samantha obviously hadn't heard his last remark. McLain watched her grab her sweater off the back of her chair and the key from its place on the key board next to the pantry door. Stupid place to keep a key, he noted. The way she left doors open, anybody could take one. Instead of telling her so, however, he opened the door for her.

Rags shot out.

Samantha and McLain had hardly crossed the terrace, when Rags disappeared, yapping off into Laura's gateway. His barking took on a quality that alarmed them both.

McLain broke into a dead run after the little dog, Samantha right behind him.

Tearing around one of the pair of huge brick pillars that marked the entrance to Laura's drive, they skidded to a halt. Just inside, a car stood idling.

Rags was barking ferociously at the driver's door.

Chapter Eleven

Slow, curling mist creeping up from the river mingled with the car's exhaust, muffling the sound of the smooth-running engine. The steady purr of it in the almost-silence was eerie.

Samantha felt the hair on the back of her neck prickle.

Rags was barking ferociously at the driver's door. Clawing frantically at the driver's door.

Samantha's mind filled with dread.

"Hey, Mutt!" McLain admonished, "That's good paint." But his voice lacked force, and he didn't look as if he was worried about the paint on the outside of the dark green Jaguar. He looked as if he were apprehensive about what he'd find inside. In two long strides he was at the door of the car. A quick glance and, "Sam! Call an ambulance. Hurry!"

As she ran past the car, Samantha saw a graceful arm, its hand limp, dangling from the driver's window. Her heart was in her throat, the car looked like Olivia Charles's!

Samantha's fear filled her voice as she flew across the gravel drive to the house. "Laura!"

She slammed into the door, twisting the knob frantically. The door was sensibly locked. With her balled fist, she pounded on it.

Laura tore it open. "Samantha! What's happened? What's wrong?"

Samantha pushed past her to the telephone. "It's Olivia." She punched 9-1-1. "Something's happened to Olivia. Colonel McLain's out there with her." She turned her attention to the person on the other end of the phone. "We need an ambulance. The address is . . ."

Laura flew out the door before Samantha finished speaking.

In a flurry of footsteps, Alison came down the butler's back stairs into the kitchen, her face full of concern. "What is it? What's the matter?"

Samantha replaced the receiver and headed for the door, urgency driving her. "Olivia Charles's car is standing in the driveway. She's been hurt."

Alison jumped down over the last three steps of the back stairs and ran across the kitchen. By the time Samantha had made it back to the gravel drive the girl had passed her.

In the dim light from the Jaguar's interior, Samantha saw that McLain had lifted Olivia from her car and placed her flat on the ground. He was tearing strips from the pretty cotton robe that Alison had had on a moment ago. Alison stood above him in her bra and half slip, transfixed with horror.

Making a pad of the strip he'd torn, McLain pressed it to Olivia's chest, looked up and ordered Samantha, "Hold this here. Press down hard."

It was then that Samantha saw all the blood. Faint with the sight of her friend's life spilling out, she dropped to her knees and did as she was told. To her horror, blood seeped up at an alarming rate, coming through the pad she held tightly against Olivia's chest.

Rags shoved his muzzle into Olivia's limp hand. When she didn't respond, he whined pitifully.

Samantha felt sorry for the little dog and would have attempted to comfort him had her own need for comfort not numbed her mind. Oh, when would help come? Her feeble effort to help her dear friend was doing nothing to halt the steady flow of blood through her own pressing fingers. Tears blurred her vision as she looked frantically toward the gate.

In the distance a siren wailed. The ambulance. Thank God!

Nerves stretched to the breaking point, she strained to hear any hint that it was approaching the scene. The sound of its squealing tires as it rushed toward them was the most welcome sound Samantha had ever heard.

Laura rushed out of the mist, back from wherever she had gone to find a flashlight. "Here. This is the one from my car. I didn't dare go into Olivia's."

"Good head." McLain praised her, making another pad. "The cops'll want to see her car."

The ambulance paused down the street

and flashed its spotlight on the facade of Samantha's house to read the number. McLain cried, "Go get 'em, Sam. Hurry!" and put his great hands where Samantha's had been on Olivia's chest.

Samantha ran out of Laura's gate waving her blood streaked arms in the glare of the ambulance's bright headlights and shouting, "Here! We need you here!"

With a squeal of tires, the heavy vehicle rocketed toward her. Before it had come to a complete halt, the Emergency Medical Team was out of it and beside Olivia. "We'll take it from here."

McLain waited until the paramedics had pressure on the stab wound, then stepped away. "Go inside, ladies. There's nothing you can do here. We'll follow to the hospital when you've gotten dressed."

Alison suddenly realized she was standing there in her underwear. She gasped, wrapped her arms around herself, and bolted for the house. Laura followed her.

"I'll get my car and be back to pick you up," McLain called after them.

"We can take my car. It's closer," Samantha offered.

"Okay. Good idea."

They turned and ran back toward Samantha's house, Rags in hot pursuit. Samantha snatched her keys off the key board just inside the kitchen door and tossed them to McLain. She knew she was in no condition to drive.

"Good girl!" McLain dragged her to the sink and made a hasty job of rinsing the blood off both their hands. Then he lobbed a vigorously protesting Rags into the pantry and slammed the door on him as Samantha yanked open the one into the garage. Together, they leapt at and scrambled into her Buick.

McLain started the engine, looked toward her and snapped, "Get your seat belt on." One quick glance and he'd located the garage door opener clipped to the visor, punched the button to activate the mechanism that lifted the door, and shifted into reverse. Before the car's hood was even clear of the door, he'd punched the button to close it again.

They hit the street with a jolt. McLain stopped the car long enough for Laura and Alison to jump in, then slammed it into drive. In a smooth rush they swept away, headed for the hospital.

Even over the snarl of her engine, Samantha heard the mournful howl set up by Rags.

It made her blood run cold.

***

In a hush broken only by the faint sounds of papers being shuffled, monitors softly humming and the squeak of rubber-soled shoes moving over well-scrubbed vinyl floors, Samantha sat with her friends and prayed. They were all begging that Olivia Charles might recover from the awful wound in her chest.

Samantha's world had turned upside down. She and all her friends had gotten over the murder of a perfect stranger and settled down again into the usual rhythm of their lives. Only a little while ago her greatest concern had been the petty annoyance of some prankster damaging gardens. Now that issue was forgotten in the horror of this attack on a well-loved friend.

Never would she be the same after seeing Olivia Charles lying there with John McLain trying to staunch the flow of blood from her chest.

They sat without speaking for what seemed an eternity. Every now and then one of them would get up and walk over to stare unseeingly out the glass window wall of the waiting room. No one spoke.

There were only three other people in the room, but they glanced toward Samantha and her friends from time to time, as if wondering what had happened to the person about whom they waited for word. They seemed curious, but were perhaps reluctant to ask because of the strained expressions on the faces of Samantha's little group. Now and again they sent sympathetic glances their way.

Finally, Alison spoke, "She *is* going to be all right, isn't she?" Alison, in a shirtdress she'd buttoned wrong in her haste, was as white as the papers carried by the nurses that moved purposefully up and down the hall.

"We don't know, dearest," Laura told her.

Samantha took one look at McLain's face, read correctly the strain on it, and knew. McLain had been in battle. McLain had known what to do to try to help Olivia. McLain had seen men wounded unto death, and McLain had seen men die.

She looked again at his stern face, and slow tears began to trickle down her cheeks.

Half an hour later, the surgeon came out of the operating room and approached them reluctantly. They all stood up as if jerked out of their chairs by a common invisible string, fearful to hear his news.

He hesitated, looking around the tense little group, his face grave. Finally he took a deep breath and said, "I'm sorry. We did everything we could."

Samantha stood closer to Laura who was shocked to statue stillness.

On the other side of her, Alison buried her face against her aunt's shoulder and sobbed.

McLain shoved his hands into his pockets as if he were afraid he'd do the wrong thing if he reached out to any of them.

He didn't get the chance.

Into their stunned silence, a deep voice spoke from the doorway. "I guess that makes it murder, then."

As if pulled by a single cord all of them turned to the speaker.

"I'm Lieutenant Nichols, Homicide," he told them. "I'll have to ask you some questions."

Chapter Twelve

After lying awake half the night grieving for Olivia and then having a nightmare that she was being roughly questioned by Lieutenant Nichols for the rest of it, Samantha finally fell into a deep sleep toward dawn. She was awakened by a phone call that sent her racing back to the hospital.

She had no recollection of how she'd made it through the heavy morning traffic. Her well-ordered life which had been, until last night, always so calm, so peaceful and predictable, last night had tumbled into panic-stricken chaos. Badly shaken, frantic with worry, she had come.

She had no idea where she'd parked the car, but she knew where she was. She knew she was standing by the bed of yet another stricken friend.

She asked softly, "How are you feeling?"

"How am I gonna pay for all this? That's the question." Pain medication blurred Jasmine Johnson's voice and slurred her speech as she gestured vaguely at the paraphernalia holding her right leg in traction.

"Oh, Jasmine, please don't worry about that now. It's all taken care of. Don't you remember we took out that accident policy on you when you first came to work for me?"

Tears spilled over. This was more than Samantha could come to grips with. Two of her friends injured in the space of twenty-four hours. One of them, sweet Olivia Charles, gone. Gone forever. Now this.

What if the car that had struck Jasmine had killed her? It would have been more than she could bear.

"Oh, yes," Jasmine was saying dreamily. "Now I remember. That do make it so I can relax a little." Her eyes closed.

The nurse said softly from the doorway, "I think if we leave now, she'll rest."

"Yes. Yes, of course." Samantha rose, leaned over the bed and kissed Jasmine on the cheek. Jasmine's eyelids fluttered and she smiled. Before the door had closed behind Samantha, the injured woman had dropped off to sleep.

"If there's anything I can do," Samantha told the nurse, "Anything she wants. Anything at all."

"We'll let you know. She'll pretty much sleep the next few days, you know. We're going to try to keep her comfortable. She has multiple contusions, as well as that fractured leg." The nurse strove for an encouraging comment. "We're lucky she doesn't have a concussion."

"Yes, yes of course." Samantha was numb. The call from the hospital had awakened her from a deep sleep—a dead sleep caused by her having cried for half the night over the loss of Olivia. Nerves tattered, she was having trouble accepting it all.

She bid the nurse an automatic goodbye, laced with thank-yous that came just as automatically, and went to the elevators. On the ground floor, she walked down the long hall to the foyer without seeing the photo gallery of those men who had contributed to the beginnings and growth of Norfolk General.

She half smiled as she mused that it would always be Norfolk General to her and other native Norfolkians who'd been born there and had had their own children there, never mind the sign outside that proclaimed it Sentara Hospital.

Turning left toward the foyer, she crossed the wide expanse of the high, glassed-in lobby to the entryway and pushed out through the heavy double glass doors.

Buildings had so much glass nowadays, she thought vaguely.

Outside, she hesitated on the curb, waiting to think again, waiting to feel something, trying to focus. Then she crossed the street to the parking lot.

Somehow she found her car.

Laura and the Colonel were waiting there next to it. Laura was still wearing her gardening clothes, standing there twisting her hands, her soiled gardening gloves stuck in the waistband of her khaki cargo pants.

The Colonel was leaning on Samantha's Buick with his hands in his pockets. Samantha thought inanely that that was very unmilitary. She wondered what they were doing here at the hospital.

Laura rushed forward. "Oh, Samantha. I'm so sorry about Jasmine. We've come to drive you home." Quickly she peered into her friend's face. "Heavens. You aren't even connecting, are you? You poor dear. Good thing the Colonel saw you screech out of your driveway and brought us here." She hugged Samantha. "We'll take you home."

The Colonel took Samantha's purse from her and asked, "Car keys in here?"

Vaguely Samantha patted both pockets of her linen blazer, then nodded.

"You drive her Buick, Ms. Fulton." He handed Laura Samantha's handbag. "I'll take her in my car and fill her in on what the cops had to say." He took Samantha firmly by the elbow and guided her to his dark blue Jaguar.

Samantha gasped and stopped dead, startled when she saw the car. Olivia, her dear, dead friend Olivia had driven the same model in dark green.

"Yeah, I know," McLain said softly, understanding. Tucking her into the passenger side, he walked around and got into his own. His voice had regained its habitual rasp when he ordered, "Fasten your seat belt."

Samantha did as she was told, took a deep breath and let it out in a long sigh. As they looped off Brambleton Avenue onto Hampton Boulevard, she stared out the car window.

It seemed odd to her that everything was the same. It seemed to her that things should change somehow when there were tragedies, but evidently they didn't. The familiar street with its huge old houses, many of them turned into doctors' offices, apartments and discreet businesses, was the same.

Twenty-first Street still swept off to the right. Next came the underpass that always flooded in heavy rainstorms.

Everything was the same, yet nothing was the same. Olivia's murder and Jasmine's accident had changed it all for her.

She gave herself a mental shake. All was clearly just as it had been the other day when she and Laura had picked Rags up from the groomer's. That familiarity brought her back to herself and she had to acknowledge that the only change was in her.

Life went steadily on in spite of all its horrors. Even though she felt everything should stop for a moment somehow, it was going to go on in spite of Olivia's murder and Jasmine's accident, and she realized that she had better get a grip.

Finally she leaned forward to check in the side mirror and saw that Laura was safely behind them in her faithful silver Buick. She took a deep breath. Her mind at ease about her friend, she turned to McLain and asked, "What did the police tell you about Jasmine's accident?"

Samantha was ready to face life again.

"They said it was an ordinary case of hit and run. Maybe some drunk."

"At seven in the morning?"

"Coming home from a binge, maybe."

"Poor Jasmine."

"She was lucky. One of the people who lives across the street ran out to help her right away. Didn't get the license number of the car, though."

Samantha took a deep breath. Then another. It finished clearing her head. She'd seemed to have been living in a fog ever since they'd found Olivia. She was relieved to be coming out of it. "I imagine the person was too busy worrying about Jasmine."

"Yeah."

Samantha flashed a glance at him. "That had undertones."

"You _are_ coming around." He shot her an approving look. "Yeah. The cops put it down to a hit and run. An accident. I figure maybe it wasn't an accident. I figure maybe Jasmine knew something about what happened to Olivia Charles that somebody didn't want her talking about."

Samantha stared at him, all the horror creeping back in, chilling her. "What do you mean?" She didn't even worry about the shock that clearly registered in her voice.

"I mean that the man who ran out to help Jasmine couldn't understand why the driver of the car didn't come back to help her, too. He said that the car had turned around as if they were going to, but then they sped off instead."

The traffic light ahead turned red, and McLain had time to swivel to look at Sam. He regarded her steadily. The expression on his face shocked her.

"You mean . . ." She couldn't finish. The words that formed in her mind refused to come out.

"Yeah. I mean I think they were gonna come back and finish the job."

Chapter Thirteen

The next morning, Samantha woke up full of determination. At least she knew of one thing that would help make Jasmine feel better, and she was going to cause it to happen. She'd said to the nurse in Jasmine's room that she'd do anything Jasmine might want and she was going to do it 'come hell or high water' as Andrew used to say.

"Yes, right now, Brenda," she said firmly into her phone. "I want to come over there right now." Samantha frowned at herself in the hall mirror as she waited for Brenda Talley's reply. For Jasmine's sake, she didn't mind being a little rude. Even a lot pushy.

"Well, I suppose if you must, you must, Samantha. Come on over. I'll go make coffee." The sharp click at the other end of the line could mean either that Brenda was annoyed because Samantha had insisted on coming over, or that she was in a hurry to make the coffee to welcome her.

Samantha frankly didn't care which it was, but knowing Brenda she didn't think it was the coffee. Unfortunately, Brenda never bothered to say 'goodbye.' That lack of social grace indicated nothing; everybody had just had to get used to it. Samantha wanted to get to Benny Stoddard both to console him for the loss of his good friend and former Sunday school teacher, Olivia Charles, and to inform him as gently as possible that another very dear friend of his, Jasmine Johnson, was in the hospital.

She particularly wanted to be the one to break the news about Jasmine. She wanted to soften this second blow before his hostess got wind of the accident. Unfortunately, Brenda had always had a lamentable tendency to be rather abrupt with bad news.

Samantha shook her head. Poor Brenda. Though she knew Brenda would resent it, Samantha couldn't help feeling sorry for her. Surely, Brenda hadn't counted on all this tragedy when she'd so blithely announced that Benny Stoddard was coming to be her houseguest. Now, instead of a guest who would have been considered a social coup, she'd have a grieving youth on her hands.

And here Samantha was on her way to put her under even more pressure. Brenda would feel the brunt of her news, even though it was her houseguest, Benjamin Stoddard Jr., that Samantha was going to tell that another of his close friends had met with misfortune.

And that poor boy. What a terrible beginning for his return home. One of the two cherished adult friends of his childhood murdered, the other injured. This on the heels of coming home from two years in a foreign prison for something he didn't do to find his parents had been killed in his absence. She sighed. So much tragedy.

Samantha's heart went out to the young man. He would have to be reeling under this series of blows.

Thank God Jasmine was only injured and would live. She, at least, would be there for him. It was so sad. Only one friend left from a past filled with loving supporters. Poor Benny.

Samantha, her thoughts in turmoil, decided to walk over to the Talleys's. Perhaps a walk would lift her spirits. She fervently hoped so.

It was a beautiful day, and she concentrated on that. The sun was bright without being hot and the breeze that wafted in off the river was gentle, ruffling only the smallest leaves on the trees.

Taking a deep breath, she savored the fresh scent of spring. Everything was budding out. She was relieved to see that the cherry trees had recovered and opened new blossoms in spite of having lost most of their earlier buds to an unexpected freeze. They'd been bolder than the other trees and budded too soon—as so often happened now that the climate was going through such peculiar changes. The Judas trees, called Redbuds everywhere but in the South, were fine, too. The dogwoods were budding and would soon be a lacy white background for the azaleas blooming at their feet.

She gave herself a little shake. She mustn't forget that she was on a mission. She was determined to convince Ben

Stoddard Jr. of the importance of his going to visit Jasmine Johnson in the hospital. Jasmine so needed cheering up, lying there helpless as she was.

Turning the corner, Samantha stepped up her pace. The Talleys's stone walkway was outlined by a stalwart battalion of daffodils. Stiffly they marked with yellow cheer the arrow-straight path from the curb to the front steps. Unfortunately, the blossoms of the crocuses interspersed here and there that might have softened the stiff effect had begun fading after the final frost of the season. She noted with pleasure, though, that the plants themselves were recovering well.

Brenda Talley opened the front door. "Inspecting my plantings as usual, I see"

"'Goes with the turf,' as Alison would say." Samantha wiped her feet carefully on the doormat. "Your daffodils are doing beautifully. So pretty with the forsythia, don't you think?"

"Yes. I suppose they are pretty together. Yellow has never been one of my favorite colors, though." She frowned at the daffodils. "So damned bright."

Samantha laughed. "I think bright's just

what we need after our long gray winter. It's dreary so much of the time here in Tidewater."

"You have a point. Come on into the living room. Benny'll be down in a minute." She went to the foot of the stairs and called, "Benny. Samantha Masters is here."

"Coming," a tenor voice responded.

The two women had just settled when a tall, slender young man entered the room. Samantha regarded him with a great deal of interest. She could see the resemblance to Ben senior in the lean and athletic way he was built, and his eyes were the hazy blue of Mimi Stoddard's.

Sadness at his loss of his parents brushed the edges of her mind. Sympathy for what he must be feeling washed over her.

This younger Ben seemed hesitant about greeting her.

"Welcome home, Benny," Samantha said, offering her hand when Brenda had finished the introductions. "I never got to meet you, as I'm a relative newcomer to Riverhaven even though I am a native Norfolkian. I . . . ."

"She's just being modest, Benny,"

Brenda interrupted. "Samantha was a Swann. Her family owned Riverhaven. You can check the deed in the deed books over in the Chesapeake Civic Center in the clerk's office if you're curious."

"Really?" Benny looked at Samantha with interest.

"Yes." Brenda smiled at Samantha. Brenda was proud of her knowledge, as if having Samantha as an acquaintance added to her own luster.

Samantha kept her gaze on Benny. She thought he must be shy about meeting older ladies. She liked that. So many young people today didn't seem shy about much of anything.

She smiled at the boy, then turned to her hostess. "I take my coffee with cream and sugar, please, Brenda."

She was used to adding her own cream and sugar, but Brenda was presiding over the silver waiter with the coffee service on it in a way that reminded Samantha of English ladies and their tea trays. "Light and sweet, please."

Calories be darned, Brenda's coffee was a far cry from Agnes Chamberlain's, and she surely wasn't going to take it black!

Samantha turned her attention back to the young man. In light of his shyness, she decided not to offer him her sympathy on the loss of his friend, Olivia Charles. Instead, she chose to tell him of Jasmine's accident and to persuade him to visit her. "I came to make a request, Benny, on behalf of someone you know. Someone who is an old friend of yours." Samantha accepted her cup from Brenda and told her, "Thank you."

"You're welcome. I hope it's sweet enough. I put in three sugars." Brenda was watching Samantha carefully.

Goodness, Samantha'd had no idea that Brenda took being a hostess so much to heart. To put her at ease, she sipped her coffee immediately. "Hmmm. Nice." She threw her a smile and got back to her reason for coming.

Turning her attention back to Benny, she saw the distress on his face and wondered if he'd already heard that Jasmine had been involved in a hit and run. She hastened to tell him, "She's going to be fine," she said first to reassure and prepare him, "but Jasmine Johnson has had an accident, and is in the hospital. I know that, more than anything in the world, she'd want you to visit her in a few days. When she's feeling better. She's been so looking forward to seeing you again. She'll be counting the days, I know."

Benny looked so shocked, his eyes wide, his mouth half open, that she feared she hadn't been gentle enough. His panicked gaze flashed to and locked on his hostess, however, so there was no way Samantha could give him a reassuring smile. Instead she offered, "I'll be happy to drive you over to Norfolk General any time you want to go. I work at home, so I'm freer to go than Brenda is."

"Th-thank you." He dragged his gaze back to her with an effort. "What happened to Ms. Johnson? Why's she in the hospital?"

"A car hit her yesterday morning. A hit and run." How odd that he called Jasmine by her last name. "We're very fortunate she wasn't hurt more seriously than a badly broken leg."

"Oh." He had paled and looked desperately upset. He put the best face on it he could. "That *is* fortunate. But it's so soon after . . . after . . ."

The boy broke off and watched Brenda

again as Samantha said, "Yes, it is awful, two tragedies almost together." She didn't add 'and right on top of you learning of the car accident that killed your parents.' She was trying to get him to pay a hospital visit, not crush him under a load of grief.

Brenda broke in, "But Jasmine is going to recover." Then she explained, "Jasmine works for Samantha now that your parents have . . . uh . . . moved away."

"I . . . I see." His voice was a tight rasp.

Brenda turned and touched Samantha on the arm. "Benny is still exhausted from his trip, dear."

Samantha felt quick sympathy—and just as swiftly recognized her marching orders. "Of course he is." She set her half-full cup on the coffee table. "I'll go now and let him get some rest." She looked over at him. "You do look tired, Benny. Get rested up, and call me when you want to go visit Jasmine, okay? She's in traction, so she'll be doubly glad for company, and while the rest of us will visit her, it's you she particularly wants to see." She rose and smiled at him. "Welcome home. We're all so glad you're safely back."

Benny flushed and stammered, "Thank

you. Thank you very much."

Brenda got up to usher Samantha to the door. "So glad you decided to come," she said as if she didn't mean a word of what she was saying and meant for Samantha to know it. "I'm sure Benny enjoyed meeting you."

"I'm glad to have met him, too." Samantha spoke sincerely, determined not to react to Brenda's goad. Then, unable to resist, she added, "I hope it wasn't too much of an inconvenience for you." For that remark, Samantha's tone was dry in the extreme.

Brenda hesitated. Finally she let her stiffly held shoulders drop and said, "Okay. So I wanted to get off to work earlier than usual this morning. So I was angry about your insisting on coming." Grudgingly, she added, "I apologize. Or you can sue me if you want."

Samantha grinned at her. "That makes it all better. I'm sorry I forced myself on you, but you know how much I love Jasmine. I just had to get my bid in to take him to visit her before he gets all booked up by the rest of the neighborhood."

Brenda sighed. "I'm hoping they won't

bother him too much." She leaned out the door toward Samantha and spoke softly. "That prison stay had a serious effect on him, it seems. I don't think he likes a lot of fuss. Not comfortable with people, you know."

"Just so he visits Jasmine," Samantha told her. "I promise not to bother him about anything else."

"Good." Brenda started to turn back into the hall, remembered her manners and watched from the door until her guest had reached the street. Then, with a wave and a cheery "Goodbye," she firmly shut the door.

Samantha looked back over her shoulder at the still quivering spring decoration on the Talleys's paneled front door and wondered how Brenda had broken the news to Benny about Olivia. Heaven knew the young man seemed to be walking around in a mild state of shock.

She was proud of Brenda for perceiving that he was shy and protecting him, but she almost wished Brenda hadn't been in such an all-fired hurry to get rid of her. Maybe she could have been of some small comfort to him.

Chapter Fourteen

Halfway home from Brenda's, Samantha saw the Dratted Colonel in the distance. She decided she must not be living right. Her luck today was certainly failing her.

Unfortunately, he'd seen her first. Rotten luck. Too late to duck between houses and get to another street. Oh, well.

McLain trotted up to her. As usual he arrived at her side without the slightest sign of breathlessness. "Well?"

She raked his lean frame with her gaze. No tell-tale darkening marked his sweatshirt. He was the most *annoying* man. He could at least have the grace to perspire—she figured honest sweat was too much to hope for—when he ran all over the neighborhood. Her voice was not exactly cordial, "Well what?"

"You went to meet the young Stoddard kid, didn't you?"

That annoyed her, too. How was it that he was always aware of her movements?

As if to answer her, he said, "Saw you head in this direction when I was shutting down my computer."

No one had ever made her feel as perverse as Colonel John Francis McLain, USMC, before. She certainly hoped no one ever would again. The man had a real knack for irritating the fool out of her.

Her conscience prickled. She really ought to admit that the irritation was something she needed to overcome. After all, she was raised as a Southern gentlewoman, and she felt obligated to overlook the faults of others. Now, she was determined to overlook his. Absolutely determined. And she would, too. Starting tomorrow.

Suddenly ashamed, she offered, "I met Benny Stoddard."

The Colonel turned his head away to hide his triumphant grin. "Yeah? What was he like?"

"Young.   Handsome.   Pleasant. And . . ."

"And what?"

"I suppose he's nervous from having been in a foreign prison."

Samantha didn't notice the grim look that came over the face of the man beside her as he said, "Yeah. I can understand that," and rubbed absently at a thick scar on his left wrist.

"He's terribly dependent on Brenda for moral support, poor boy. He keeps his eyes glued to her. As if somehow she's his lifeline."

"That can happen when you first get out and back to the real world."

"The real world? I can't imagine a world much more real than a foreign prison."

"You've got a point. Ours are more like country clubs by comparison. A helluva lot more like country clubs."

They turned the corner onto Samantha's street. She looked at the strained expression on his face and found herself saying, "Why don't you come in? I've made a pitcher of iced tea."

"'The house wine of the South'."

"Yes. It is rather like that isn't it?" She smiled up at him. "Now where did *you* learn that?"

"How do you know I'm not a Southern boy?"

She laughed in his face. "Chicago. No doubt about it."

He conceded it with a wry smile as they walked up her driveway. "Dolly Parton told me." The wry smile turned into a grin. "In *Steel Magnolias*."

"That's right. I'd forgotten. She said it when she was serving iced tea at the fair. That movie certainly developed a following quickly."

"Yep."

Samantha pulled her door key out of her pocket.

Snarling fury erupted as the door opened. Rags attacked. Flying out the instant Samantha opened the door he grabbed the cuff of McLain's pant leg and shook it, growling fiercely. McLain looked down and snarled back, "Knock it off!"

Samantha stooped and snatched the little dog up, disengaging him from the khaki fabric of McLain's trouser leg by wiggling a fingernail between the dog's teeth. "Stop it, Rags! That's enough!"

"Too damned much if you ask me. What ails the blasted dust mop?"

Samantha straightened and glared at him. "He's protecting me."

"Ha!" He meant it as an expression of disbelief, but the thought of the six pound clump of hair defending anybody got the best of him. He roared with laughter.

Samantha was determined to ignore his rudeness to her pet. It *was* time that Rags understood McLain was a friend, after all. Samantha might wish him anywhere but here, but he *had* done some very thoughtful things for her. She gave the little terrier a shake and scolded, "Friend, Rags. Colonel McLain is a friend."

Rags looked at her with narrowed eyes. "Friend," she repeated firmly.

Rags slanted a look at the tall man. One lip lifted. A low growl emanated from his tiny frame. Rags was percolating again.

"Doesn't look like he agrees with you, Sam."

She took a breath to scold McLain this time. How many times did she have to tell him she hated being called Sam? Maybe she'd *let* Rags bite him.

"Maybe that's it," McLain said, his own eyes narrowing in thought.

"What's it?"

"The fact that you don't feel very friendly yourself where I'm concerned."

"I . . ." she began hotly, only to trail off as she realized he was right. ". . . will get the tea." She turned away, leaving him to seat himself at her kitchen table and busied herself getting their iced tea. When she had two tall glasses chock-full of ice and brimming with sun-brewed sweet tea she said, "All right. You may have a point."

McLain opened his mouth to blast the moderation of her statement, then shut it firmly.

Samantha put the glasses in place on the table, gave him a brightly colored linen napkin and sat down across from him. "All right," she repeated. "I'll try not to let you annoy me."

The Colonel's eyebrows shot up, he opened his mouth, then closed it again. When he spoke, it was with quiet calm. "Thank you." Samantha could barely hear his teeth click together at the end of his two word sentence.

"Now." Samantha spoke into the silence between them. "Tell me what you're writing on your computer."

"I'm writing a history of the Corps."

"How nice. What are you calling it?"

"*America's Finest Fighting Men: The United States Marines.*" His gaze held hers, warning her to be careful.

She was. Quietly she said, "That's quite an undertaking. It will keep you busy for a long time."

"Yep," he agreed briskly. Then, eyes steady, he added quietly, "In the meantime, though, I intend to catch this vandal and to find out if he's responsible for the death of your friend."

Chapter Fifteen

The lovely sunny promise of the morning had disappeared, and now a steady drizzle fell from lowering skies. With a sigh, Samantha attempted to make the best of a damp situation. "A good day to be indoors, at least, isn't it?" she asked her small companion. "Good thing I made my Commissary run yesterday."

She rushed to put the finishing touches on the card tables. The Bridge Club would start arriving any minute now. "Where did the week go, Rags? Honestly, time seems to rush past like an express train."

"Yap." Rags ran and jumped up on one of the wing chairs, turned three circles and settled down.

"You know you'll have to get into your box."

"Errr."

"Don't growl at me. You can bet your best plush chew toy that I can stand your disapproval a lot easier than I can handle Agnes's comments if she finds you running loose and 'scattering dog hair everywhere'."

Rags dropped his muzzle to his paws and did his best to look pitiful.

"Stop that. It won't work."

"Yurpf." He jumped to the floor. With measured tread and immense dignity, the Yorkshire made his way past his owner and into the kitchen. With a huge sigh, he plopped down in his box.

Even over her own movements, Samantha could hear his tiny body slam down on the floor of his roomy airline kennel. She hadn't time to feel guilty, however. Today was her day to host the Bridge Club. She gave her preparations a last glance.

The queen-size card tables cut across the center of her spacious living room, the dining room table held a tempting selection of goodies, and two silver-plated electric urns showed the red lights that proclaimed that both the coffee and the hot water for tea were set to go. Sugar, the creamer waiting for the actual cream to be poured into it at the last minute, and a really nice selection of tea bags were there. All was in readiness. It was safe to go change.

Half an hour later, Samantha was pushing her fingers through hair still damp from her shower as she rushed to answer the first ring of the door chimes. Olivia Charles's cousin was standing on the doorstep lowering her umbrella. "Janet. How nice that you could play today."

"Thank you." Janet Wilson's smile was tinged with sadness. "But I just hate the fact that losing Olivia is what makes room for me to play." Tears filled her eyes. "She was so much more to me than a cousin. She looked after me, you know."

Samantha took a deep breath and put her hand on her guest's arm praying for the right words to put the girl at ease. In a society suffering from a surfeit of words, why did the right ones have to be so hard to find? "Life goes on, Janet," she said softly. "And we go on with it. It's difficult and unfair and even horrible sometimes, but it doesn't stop just because we're grieving."

She took a deep breath and continued even more gently. "Please don't feel you're taking Olivia's place, dear. Nobody could replace her with us anymore than they could with you. But now, you're going to play Bridge with us, and we are glad to have you here. In your very *own* place."

Janet put her own hand over Samantha's and gave it a little squeeze. "Thank you, I . . ."

The door chimes interrupted whatever Janet had been going to say. The door swung open an instant later and Laura Fulton and Anne Stuart came in together, Anne crying, "Knock, knock!"

Agnes Chamberlain was behind them on the porch, Emilee Twiford was halfway up the walkway, and beyond them, Samantha could see Tyler Brokenborough just parking her car. Behind her several other members of the group hurried through the gentle rain. 'The girls' were gathering.

Brenda Talley called from where she was locking her newly acquired Lexus, "Hello everybody!" She laughed. "You all look like a drab flock of khaki-clad pouter pigeons. See me! Here comes a red bird!" She pirouetted to show off her bright red, hooded raincoat.

Samantha laughed, "That's Cardinal, Brenda. We call them Cardinals here in Virginia, not red birds."

"And we'll just have to call *you* Little Red Riding Hood if you dare call us khaki-clad pouter pigeons ever again, Brenda Talley." Laura was pretending to frown at the woman in the red raincoat.

Brenda pushed her way in and kissed the air beside her cheek. "Don't frown, Laurie. It makes wrinkles." She slipped out of her coat and Samantha took it. "Everything looks beautiful, Samantha."

"Thanks." Samantha headed for the bedroom to put the four coats she'd collected on her bed. There'd be too many to hang in the guest closet. By the time she got back, the entire Bridge Club had arrived. Laura passed her carrying the rest of their coats back to Samantha's bedroom.

As Samantha re-entered the living room, she decided it was time to make an announcement about their Bridge partner. She smiled brightly around at them. "Did all of you know that Emilee is going to move to one of Alison's condominiums?"

Brenda Talley's lips tightened.   It irritated her that everyone there thought of the elegant condominiums as Alison's condominiums just because Laura's niece was chief salesperson there.

Only Brenda, whose husband had gone to great lengths and considerable financial strain to build those condos, frowned at them being called Alison's. Her husband's straitened financial condition had resulted in the curtailment of her shopping trips to Richmond and to Tyson's Corner and all the outlet malls near D.C. and she resented it.

Nobody   noticed   Brenda's   frown, however. Everybody was too excited for Emilee. Delighted cries rang throughout the room.

"Oh, what wonderful news." Laura was the first to comment.

"No! You don't mean it," came from Anne Stuart.

"Oh,   Emilee,   how   nice."   Tyler Brokenborough was all smiles.

"It's about time you got rid of that albatross of a house. If you'd kept it hanging around your neck much longer, it would have been the death of you." This last was from Agnes, and for once

Samantha wholeheartedly agreed with her.

Emilee sat and beamed, her hands tightly clasped in her lap to keep them from flying around to express her happiness. "Yes, it *is* wonderful, isn't it? Brenda's Herb got me a very good price for my place, and Alison sold me a delightful condominium. A corner one. With room for a small garden."

Brenda's displeasure dissipated to see that everyone took for granted Herb's involvement with the sale of Emilee's house. Fiercely possessive of her handsome mate, she basked in any praise of his abilities.

Emilee wiggled in her seat like a happy puppy. "And it was all Samantha's idea." Instantly, everybody turned to her benefactress. "Oh, good for you, Samantha."

Samantha calmly accepted their compliments for having thought of the condos for Emilee. She only regretted that she hadn't thought of them earlier.

Everyone returned to their seats, smiling. With all the bad news they'd had lately, they were especially joyous to have this bit of good.

Agnes Chamberlain broke into their happy murmuring to announce, "I hope you've made your apricot pound cake, Samantha. Bridge at your house wouldn't be worth the trouble without it."

Samantha burst out laughing. "Agnes, I'm glad you like my pound cake so much." It would do no good to hint that Agnes might have left off her second comment.

Everyone agreed that Agnes Chamberlain was hardly the soul of tact. It was no secret that Agnes had long ago decided that tact was a waste of her time.

Anne Stuart couldn't resist. "As for me, I hope you *haven't* made your apricot pound cake." She glanced down at her voluptuous figure. "You know I can't resist it, and if I gain one more ounce I won't be able to get into this dress."

Agnes took this as a direct attack on her chance for apricot pound cake, bristled and retaliated. "Well, I don't see why that has to interfere with *my* enjoyment of dessert." She lifted her chin and delivered the *coup de grace*. "Next time buy your dress in a size that fits you."

"Agnes!" Samantha almost shouted. "Don't worry about a thing." She put a firm hand on Anne's shoulder and shoved her back down in her chair. "I *did* make apricot pound cake!"

From her place at the farthest table, Brenda Talley hooted with laughter.

Tyler Brokenborough, always intimidated by Agnes and fearful that the impossible was going to happen and an actual fight between Anne and Agnes break out, tried hard to find something to distract them. "Oh, dear," she called out in a tremulous voice, "I've broken a nail."

She held the finger up for them to see. Everyone jumped on the silly diversion with little murmurs of sympathy, but it was Janet who saved the day. She said, "Here, I always carry a nail kit in my purse." She dug for it and handed a small leather case to Tyler. "It has all you'll need. File, scissors, the works."

Smiling broadly, Tyler thanked her and took it. Battle had been averted.

Samantha took a deep, relieved breath and said, "Ladies! It's past time to start. Please, let's play Bridge!"

***

When the others had left, Laura Fulton wiped tears of merriment from her eyes.

"I thought you were going to actually leap on Agnes when you shouted, I *did* make apricot pound cake!"

Samantha chuckled. "I wanted to, but I had all I could do to hold Anne in her chair. She was the one who was about to do the leaping on Agnes."

They both sat smiling for a while, companionably sipping their tea. Then Laura said, "Did you notice that Anne ate the strawberries you'd fixed for the diet conscious among us . . . *and* the apricot pound cake."

Samantha opened her eyes wide under lifted brows and refused to comment. An instant later they were both laughing again.

Nothing was really that funny, but they needed laughter to release the awful tension of the last few days. When their laughter died down, things were a little more in proportion.

Samantha wiped the corners of her eyes with her napkin, and said quietly, "You know, we're certainly a diverse group. It's a wonder we get along as well as we do."

"Yes, it is." Laura sipped her tea. After a moment she said, "Janet Wilson fitted right in, didn't she?"

"Well, she always has, the few times she's subbed."

"Yes, but you know people change sometimes when they become regulars." Laura twined two fingers in the hair beside her right cheek.

"It was sweet of 'the girls' to ask her to be a regular so soon. I suppose it had a lot to do with . . ." It was still hard for Samantha to talk about Olivia's death. ". . . her loss of her cousin."

Laura twisted her hair. "Yes. That's got to be difficult for her. Olivia was the one who brought her here, and who got her the job with Herb Talley at Greater Tidewater Realty, too. It's no wonder she's a little quiet just now."

Samantha took a sip of tea.

"Several of 'the girls' remarked on how friendly and easy to get along with she was. She seems to be fitting in without any effort." Laura grimaced. "I guess we're lucky Janet survived Brenda. Poor Olivia almost didn't when she got Herb to agree to hire Janet. Remember? I thought Brenda was going to wring Olivia's neck over that. She didn't like having such a pretty young woman come into the office to be near her precious Herb one little bit." She sighed. "Brenda's so darned possessive of him. She was pretty cool to Olivia for quite a while as a result."

"I'm certain she's sorry now." Samantha refused to give in to the sadness that came over her.

"Yes, I'm sure she is. Brenda may be a little hard, but she's not totally without feelings."

"Hard?" Samantha gave that a moment's thought. "Yes, I suppose that does describe her. Has she always been?"

"She was certainly tough when Herb was just starting out. She got listings for him by absolutely refusing to take 'no' for an answer. She was the driving force that built that brokerage."

Samantha smiled. "Really? I wasn't here then. They were well established and quite successful by the time Andrew bought our property through them. But I can see how it would be. Herb was the charmer, Brenda was the sledgehammer?"

"Yeah, and it worked." Laura looked into her empty tea cup.

"And very well, too. They're doing fine now."

"Yes, and Herb just paid a fortune to build the condos Alison is selling, so they must be even more successful than we thought."

"I don't know, Laurie. Brenda gripes about not being able to whiz up to D.C. to shop at her favorite places as much as she used to." She looked at her friend's empty cup. "Want some more tea?"

"No, thanks." Laura sighed, got up and went to put her tea cup on the counter beside the sink. "Alison's due home any time now, and she's been a little depressed lately. I'd better be there for her."

Samantha sat up straighter. "It's not like Alison to be depressed." Samantha's voice held a note of concern. "Let me know if there's anything I can do."

"Don't worry, I will. She listens to you." Laura sighed again.

Samantha interpreted the sigh. "That's because you've always been like a mother to her, you know. Sad to say, at Alison's age, nobody listens to their mother. If you think she needs to talk, and you'd like to, just send her over. I can't imagine that she's holding back anything from you, though."

"Okay. I will. Maybe she's just tired. That ghastly man she was dating—that Randal Hale—seems to have fallen by the wayside, so she isn't keeping late hours. I haven't a clue what's wrong between them. If anything. I'm just glad he's gone." She moved through the kitchen. "Thanks for the tea." With a flip of her hand, Laura disappeared out the kitchen door.

Samantha got up, let a resentful Rags out of his box, and went to find her apron. It was one of the rules of the Bridge Club that the hostess must refuse all offers of help from the players. It was a good rule. It cleared the decks for the hostess to clean up as she pleased, and to take care of any family duties. It also got 'the girls' home in time to cook a decent supper for their own families and thus avoid having to drop out of the group because of husbandly discontent.

Samantha thought about that as she tied her apron strings. Husbandly discontent. Even with all the advances made by the feminist movement, it still existed. Hmmmmm. There were worse things, she decided, than being a widow.

She was up to her elbows in soap

suds—never would she trust her fine china to the dishwasher, no matter what the manufacturer said about the gentle cycle—when the phone rang. Quickly she wiped her hands.

"Hello?"

"Sam." It was the Dratted Colonel, of course. Nobody else was rude enough to call her Sam. "We need to get together and make some plans."

"About catching the vandal?"

"Absolutely."

"Very well. When would you like to meet?"

"How about now?"

"Colonel McLain. It's supper time."

"So?"

"So I'm going to eat supper before I meet with you."

"Hey. How about going out to eat? Do you like Chinese?"

Samantha was hesitant. Why did he have to say Chinese? If only he hadn't said Chinese. She didn't want to encourage this man to think of her as anything but a neighbor. She certainly had no desire to graduate to dinner partner—even if she was an absolute pushover for Chinese food. But she had, after all, insisted that she was going to be part of the plot to catch whomever was ruining gardens.

It mattered even more, now that the situation had escalated far beyond mere vandalism. Now it was murder. Olivia Charles had been *murdered*. That opened the door for a lot of questions. Was Olivia's death tied to the murder of the stranger that the police didn't seem to be making any headway with? Or was Olivia's murder tied to the vandalism they'd been experiencing.

Now that there was the distinct possibility that the same person who had been vandalizing the gardens of Riverhaven had been seen by Olivia and she had consequently been killed by him, there was no way she was going to chicken out. She was more determined than ever to catch the vandal if by doing so she could bring to justice Olivia Charles's murderer.

"Come on, Sam! What's the holdup? Will you go or won't you? I know a great little Chinese restaurant out where Chesapeake and Portsmouth run together. The drive'll give us time to talk."

"Give me fifteen minutes."

"Be sure to cage the mutt."

As if she'd forget to do so. She always put Rags in his airy indoor kennel when she left the house for any length of time. That way, if a fire should break out, the firemen knew exactly where to find him. Every Christmas, she took a big plate of cookies to the station house and when she did, she never failed to remind the firemen there of just exactly where Rags would be found and to impress upon them that he must be saved.

"Does Rags make you nervous, Colonel?"

"Yeah. I'm wearing good slacks."

"All right. I'll put him in his kennel." From the floor at her feet, Rags began to percolate. She'd said the 'k' word.

As if he could hear the little dog, the Colonel said, "Don't forget to padlock it."

Chapter Sixteen

Samantha absolutely loved Chinese food. She rarely got to eat it because she hated to go out alone for dinner. Laura, with whom she usually went out whenever Laura's pilot husband Bob was away, was certain that all Chinese cuisine was loaded with monosodium glutamate and wouldn't touch it. It had therefore been a real treat tonight to eat Broccoli Beef, Pepper Steak and Cashew Chicken to her heart's content.

Dinner had been wonderful. On the drive home, Samantha was fairly content with the Dratted Colonel. Until he drove into the oncoming lane.

"Well, that's the list. I . . . Ooooh!" Samantha cringed back into the expensive leather bucket seat as McLain swerved back into the right lane. The red Mustang he'd almost met head-on flew past with a blare of its horn. "Will you *please* be careful!"

"Had to get around that old fart in the Lincoln. He was five miles under the speed limit."

"Kindly watch your language! And, for your information, that man was a full decade younger than either one of us, Colonel McLain."

"Well if he's so damn young, he ought not to drive like an old fart."

Samantha clamped her lips together and ignored him. Such behavior on a multiple-laned thoroughfare was beyond her comprehension. What was *not* beyond her comprehension was the fact that Colonel John Francis McLain enjoyed shocking her.

She thrust the list she been going to go over with him back into her purse and sat looking resolutely ahead. Time for a little payback.

McLain zipped off Interstate 64 right after Forest Lawn Cemetery, and they were all the way down Terminal Boulevard to Naval Station Norfolk before he said,

"You wanna go over to her house and run all this by your friend Laura?"

"It's late."

"Now you're being picky. It's not even eight-thirty yet."

"It will be by the time we get there."

"Naw." He shoved the gas petal down and the Jaguar growled as it leapt forward. "We'll make it in plenty of time. Even prissy ladies like you don't mind calls before nine."

"That's telephone calls, not personal appearances."

"It's all the same. Ms. Fulton's a class act. She won't mind."

He wove in and out of traffic until he was at the head of the pack waiting for the signal light at Sewell's Point Road to turn green, revving his engine impatiently.

"Will you stop that! You act like a teenager trying to race off a stoplight."

"Yeah, I do, don't I?" He grinned at her. "I've always found that being first off the light gets me ahead for the next one. Do it enough, and you can make pretty good time—for being in town."

"This fine car is wasted on you, Colonel," Samantha said scathingly. "You should have gotten one of the little ones that everyone expects to zip around like a water bug."

"Thanks for the suggestion. Maybe I will get one."

He made the turn into Riverhaven with tires screeching and shot down the slight hill past the Yacht and Country Club.

"I wish you'd slow down. There are children and pets in this neighborhood, you know."

"Leash law."

"*Not* for children."

"More's the pity. Besides, by this time of night they're all in bed."

He whipped around the dogleg past her house, braked on the last of the asphalt and entered Laura Fulton's gravel drive with care.

Samantha muttered, "Well. Nice to know you can be considerate about something."

"What's that?"

"Nothing."

"Do you mutter a lot, Sam?"

"Never before I met you. And do *not* call me Sam."

"Don't get surly, now, Sam."

He let the car roll to a stop and set the brake. "Lights are on downstairs, and they already have company." He nodded toward a dark car parked a little further on.

"Maybe we shouldn't intrude."

"Why? Haven't you ever heard 'the more the merrier'?" He was already out of his side and coming to open her door.

Before Samantha got out of the Jaguar, Laura swung her front door wide. "Samantha! Colonel McLain. I thought I heard a car. Come on in."

Samantha wondered why Laurie was so glad to see them. Her tone of voice made them seem like a rescue mission. Whoever her company was, wasn't she enjoying them? Walking sedately into the living room, Samantha hid her burning curiosity to see whom she'd find there.

Janet Wilson sat in one of the wing chairs bordering the fireplace. She shot to her feet as they walked in. "I should be going."

"Oh, no. Please don't let us chase you off." Samantha smiled warmly.

Laura put in, "Do sit back down, Janet, it's early yet." She gestured toward the sofa the bulk of which marked off the conversational grouping there at the fireplace. "Won't you and the Colonel sit there, Samantha? Then we'll all be close."

Considering the cavernous size of Laura's living room, the suggestion was a sensible one. Samantha sat, and McLain folded his length down beside her on the opposite end of the couch.

When all the fuss of who wanted coffee, who wanted tea, and would the Colonel prefer a Bourbon? Whiskey? Scotch? was over, Laura looked straight at McLain and added the final enticement, "I have Wild Turkey, if you'd like some."

"Coffee'll be fine, thanks."

While Laura went about playing perfect hostess, Samantha noted that McLain was watching Janet Wilson with a great deal of interest. Good. She was certainly a lovely young woman. Blonde and beautiful, perhaps she'd engage the ex-Marine's interest long enough for Samantha to get on with her plans for the entrapment of the vandal without him. She could only hope!

"The Colonel and I have made up a list of all the neighbors who might be of assistance in trapping our vandal . . ."

There was a slight noise in the foyer, and Alison stood in the archway between it and the vast living room. She peeked in hesitantly. "Am I interrupting anything?"

"No, dear, of course not." Laura and Samantha spoke in unison. All of them laughed and Alison came just into the room.

Samantha looked at Laura. Laura deferred to her with a wave of her hand, and Samantha began explaining. "We're making plans to catch the vandal. Damaging the gardens was bad of him. But now the possibility arises that he may have . . . may have . . ." Samantha couldn't finish her sentence. Not with Olivia Charles's cousin sitting there so quietly.

"Please." Janet's voice was husky with repressed sorrow. "Don't let my presence matter. I am as anxious to hear your plans as any one of you."

Of course she was. Samantha should have known that Janet wouldn't rest until she'd found out who'd killed her cousin. Hadn't Olivia been the one to bring Janet to Norfolk to work? Persuaded Herb Talley to hire her for Greater Tidewater Realty? And hadn't Olivia often said that she had been Janet's 'keeper' almost all the younger woman's life? Looking at Janet's strained face and the way her hands twisted in her lap, Samantha could easily understand that protective attitude in her late friend.

Poor Janet. If Samantha felt bereft at the loss of Olivia Charles, what must Janet Wilson feel?

McLain said, "Come on in, Alison."

After an instant's hesitation, Alison crossed the room and curled up in a chair just out of their circle. Laura queried her with a raised eyebrow then handed her a cup of tea with two sugars.

Alison smiled her thanks.

Samantha took her notebook out of her handbag again. "Colonel McLain and I have made a list of all the neighbors we think could help us trap the vandal."

Alison's tea cup rattled in its saucer. She steadied it with her other hand as she placed it on the table beside her chair.

McLain turned to smile at her. He received a small nervous smile in return.

Samantha sighed. Everybody was uptight just now. She was, too. "We decided that the best idea was to choose women living alone who had couples on either side who would be willing to take turns watching the woman who is alone's garden." She frowned at the way her sentence sounded, gave it up and went on. "Standing watches, the Colonel calls it—in order to call the police in the event that the vandal shows up."

"The Colonel is going to ask the police to please have a unit—that's a police car—near Riverhaven at all times. Those of our neighbors who possess firearms will hold the vandal until the police can arrive."

"What if he strikes where there isn't a gun owner?" Laura wanted to know.

"That *is* a problem. Guns have become so unpopular lately."

The Colonel interrupted with, "Yeah. In spite of the FBI statistics that clearly prove that the more gun permits there are in a given area, the less crime there is in it."

Samantha couldn't help it. Even knowing that decent people having gun permits lowered crime rates, Samantha didn't like guns. She had to struggle to be fair when the subject came up.

Amusement in his eyes, McLain went to her rescue and changed the subject. His voice rumbled, "Of course, we may have seen the last of the vandal now that he's committed murder."

"That's true." Laura wrapped her arms

around herself.

Alison shuddered.

Samantha tore a sheet out of her little notebook. "Here." She handed the paper to Laura. "I've divided the list between the two of us, giving each of us the people we know best. Though there are a couple on it that neither of us knows at all yet. I'm sure they'll want to help anyway, don't you think?"

"Of course they will." Laura was certain of it. "It's their neighborhood, too."

McLain said, "They'd be damned poor neighbors if they didn't." He chuckled. "And I bet between you and Ms. Prissy, they'd be made pretty miserable if they didn't help."

Laura looked at him blankly. "Mrs. Prissy?"

Samantha glared at the Colonel, then turned back to inform her hostess, "Colonel McLain finds humor in being insulting. He calls me prim, proper and prissy."

"Oh," Alison cried, "I don't think you're prim or prissy at all."

Samantha threw a smug look at McLain. "Thank you, Alison."

McLain muttered, "She didn't say you

weren't proper."

Samantha turned back to Laura, ignoring him. "Anyway, you call your list tomorrow and I'll call mine. We probably won't be able to get everybody the first day, so let's give it two. Then we'll set the trap and hopefully catch our culprit."

"All right." Laura was twisting a strand of her hair. "There are no meetings on my schedule for tomorrow, and the evening is free to call the ones who work or play golf."

"Doesn't look as if they'll be playing much golf tomorrow." McLain nodded toward the two large windows at the end of the room. A flash of lightning shot across the sky. An instant later they heard the crash of thunder. In the next flash they could make out broad ribbons of rain falling from not-too-distant clouds across the river, then all the panes were black again.

"Oh, dear." Samantha placed her tea cup carefully on the tea tray as she rose. "I have to get home and take Rags out before that storm gets here!" She turned to McLain. "I can walk home, Colonel. Don't disturb yourself."

"Fat chance I'd let you." He rose. "Thanks for the coffee Ms. Fulton."

"Laura." She smiled warmly at him. "Please call me Laura."

"Thank you. I'm John."

"And *I'm* in a hurry," Samantha interjected. "If you are going to insist that I wait until you drive me home, please come now. I don't want to get drenched seeing to my dog!"

"Samantha! Behave." Laura shook her head apologetically at her male guest. "She's usually lovely, you know."

McLain threw her a look that told her what he thought of *that* statement.

"Really," Laura insisted.

"I know." He relented. "I just rub her the wrong way."

"*Will* you come on!" Samantha was half way to the door.

Just to aggravate her he turned to Janet Wilson and offered, "Would you like me to walk you to your car, Ms. Wilson?"

"No. No, thank you. I'll be fine. I'm leaving with you anyway. Thank you so much for the tea, Mrs. Fulton. And for the talk. I feel so much better, knowing what's being done." She moved toward the foyer gracefully, passing Samantha.

Samantha stomped along behind her,

passed her and ripped open the door. "Goodnight, Alison, Laura. Thanks for the tea." She didn't speak to McLain until he had opened the car door for her in her own driveway. Ignoring the hand he offered to help her out, she said, "Thank you for bringing me home, and thank you very much for dinner."

Suddenly she realized how surly she was being. She sighed, trapped by 'proper behavior' again. "And thank you for helping with the vandal list," she said with more warmth.

He raised an eyebrow. "Yeah," he told her generously, "No problem." With that, he got into his car and drove off.

Samantha watched him hesitate in the street until she got her door open and waved. She watched him start away as she closed her door. Then she called, "Rags. I'm home."

There was a welcoming "Yap!" Then the little terrier began digging frantically at the bars of his kennel door, desperate to get to her.

Samantha let him out, swooped him up to give him a quick hug and put him down again. His toenails clicked across the kitchen vinyl. "Ruf!"

"I know, I know. Don't scold. I didn't mean to be so late. Just let me change my shoes." She kicked off her good pumps and slipped into the loafers she'd left for that purpose. Pocketing her keys, she plopped her purse in a kitchen chair and started to open the door again.

"Yap!" The Yorkshire sat.

"Don't you want to go out?"

The terrier started down the hall, looking back over his shoulder.

"Rags. Come back here. It's going to rain, we have to hurry."

Reluctant, he stopped and looked toward her bedroom. Then he sat and looked at her.

"No, you don't want to go to bed. You want to go out first."

Rags looked at her with an expression Samantha could only interpret as scornful. Taking charge, she told him, "Come on. You have to make your last duty call. Fool dog. I won't let you get wet. Come on!"

With a last, low growl toward the other end of the house, Rags rose, sighed, and followed as his mistress commanded.

Chapter Seventeen

A quarter of an hour later, Rags and Samantha were in the house to stay at last. Thank heavens! Samantha couldn't believe that she had been Bridge hostess only that afternoon. "It's been a long day, Rags." She smiled down at her tiny companion. "I'm weary."

Surprised at the discovery, she made an extra effort to straighten her shoulders. In her head, she could hear her mother's gentle voice. *Ladies do not beg the world for sympathy by exhibiting their weaknesses, Samantha. Never Slump.*

"Yes," she muttered, "but I don't see why that has to apply to my *dog*."

Rags looked up at her and yapped.

Samantha burst out laughing. "Great Scott. I *am* tired, Rags. Sleepy, too. Let's get to bed."

At the mention of bed, Rags ran ahead. Instead of leading the way into her room, however, he stood across the threshold of the bedroom as if to bar her entry. "Grrrrr."

Samantha halted in astonishment. "What in the world's the matter, Rags?" She bent and scooped him up.

The phone rang. Moving to the bedside table with the squirming Yorkie under her arm, she lifted the receiver. "Hello?"

Rags squirmed even harder to be free. "Yap. Yap!" He threw his head back and forth in a determined effort to gain his freedom. With a mighty shove of his hind legs against her hip bone, he flew out of her arms onto the bedspread in the middle of the bed.

Braking his forward momentum by digging his front claws into the spread, he backed to the foot of the bed so fast he would have fallen off the end if it hadn't been for the quilt rail at the bottom of the four poster. As he backed away from the pillows, his outcry became all the more fierce.

"Hush, Rags! I can't hear!"

Rags stopped barking and settled into his on-going, low growl. His bright button eyes swiveled from her face to the head of her bed frantically.

"Oh, hi, Laurie. Yes, I *was* wondering what Janet Wilson was doing over there. Is she finally trying to make friends in the neighborhood?" Rags wouldn't let Samantha sit on the edge of the bed—he kept darting at her and snarling—so she gave up, went to the slipper chair and sat to take her shoes off.

"At least she's facing her loss. That's healthy. And it's nice she's taking such an interest in catching the vandal. We need everyone to be interested, and it should help keep her mind off her loss." She reached down and pulled off a shoe. "Of course, I wanted to talk to you about what you thought Lieutenant Nichols would think of what we're trying to do, but I couldn't in front of Janet. It would have reminded her about Olivia."

"What?" She'd missed Laura's last remark. Rags was barking again. Samantha was afraid he'd wake the neighbors. "Heavens!" She turned to him and said, "Rags, be quiet! I'm afraid you'll wake the *dead!* Hush!" She reached for him. Her fingers only brushed his taut little frame.

Rags kept up his clamor as he evaded her. "Yip, yip! Grrrrr! Yap! Yap! Yap!"

"Oh, for Pete's sake, Rags, pipe down! Hang on, Laurie. I don't know what his problem is, but I can't hear a word you're saying. He'll calm down in a minute, I'm sure." She reached for the edge of the bedspread to flip it down to fold away as she chatted. She wanted to get to the serious business of sleeping as soon as she and Laura had finished catching up.

Rags darted at her wrist and slammed into it with his bared teeth.

"Rags!" Had he lost his little mind? She rubbed her wrist as her mind flew to the plants in her garden that he might have nibbled. She knew darn well she didn't have any loco weed. No, nor anything like it. What was the matter with Rags? Taking a steadying breath, Samantha crooned, "There, there, darling," and reached for him.

As she did, she thought she saw the bedspread, where it stretched between her two pillows, stir. She froze.

Rags leapt into her arms.

Samantha caught him by sheer reflex.

The phone fell from her grasp. Samantha didn't even notice. Her gaze was riveted to the slight space between her two down-filled pillows. As she watched, she felt her eyes go as round as saucers.

A sleek head appeared over the edge of the spread. Triangular, smooth, black as death, it advanced, its tongue darting in and out of its mouth as it sensed the air, searching for the heat of any warm-blooded presence.

Samantha stared, anchored to the floor beside the bed by sheer horror, as the thick black body of the water moccasin slowly uncoiled from the space between her pillows. From between the pillows on which *she* would have lain her head by now if Rags hadn't been making such a fuss.

"SSSSnake!" Samantha screeched. "That's a snake!"

The receiver of her abused phone screamed from the flokati throw rug beside her bed as, "What snake?" Laurie screeched in her turn. "What's happening? Are you all right? Samantha! Hang on! I'm coming!"

Samantha rushed to her closet and

grabbed her umbrella. She knew the snake could find a place to hide if she went out of the room for a poker—a rake—a shovel—an *axe*!!!

Ohhhh, God! Why didn't she keep an axe in the house? In her bedroom!! She hated snakes! It was all she could do to tolerate the good black ones that kept the bad ones away! And this was a *bad* bad one.

Looking at the bulging poison sacks on either side of its head, she knew they were full of venom. The snake would probably kill her if she were bitten. Surely it would kill a little dog like Rags!

Rags was squirming to get down again. Barking furiously at this threat to his mistress, he was ready to sacrifice himself to save her.

Samantha tightened her grip on her friend. Beyond a shadow of a doubt, she knew his tiny frame would never survive an injection of so much venom.

Rags had to stop barking. Samantha had crushed him to her so hard, he couldn't get enough breath to go on.

Samantha brought the crooked handle of her favorite umbrella down on the snake.

Unaffected, it fixed its gaze on Samantha and began to coil into striking position. As it did, it hissed. Its jaws opened wide showing the white interior of its mouth, white as snow—Cotton Mouth, the Southern nickname for the water moccasin. And its fangs! Dear Lord, its fangs looked three inches long!

Samantha drew the umbrella back for another blow. Oh, why didn't she keep her gun handy? She didn't care if she did shoot a hole in her expensive queen-sized mattress. She didn't even care if she shot her solid cherry four-poster into kindling. All she cared about was killing that snake!

Rags began to gasp for breath.

The kitchen door slammed back against the wall so hard that Samantha could hear it all the way here on this side of the house. An instant later Laura Fulton ran into the room, the spare key to Samantha's house in one hand, the poker from her fireplace in the other. She began slamming the later into the snake.

Suddenly, "All right!" McLain's voice roared at them. "Stop that before you make a mess!" Without taking his eyes off the coiled snake, he told Samantha, "Let the dog breathe, Sam."

Samantha gave a startled look at her canine friend. He was limp! She eased her death grip, and saw the little hero desperately gulp air. Dropping her umbrella she shifted him to lie over her shoulder as if she wanted to burp him and patted air back into him.

Her attention, though, was all on the Colonel. Thank God he'd come! She was so thankful to see him that she didn't even wonder how he'd gotten here.

McLain was approaching the awful thing on her bed. With one hand, he commanded its attention by wiggling his fingers until the snake's cold gaze was locked on them. When it struck at that hand, the hand was no longer there. McLain's other moved in a blur.

"There." His voice was full of calm satisfaction. His hand was full of riled Cotton Mouth.

Laura and Samantha clung weakly to each other and looked away. Then both of them stared at the writhing snake McLain held so casually. It hissed and thrashed for all it was worth. McLain reached into his pocket for his Swiss Army knife, put it up to his mouth and opened the largest of its blades with his teeth. "Ms. Fulton, if you would be so kind as to open that door for me," he nodded to the French doors in the end wall of Samantha's bedroom, "I'll just take this little snake outside. I don't think you ladies want to see this." He raised the knife significantly. "Sam. You go make us a pot of coffee. We need to talk."

Neither of the women could think of anything to say. Neither of them could have found the breath to say it if they could have. Samantha didn't even mutter "Don't call me Sam!"

Laura, shaking like a leaf, opened the door for him.

Samantha went to make coffee.

Rags just kept breathing.

Chapter Eighteen

The windows rattled in their frames as thunder crashed on the heels of a bolt of lightning that lit Samantha's kitchen with garish blue light. An instant later the heavens opened, and rain drummed down blotting out all other sound.

Samantha ran to close the kitchen door. Laura and the Colonel had left it standing open in their haste to come to her rescue. Just as she reached it, the Colonel ducked in. One hand raked raindrops out of his hair. The other he held behind his back. "Got a plastic bag?"

"Certainly. What for?"

"Don't ask."

Samantha stopped rummaging for a bag for him. "You don't mean it's for that snake?" She already knew what it was for.

Where was he going to take it, and why?

"Sure I do. They're good eating."

"*That's repulsive!*" She quivered with indignation.

Laura came in. Not wanting to further upset her friend, she'd been hiding in the bathroom pretending to freshen up until she could stop shaking. "What are you yelling about, Samantha?"

The Colonel was tying a knot in the top of a heavy plastic bag from Samantha's favorite shoe store. "Mind if I put this in your refrigerator until I leave."

Samantha's mouth dropped open.

Laura, in total ignorance of the bag's contents, answered for her friend. "Of course she doesn't mind."

Samantha just stood trying to catch her breath and get her eyes back behind her eyelids.

Laura, mistaking her friend's explosive state for delayed shock over her close call with the water moccasin, told her, "You just sit down, dear, I'll fix the coffee."

Samantha went to the table, sat as she was told, and closed her eyes.

"Snap out of it, Sam. It won't hurt anything, and Frank will be forever in your debt. He loves 'em."

Laura asked, "Frank is your cook, isn't he?"

"Cook, valet, butler, chauffeur . . . you name it, that's Frank." He peered at Samantha. "Come on, Sam. We have a lot to talk about here." When she neither replied nor opened her eyes he asked, "You okay, Sam?"

At that, her eyes snapped open and shot daggers at him. "I am fine, thank you, Colonel McLain. I am just fine! I *always* keep water moccasins in my refrigerator!" Her voice held a note of hysteria.

McLain stepped a little back from her. Hysterical women made him nervous.

Laura left the coffee maker to do its job and joined them at the table. "What a silly thing to say, dear." She patted Samantha's hand. "You're just in shock. And who could blame you," she soothed. Her dark hair swung forward as she bent to peck Samantha on the cheek.

"Actually . . ." McLain began to confess.

"*Not a word!*" Samantha commanded, her eyes narrowed and blazing. She wasn't going to let him upset Laura. "*Not one more word!*"

"Okay, Sam. Don't get your knickers in a twis . . ."

"Be silent!" Both of the others could hear Samantha's teeth click together on the 't' at the end of the word. The Colonel was instantly silent, both eyebrows approaching his hairline. Gingerly, he sat down across from Samantha.

Laura looked from one to the other, her gaze bewildered.

Samantha sat breathing deeply and rhythmically. After a long moment, she said, "I'm all right, now. I'm all right. We can talk."

McLain appraised the calm voice and decided to accept her rigid control as normal behavior. Sheeeesh. So he put a little snake meat in her fridge. What did she want him to do, waste it? Women!

Outwardly, McLain curbed his disapproval of her peculiar attitude. Perhaps it was better that she was on her high horse anyway. There were far more important things to be concerned about, and the most important was the fact that somebody had obviously just tried to kill Samantha Masters.

"Listen, Sam . . . antha."

Samantha's head swiveled toward him. Had he really said her full name? Either she was more in shock than Laura thought or she was hallucinating. Eyes wide she asked, "Did you just call me 'Samantha'?" Her voice showed she was incredulous.

"Don't get used to it, lady."

"I didn't even *hope* it would last." She cocked her head, considering him a moment. "You must really be worried about me."

"Damn straight."

Samantha didn't even flinch at the profanity.

McLain shot a glance full of concern at Laura. "Laura?"

"Yes, John?"

"Would you take Samantha home with you tonight? I'd like to do a sweep of the house with Frank before I let her stay here again."

Samantha didn't even challenge the absurdity of his thinking that he had anything to say about where she stayed. It hadn't previously occurred to her there might be more than one water moccasin in the house.

One thing was certain, the mere

suggestion that there might be another snake made her extremely amenable to his suggestion that she spend the night elsewhere. She hadn't the foggiest intention of objecting to him bossing her around at this particular time. The idea that *he*, not she, would be the one to find any residual reptiles appealed to her too strongly.

Laura didn't notice. She just drew her sandaled feet up away from the floor and clasped her arms around her legs, her feet in the chair. Obviously, she hated even the idea that there might be more snakes.

"Not to worry," McLain told her. "The mutt's under the table."

Samantha shot him a poisonous look.

"Okay. The *hero* mutt's under the table."

Laura put her feet back on the floor. It was an extremely tentative movement.

"Look, you two. What we need to discuss is that this was an obvious attack on Sam."

There it was again—Sam. Samantha'd known it wouldn't last.

McLain watched her closely. "Can you think of any reason the vandal would want to harm you, now?"

Samantha shook her head. "No. No I can't."

Laura kept looking down at the floor under the table.

"I've talked to Lieutenant Nichols, and he said they haven't made a connection between the first murder and Mrs. Charles's murder. Maybe there isn't one, but I can't help feeling that there's got to be one between Olivia's murder, Jasmine's accident, and this attempt on your life."

"I might not have died."

"Lady, if you'd put your head on one of those pillows, you'd have died. Hit in the neck, the venom would have gone straight to your brain and you'd have shut down in a matter of minutes."

Laura gulped and turned pale.

"Oh, Rags." Samantha had only thought of how brave her little friend had been. Now the full realization hit her that without his intervention, she'd be dead. She bent to scoop him up.

Laura spoke sharply. "Just leave him on the floor right now, please. I'll buy him a big sirloin steak tomorrow. I promise. Just please don't move him from guarding my feet."

"Yeah, Sam. Leave him in case there's anything else here."

Laura burst out, "*That's* done it! Get your raincoat, Samantha. Any intelligent conversation you expect from me you're going to have to come to *my* house for. I'll lend you a nightgown and a toothbrush."

"Geeee, thanks." The Colonel couldn't resist.

"Not *you!*" Laura glared at him. "I was offering Samantha."

Samantha looked at her friend from under frowning eyebrows. "I'm not leaving Rags."

"Of course, you're not. Rags must come, too."

Samantha was speechless. Laura must really be upset. She'd never let Rags, whom she always referred to as a destructive little monster, into her perfectly appointed home if she weren't desperately concerned for his mistress's welfare. And maybe her own sandaled feet.

"Right! Sounds like a plan." McLain was approving. "Now let's get it in gear. We need to talk, then you two need to get a good night's sleep. It's time to stop playing with this damned vandal and get down to business." He opened the door and waved his hand. "Out!"

Samantha and Laura didn't need another invitation. Huddled together under Samantha's raincoat, they ran across the lawn to the gates of Laura's estate like Olympic sprinters. McLain loped along after them with the protesting Yorkshire terrier under one arm, his hand clamped around the dog's muzzle.

"Wow! That's really coming down." On Laura's side porch he shook his head and raindrops flew. "You girls all right?"

"Fine," they said in unison, stumbling together into Laura's brightly lit kitchen through the door Alison held open.

"Okay." He took Samantha's raincoat from them and snapped it vigorously outside the door to get most of the wet off.

"I'll take that." Alison, her eyes huge in a pale face, took it and went to hang it up.

"Quick thinking of you to ring me, Al," McLain called after her.

"I couldn't think of anything *but* calling you." The girl raised her voice as she moved toward the closet. "Every other thought flew right out of my head when Aunt Laura dashed out of the house with a poker in her hand shrieking 'I'm coming, Samantha!' I didn't know what the trouble was, but I knew *you'd* be able to fix it."

"Wasn't much. Just these two annoying the hell out of a water moccasin."

Alison reappeared as if by magic. "What!"

"Yeah," McLain was watching her carefully. "Somebody had put it in Mrs. Masters's bed."

Alison cried, "Oh, how awful! I should have gone!"

"Why?" he asked. "They were making it mad enough without your help."

Alison looked stricken. "That's *not* funny!"

"No," he admitted after a moment. "I don't guess there is much funny about this damned vandal. I apologize."

Alison looked close to tears. She went to Samantha. "I'm so sorry I didn't come, Aunt Samantha. I thought Aunt Laura was just being hysterical, and I pushed it off on the Colonel because I had an important telephone call to make."

"Well, thank you, Alison!" Laura was offended.

Samantha put an arm around the girl.

"It's all right, darling. Really, the only one of us who did any good was Colonel McLain. If you hadn't called him the whole thing would have gotten out of hand." She hugged her hard. "You did just the right thing. I'm grateful that you were here and that you thought of him. He took over and saved the day."

She began to smile. "Someday, when it is not so fresh in our minds that we can't get around our terror, remind me to tell you just what your aunt and I were doing when the Marines . . . Marine, singular . . . landed. A slapstick comedy has nothing on us!"

"I'll say." McLain tried to put the tense girl at ease. "If you ever need any bedclothes annihilated, call these two."

A giggle escaped her first, then Alison burst into tears and buried her head on her aunt's shoulder. "I'm just so g-glad you're both safe. It must have been h-horrible!"

Samantha, frowning slightly, left Alison crying it out with Laura to comfort her and went to pull out Laura's coffee maker. Lost in thought, she started making coffee. After a moment, she shook her head and put her mind back on her present chore.

There was already a pot of coffee made, she knew, fresh-brewed and sitting on her kitchen counter. So this one was an extravagance. Too bad. Wild horses couldn't have dragged her back across the street to get the coffee Laura had just made in *her* kitchen!

***

McLain left to go tell Lieutenant Nichols about what he called 'this latest development,' and the three women went to bed. Samantha was more somber than she had ever been in her life as she tucked herself into one of the twin beds in her friend's elegant guest room.

An attempt had been made on her life. Try as she might, she could hardly believe it. The proofs Colonel McLain had offered had been unarguable, however. She'd finally had to admit he was right. There was no way the snake could have gotten into her house without the help of a human being. Even the most talented reptile could hardly open a locked door.

There was nothing else to conclude. Colonel McLain had pointed out that someone in her Bridge group must have unlocked the outside French doors in her bedroom. They'd have done it when they went to one of her bathrooms, he'd said.

That man could be so indelicate!

Most of 'the girls' had gone to use one or the other of her bathrooms, of course. How could they not have with all the coffee they habitually drank as they played?

It was impossible to guess who might have unlocked the French doors to the bedroom patio, though. It was equally impossible to imagine any of them having done it. They were all her friends. Surely none of them wanted to harm her, much less *kill* her?

None-the-less, John Francis McLain had convinced her that the water moccasin could have gotten into her bed only if someone had re-entered her house and put it there. The odds against a snake placing itself under the bedspread in just the right location to strike at her unguarded throat were past astronomical.

Oh, Lord. That kind of evil transcended even a reptile's instincts.

She sighed, the sound oddly strangled by the tightness of her throat. She was tense all over. Horror gibbered at the edges of her mind.

More than anything, right now, she wanted to be able to refuse to face the fact that there had been someone in her house—her *home*—this very day who meant her harm. Someone who helped arrange things so that they, or maybe even someone else who had the intention of killing her, could gain access to her bedroom. Striving to deny it, she turned over and stared at the drapery-covered window.

Lightning flashed behind the damask covering the panes; thunder rumbled shortly after the flash. The storm was nearby and lingering.

Samantha's unsettling thoughts were lingering, too. Suppose it wasn't merely that someone who was present had unlocked the door? Someone who'd thought the person who'd asked her to do it had meant no harm? Or suppose, instead, that the very person who wished her ill had sat in her living room all afternoon smiling and playing Bridge? Samantha couldn't stop the shudder that went through her. And suppose that that person was a cold-blooded killer bent on *her* destruction.

Samantha turned again to face the

door of Laura's guest room. Hugging her sleeping terrier, she shivered. She didn't want to think about any of this, but unfortunately, McLain was right. Even though the four of them had sat up half this night trying to figure out a reason for the attack on her and been unable to do it, her life *was*, most definitely, in danger.

Her flesh crept at the thought. The back of her neck prickled as if there were danger behind her in this very room.

Resolutely, she turned her mind away from it. She thought instead about Alison. The girl had seemed so on edge. Her face had been truly pale, as if she were ill . . . or desperately afraid. What could possibly be the matter with her? She was usually such a happy girl. She . . .

Outside in the hall, a soft step sounded.

Samantha shot bolt upright. Then she sagged back into her pillows. Oh, really. How foolish! She was perfectly safe here. This was Laura's, and she knew how carefully Laura locked up at night. Whoever it was passed her door, of course.

Her every sense was stretched to the breaking point now, however. The slightest noise was amplified by her fear, and she heard Alison enter her Aunt Laura's room. Shortly thereafter, she heard the sound of someone beginning to weep.

Moments later, Alison Fulton was sobbing as if her heart would break.

Chapter Nineteen

The next morning broke sunny and clear, the landscape washed clean by the storm. Samantha refused breakfast at Laura's, and came home. Here she didn't have to worry that Rags might commit a doggy *faux pas*. Nor, thank heavens, did she have to eat the odd, grain-based things that Laura considered a healthy breakfast. Eggs, bacon and toast were a proper breakfast to Samantha, and devil take the cholesterol!

Now that the Colonel had assured her that he and Frank had gone over her house carefully and that there were absolutely no more snakes—or, for that matter, any kind of danger—Samantha wanted to be in her own home. Not that she wasn't grateful for the good night's sleep that she'd gotten at her friend's, for she was. Very grateful.

The idea of sleeping in her own familiar bed after finding that water moccasin in it had been unthinkable. Even with the bed stripped and remade, she knew that tonight it was going to take an act of courage to lie down on it.

When, just a little while ago, she'd looked into her bedroom and seen that some kind soul—obviously Frank Takamoto—had changed her sheets and her blanket, she'd been very much relieved.

By tonight, she imagined, she'd be able to go to sleep there without too much trouble, in spite of last night's ghastly experience. Once she'd forced herself to get into the bed it would be all right. She took a deep, steadying breath. And she'd do that only after she'd picked up her pillows—probably with a yardstick, or her faithful favorite umbrella—and inspected under them.

She got up to get a second cup of coffee and had just reached for the pot when the phone rang.

"Hello?"

"You must come right away, Samantha!" It was Laura, and she sounded more upset and insistent than Samantha had ever heard her. "I've already called Colonel McLain, and he's on his way over. Please hurry, I don't know how much more of this she can stand!" Laura hung up on a sob.

Samantha left her coffee sitting on the counter beside her coffee maker. She all but sailed her breakfast dishes into the sink full of soapy water in which the frying pan was soaking free of her scrambled eggs. Then she grabbed her door key and ran. Whatever the matter was, it must be pretty serious for Laura to have lost her habitual poise.

Samantha was in such a rush to get to her distressed friend that she didn't even notice what flowers were blooming along Laura's drive! Running all the way, she arrived completely out of breath.

"What . . . is it? What's . . . wrong?" she panted as she burst into the house. She stopped in mid-stride. "Art Chamberlain! What are you doing here?"

"Sit down before you fall down, Sam." McLain took her by the arm and started to lead her toward a chair. "I told you you needed to take me up on my offer to start you on a fitness program."

Samantha shook free, blew the hair out

of her eyes and glared at him.

McLain grinned back.

Laura, calm now that everybody'd arrived, took charge. "Thank you for coming so quickly, Samantha." She gave McLain a subduing look. "Suppose we all go into the living room. We need to be comfortable. Alison has something important to tell us."

Samantha shifted her gaze from Art Chamberlain to Alison. She studied the girl as the group made their way to chairs and sofas in front of Laura's living room fireplace. What she saw worried her.

Alison was even paler than she'd been the previous evening when they'd been discussing ways to stop the vandal before he could attempt another murder. Poor girl. Whatever had had her so upset last night when she'd gone to her aunt's room was certainly taking a terrible toll on her. As soon as everyone had settled, Samantha said, "Alison?," Her voice was full of the concern she was feeling for her precious young friend.

"I have something to tell you." The girl drew a quivering breath. "Something that I must tell you." Tears filled her eyes. "Aunt

Samantha, I'm the vandal." The words tumbled out. "It's me. I ruined your tulip tree, and I tore up Mrs. Twiford's garden, and the Hathaway's and Turner's before that. But I *meant* well," she pleaded for understanding. "Really, I truly did. My intentions were good. I thought that by tearing up her flowers, I'd help Miss Emilee decide to move."

She jumped up and looked wildly around at the others. "She couldn't go on with that huge old place much longer, she just couldn't. You all know that. She needed to go somewhere that wouldn't work her to death." She whirled to face her aunt. "And that time when you brought her to see me at my condos, she really yearned over them. Remember?"

"Yes, I do remember," Laura answered, "but . . ."

"There! You all know how it was. Miss Emilee was working herself to death . . . and she just drooled over the condos and how easy everything was in them. When I saw that, I just had to get her to decide to move. After I saw that she would love to have been in one of them, I simply couldn't stand the way she worked and worked and skimped all the time."

"So you played vandal," McLain said softly.

"Yes! I did." She faced him, her eyes defiant.

"I wondered. You were pretty upset the other night." He smiled at her gently. "I figured we were making you sorta nervous."

Samantha rounded angrily on McLain. "What other night? What *are* you talking about?"

"The night we came over with the list and found Janet Wilson here." McLain was talking more to give Alison time to calm down than to answer Samantha.

"Oh." Samantha subsided, thinking back. Alison *had* seemed nervous that night, but she hadn't connected it with the list she and the Colonel had made of neighbors who might help in their plans to catch the vandal. McLain had, though. Samantha frowned. She should have been more observant, more sensitive. After all, he wasn't as close to Alison as she was.

McLain prompted Alison. "So you took on the job of convincing her she'd be better off moving, and tore up a coupla gardens and hers. Then you vandalized your Aunt

Laura's greenhouse and tore up Sam's tulip tree to give more credence to the vandal idea after Miss Emilee's."

"Yes." Alison nodded vigorously. "And Mr. Chamberlain caught me." She flashed a shy smile at her elderly neighbor.

"Ah, yes," Art Chamberlain began tentatively, as if testing the water to see if anyone would listen to him before he went further. It was a habit that living with Agnes had fostered in him. "Yes, yes, I did see Alison. We rather bumped as I cut across your lawn, Samantha. Coming back from . . . er . . . my . . . hmmmm . . . errand at Laura's greenhouse, don't you see." His eyes begged the Colonel not to divulge the nature of his errand. "I was shocked, I can tell you. It was so unlike Alison to do such a thing, especially since she loves you. She was tearing blossoms and small branches from your tulip tree. I scolded her severely. I had to scold her in a whisper, of course.

"Even so, Rags began to bark, and then your outside spotlights came on and . . . Oh, dear, that gave me an awful start! I'd forgotten you had them—the lights, I mean— because you'd never turned them on before. They surprised Alison and me both."

"They certainly did!" Alison agreed. "Then we ran like rabbits when we heard your phone ring, Aunt Samantha."

"And then I told Alison that she must tell you, Mrs. Masters, and you, Mrs. Fulton, exactly what she had been doing, and why. I was very firm with her about owning up to what she'd done. I told her that I would be there for her if she needed me . . ."

Alison interrupted him. "That was the important phone call I had to make last night. I knew where Mr. Chamberlain had gone, and I had to tell him he had to come home right away."

Mr. Chamberlain smiled at her and continued as if she hadn't spoken, " . . . but that I was going to go visit a friend out of town until she had confessed." He looked around the intent circle of faces. "I had to get out of town, you see. At least until Alison had cleared the vandal matter up to her own satisfaction. It was the only thing to do, you know. Otherwise, Agnes would have seen something wasn't right with me." He sighed. "Agnes never misses a thing. She would have had Alison's secret out of me in an instant, and the fat would have been in the fire."

He looked around at them, his eyes begging them to see his reasoning. "You know how Agnes can be. I had to leave to give her time. Alison, I mean, not Agnes." He blinked at them. "You *do* see, don't you?"

Nobody said anything, they were all too busy absorbing the facts that the pair of accidental conspirators had just given them. Each of the listeners came to the same conclusion. It was obvious. The expressions on their faces showed they were all in agreement.

Things were much worse than ever before now.

For if Alison had been the vandal . . . then *who* was the murderer?

Chapter Twenty

Still uneasy about the conclusions they'd all been forced to draw by Alison's confession the other night, Samantha glanced out the large, side-by-side windows that made up the front wall of her living room. This was the evening they'd agreed to meet to discuss the tragedies that had befallen them, and it looked as if the weather was going to be as dismal as their meeting was apt to be.

Twilight crept across the river and slowly turned the silvery haze that hung there to a misty lavender. Beyond that deceptively tranquil haze, however, ominous black clouds hung low in the sky.

Now and again, lightning lit the interiors of those clouds with brief silver flashes, and even with the windows closed and the storm still so far away, Samantha could hear the low grumble of thunder. "Hope everybody brings raincoats, Rags," she told her little shadow.

Rags cocked his head, ran to the sofa, jumped up onto and trotted along the back of it. From there, peering out at the magnificent sky, he answered Samantha with a single, "Ruf!"

She started for the kitchen. "Come on, boy. It's time to put the coffee on, our guests will be arriving soon."

Before they'd left Laura's the other night, they'd decided they were going to meet to discuss what they might possibly do next. It didn't matter to them that Art Chamberlain had insisted that murder was best left to the police, though certainly what he said did make sense. None of the others who'd been at Laura's that night were content with that, however. Too many homicides went unsolved these days. Just look at the murder of the man that had been found in the Formosa azalea bush. The man with his fingerprints removed. Samantha shivered with revulsion. No progress had been made on that case yet. The police were inundated with unsolved crimes.

Besides all that, Olivia Charles had been a friend. A dear friend. All of them had loved her. As a result, her murder had touched their lives too deeply for them just to stand idly by and wait for the crime to be solved.

There would be five of them tonight. Laura, Alison, the Colonel and herself had set up the meeting, but Janet Wilson had phoned Laura just this afternoon and asked to be brought into any plan to help identify her cousin's murderer. Of course, they couldn't exclude her. Who had a better right to be present?

Samantha's mind was on the girl as she counted out dessert plates, cups and saucers. *Poor Janet,* Samantha thought as she poured the contents of the coffee maker into her pre-warmed silver coffee pot. *The girl really had no one else in the world. Olivia, excited at the prospect of having her cousin with her again, had told the Bridge group that she'd been responsible for her ever since Janet's parents had perished when their house had burned.* Aloud, Samantha murmured, "Now, Janet has no one." She looked down to where Rags watched her, bright-eyed. "It's sad isn't it, Rags?"

"Errrr."

Samantha gave him a quick pat and tried for a lighter tone. "I made another apricot pound cake. Surely that's enough for just the five of us." She put the cake on one end of the large silver waiter that held the dessert plates and forks, then put the coffee pot on the other end of the tray with the cups and saucers.

Rags wagged his stumpy tail and watched with approval as she took out the tea napkins. When she returned to the tray with them, he trotted after her, then followed as she took the heavy waiter into the living room and deposited it on the coffee table.

The room was dim now, and Samantha drew the drapes. She loved the light and opened the house to it every morning, but darkness was something she blocked out. She hated the way night turned the multi-paned windows of every room into black mirrors.

She didn't like having her reflection popping up at her in odd places, startling her. Now, with her nerves on edge from all that had happened recently, she liked it even less. Especially since she'd recently added the thought that someone outside could actually be looking in.

"Grrrr." Rags started for the front door.

"Oh, that must be the Colonel." She chuckled. "I know how much you like him." She smiled down at the terrier and went toward the front door. She had almost reached it when the door chimes sounded. Opening it, she said, "Good evening, C..." She coughed and hastily changed her greeting to "Janet." Continuing smoothly, "Won't you come in?"

"Thank you, Mrs. Masters. I hope I'm not intruding. It's just that I . . ."

Samantha interrupted the girl to put her at ease. "Nonsense. Of course you're not intruding. Everyone understands that you're anxious to help. And rightly so, dear." She led Janet to a place on the sofa. "Everyone knows that Olivia and you were very close."

"Yes. Olivia was my guardian, as well as my mentor. She was only a few years older, but everyone knew she was so much wiser. Olivia always knew what was best. What I should or shouldn't do." She stopped speaking abruptly and stared down at her tightly clasped hands. Her shining blonde hair fell forward to veil her face.

How Samantha's heart went out to the girl. Now that she didn't have Olivia, Janet would be forced to grow up. Samantha regretted that thought the instant she had it. Chiding herself for being unkind in even thinking that Janet had a sort of immaturity about her, she forced a smile and offered, "Would you care for coffee?"

"Yes, thank you." She accepted the cup Samantha poured, added cream and sugar and sat back. "Samantha?"

"Yes?"

"Do the police have any clues, or do *you* have any idea who could have . . ." Janet broke off as the door chimes rang.

"Excuse me," Samantha rose and went to the door. Before she reached it, Colonel McLain opened it for himself and entered the foyer.

"Lousy weather coming in." He slid the raincoat he had slung over one shoulder off and hung it in the guest closet himself.

"Yes." Samantha wondered if she ought to thank him for making himself so at home, then decided it would serve no useful purpose. There was no way she was going to retrain the man. "I saw the storm building up across the river before I drew the drapes."

He nodded at Samantha and greeted the other guest. "Hi, Janet." Then, "I didn't know you were coming."

Samantha scowled at him for his tactlessness. "Laura invited her, and I'm sure we're all glad to have her."

"Yeah." He was totally unrepentant for having been less than welcoming.

Samantha shook her head. The man had absolutely no social graces.

There was a quick tap at the door, and Laura and Alison came in with their raincoats over their arms.

"Here." Samantha smiled as she embraced each in turn. "I'll take those." She hung the coats in the guest closet while Rags tore frantically around Alison until the girl bent down and took him up to hold him. Then he tried his best to lick her chin. Alison held on to Rags as if he were a lifeline.

"Alison. Don't let that dog lick your face." Laura spoke vaguely, out of motherly habit, certain she was talking to the wall for all the good it would do. She asked Samantha, "Anything I can do?" When her hostess shook her head no, Laura went to sit in one of the wing chairs that stood in front of the windows.

Alison, subdued since her confession, nevertheless let Rags's little tongue touch her face once before she held him away. Her voice lacked its usual cheery enthusiasm as she told him, "Thank you for that nice doggie kiss, Rags."

Worried about this change in his friend, Rags squirmed in her hands and stretched his neck as far as he could toward her, his tongue stretching, too.

"No, thank you!" Alison laughed a little and gave him a quick hug. "No more kisses, or I'll put you down."

"Rhhrrr." Rags searched her face anxiously with his button-bright gaze, sighed deeply, then dropped his head, admitting defeat.

Alison plopped into the other one of the wing chairs. When she did, Rags grunted at the jolt and sent her a single reproachful look but made no move to leave her arms.

The Colonel took the big leather chair that had been Andrew's favorite. He crossed his ankles and sighed as he lifted his feet to the matching ottoman.

Samantha poured coffee for everyone, adding cream and sugar to their specifications, and Laura passed the cups around. "Does everyone want apricot pound cake?"

She didn't have to ask the Colonel twice. "You bet."

"Janet?"

"No, thank you."

"Alison?" Samantha asked as she began to slice the golden, sugar-glazed round.

"Please. I never miss your apricot pound cake. I've never tasted anything I thought was better."

Samantha looked at her sharply. The words were Alison's, but the listlessness was not. The poor child must be suffering terribly. Samantha's heart went out to her.

"Well. What are we trying to do here?" The Colonel's voice was a welcome rumble.

Samantha, feeling the meeting called for some sort of notes to be taken, pulled her pad and pencil out of her purse.

"As I see it, we've lost our prime

suspect." He smiled kindly at Alison and added, "We know our vandal was certainly not responsible for Olivia's death."

Samantha winced for Janet, but the girl seemed to have herself well under control.

"True," Laura said, "but have we any idea who could have done it?"

"Couldn't have been robbery. Her purse was there, so were her rings and that pearl necklace she always wore."

"Perhaps we frightened the would-be robber off," Samantha offered. "After all, Rags did kick up a fuss and get us out the door fairly quickly."

"True." McLain was careful not to add that Olivia's heart had still been pumping blood from her wounded chest when they arrived beside her.

"Our theory that she might have seen the vandal, who then might have wanted to silence her, doesn't work anymore either. Not since the attempt to kill Samantha with the water moccasin."

"No."

"What if . . ." Janet Wilson began and just as quickly stopped.

"Go on, Janet," Laura prompted. "What if what?"

"What if someone killed Olivia because she knew something they didn't want disclosed?" She looked around at them, her eyes searching.

"But what could that have been?" Samantha frowned. "Olivia was such an open person. If she knew anything dangerous, she probably didn't have any idea that she knew it."

"I'll buy that." McLain took his feet off the ottoman and sat forward, his elbows on his knees, his hands clasped. "And I'll propose that whatever it was, there's a very good possibility that Jasmine Johnson knew the same thing. Or something closely related to it."

Janet Wilson looked startled. "Why in the world would you say that? My cousin Olivia and Jasmine Johnson hardly moved in the same circles."

Samantha shot a glance at the girl. Surely she wasn't upset to think that Olivia and Jasmine might have had something in common. Jasmine was as much a part of their neighborhood as any of them.

Laura was on the edge of her chair. "Why in heaven's name do you think that Olivia being attacked in my driveway has anything to do with poor Jasmine having been the victim of a hit and run?"

Samantha said, "There have been too many things happening lately for them not to have been related."

"I hate to keep saying 'true'," McLain said, "but there you have it. As I understand it, this neighborhood has never had anything happen but the occasional attempted burglary, and here we are with two homicides *and* two attempted murders."

Laura jumped up out of her chair, staring at him, aghast. Her voice trembled as she demanded, "I understand about the snake, but you don't mean that you think someone tried to *kill* Jasmine."

"Yes, I do."

"But that's absurd. That was just an accident. Jasmine doesn't have an enemy in this world."

"Would you have thought that Olivia Charles had?" McLain asked her quietly.

"No." Laura looked confused. "No. Of course not." She looked around vaguely, as if wondering what she was doing out of her chair, smoothed her skirts under her and sat again, deep in the chair this time, as if seeking shelter.

"All right, then." The Colonel's natural leadership, honed to perfection by his years in the Marine Corps, was taking over the discussion. "We can't forget that I said two attempted murders. That snake in Sam's bed was playing for keeps. I'd say that our first and foremost consideration is to discover just what it is that Olivia Charles and Jasmine Johnson *and* Sam either had in common, or all three knew." He sat back in the chair. "It looks like we need more time to think about this, in the light of the attack on Sam."

There was a soft current of agreement.

"Remember, it doesn't matter if it seems important to you, just wrack your brains. Just dredge up anything that might be even vaguely pertinent and bring it to our next meeting, okay? Anything that turns out to seem to fit, we need to pass on to Lieutenant Nichols."

There were more murmurs of ascent as the others acknowledged the wisdom of his proposal.

Samantha closed her notebook and put her pencil away, as disappointed as the others that they had achieved absolutely nothing. "Well, if that's all we can accomplish for tonight, would anyone else care for another slice of pound cake?"

Before she stopped speaking, lightning sent blue radiance through the room in spite of the drawn draperies. Thunder crashed and rattled every window in the house. An instant later the heavens opened and heavy rain drummed down into their despondent silence.

Chapter Twenty-one

Samantha sat with her friend Laura Fulton on a rustic bench that overlooked the river at the edge of Laura's property. Gulls mewed overhead, sunlight glinting on their wings as they wheeled and soared against a bright blue sky, their eyes eagerly searching the water for their breakfasts. The grass still had the damp of morning dew, but the sun was strong, and the humidity was no more than was usual for a spring morning in Tidewater.

Laura had been lifting some bulbs for Samantha to take over to Emilee Twiford's new place in Greenbrier, and had just finished getting the last of them out of the ground when Samantha arrived with a thermos of tea and two cups.

"I don't think it'll hurt to take them up

now," Laura told her. "I was careful, so they'll probably still bloom this season." She tucked the newspaper on which she'd sat the clumps of flowers around them as gently as if the tulips were sleeping babies. Then, together she and Samantha packed the parcels that she'd made of them into a basket.

"I hope so. I'm sure you've gotten enough earth with them to keep them from feeling too much shock if they're quickly replanted. You know Emilee will have them in the ground before I even get them out of my car."

"Good trick if she can do it."

Samantha uncapped the thermos and poured tea into the cup Laura held out to her.

Laura grinned, deliberately sly. "It's kind of you to take the time out of your newly crowded social schedule to drive these out to Emilee."

Samantha looked at Laura, startled, then laughed. "So you noticed."

"How could I help it? I'm out here in the yard digging around all day, and I can't help but see Janet's car in your driveway."

"She *is* becoming part of my life, isn't

she?" Samantha didn't sound as if that prospect gave her a great deal of pleasure.

"Hey, don't fight it. She has to come on her lunch hour, and I'll bet you make the poor woman go with you to eat Chinese every time she does."

Samantha chuckled. "You bet I do. Janet likes Chinese food as much as I do, and I'm certainly not going to let an opportunity like that slip by. I've given up trying to get you to go."

"Just be thankful I'll eat Mexican with you."

"I am, believe me."

"And pizza."

"Don't cheat, Laura Fulton. You've always liked pizza."

"It was worth a try. I need some leverage to get you to the new Vietnamese Restaurant."

"No thanks. Too exotic for me." Samantha sipped her tea.

After a moment Laura said quietly, "Seriously, Samantha. I know you're doing Janet a world of good. She must be terribly lonely without Olivia."

"Yes, I think she is."

They sat quietly, watching a lone

destroyer making for the Destroyer Piers and sipping their tea. The breeze from the river ruffled their hair.

It was true about Janet. In the week and a half since the meeting at Samantha's the night of the thunderstorm, the poor girl seemed to have become part of Samantha's life. She called on the phone almost daily, and they'd already been to lunch twice. The young woman was pathetically eager to help with any plans to find out who had murdered her cousin. Samantha knew in her heart that Janet must have vowed she wouldn't rest until they'd solved Olivia's murder.

Today, Janet had taken time off to go to the hospital to visit Jasmine with her, and Samantha was grateful. Jasmine was better now. Everything but her leg had healed, and she was fretting at being stuck in a hospital bed. Samantha knew it had to be awful waiting to get out of traction, and was trying hard to keep her friend occupied and entertained. After she took Emilee's flowers out to Greenbrier to her, she was going to meet Janet in the hospital parking lot and take her up to visit Jasmine.

She glanced at her watch. "Oh, dear. Look at the time, Laurie. I better get going. Janet's meeting me at twelve fifteen."

"Okay." Laura grinned up at her as Samantha stood. "I'll help you out by finishing off the tea."

"Thanks a lot, Laurie Fulton."

"Hey. I'll even wash your thermos. Cups, too."

"That'll be good. I'll see you this afternoon when I get back, okay?"

"Great. Look for me in the peonies. They need more feeding, the pigs."

"Peonies surely are, aren't they? But look how they pay us back with all those extravagant blossoms."

"Plus a great smell. *If* you don't inhale an ant." Laura wrinkled her nose.

"That's a definite risk. The little pests really like Peonies. I think they feed on the aphids in the blossoms."

"To borrow a word from our friend the Colonel, 'true'." Laura grinned at Samantha's instant frown. "See you later."

Samantha picked up their basket of plants and left Laura to finish the tea.

At home she put the flowers in a shady spot and hurried in to dress. She could hardly go to Norfolk General in her blue jeans. It was already nine, and Greenbrier was a good half hour away—if the traffic wasn't bad, longer if it was.

All the water in the Norfolk-Virginia Beach area made it impossible to add more highways, and the region was really crowded now that so many people were moving into it from New York and New Jersey.

Greenbrier and Great Bridge in the City of Chesapeake, which Samantha remembered used to be lovely, quiet country, were both packed with new homes now. Even Virginia Beach was feeling the pinch and talking about moving the Green Line that protected the farmland on the other side of it from encroachment. Samantha really hoped they wouldn't.

As she rushed into the house, Rags greeted her and followed her back to her room. Samantha was shedding her gardening clothes as she walked. Standing in her closet she asked him, "What shall I wear, Rags?"

Rags put his head on his paws and moaned.

"Honestly. You're no help at all."

The tiny dog's head shot up.

Samantha grabbed a blue-striped shirt with a buttoned-down collar, a navy linen blazer and a pair of light tan slacks. "There. That ought to do."

She looked around the floor of the closet because the cubby hole that usually held her navy blue loafers was empty. After a fruitless search she muttered, "Oh, Glory I miss you, Jasmine." Guilt hit her and she added as if Jasmine was there to be placated, "Not just because you keep everything in order, of course, but that part surely is nice." She searched the closet floor again. "Now where are my loafers? Did I kick them off somewhere?"

She knew that in the evening if she was tired she often forgot to put things back where they belonged. And with as little sleep as she'd been getting lately, she was frequently tired. Without her wonderful Jasmine to keep her in order . . . "Where *are* my shoes!"

She came out of the closet to find Rags sitting with one of her loafers in front of him.

"Oh, Rags. Thank you, dear." She bent to give him a pat. "Where's the other one."

Rags whirled around and led the way to the slipper chair next to the phone. Poking his nose under it he indicated Samantha's other navy blue loafer. Sitting back, he looked immensely pleased with himself.

"Yes, you're a wonderful dog. Good boy."

She could swear she saw Rags smirk.

Samantha smoothed his head. "I must have left it there when I was talking to Laura."

"Yap."

"Thank you."

"Errrf."

She blew her bangs back and grimaced. "Rags, I really must stop this. First I begin forgetting where I put things when my mind is otherwise occupied, and now I think I'm actually having a conversation with a dog. I . . ."

The phone rang, interrupting her thought.

"Hello?"

"We still on to go to the hospital?"

"Yes," Samantha gave her caller the name she'd neglected to supply, "Janet. I'm getting ready to run some plants over to Emilee Twiford in Greenbrier, then I'll meet you there in the parking lot. Twelve fifteen, right?"

"Good." Janet Wilson hung up without saying 'goodbye.'

Samantha frowned at the handset. "So many young people are doing away with the traditional courtesies these days, Rags." She shook her head. "I wish I didn't mind."

Rags cocked an ear her way.

"I'm just going to have to learn to overlook it, I suppose. Glory! It makes me feel like a dinosaur. Thank heaven Alison isn't that way."

At Alison's name, Rags perked up and yapped.

"Me, too, boy. She's a honey." She sighed. "I hope she's feeling better about that vandal business. She was feeling so guilty. All of us understand why she did it. And none of us mind a bit now that she's explained. But she was so solemn last time we saw her wasn't she?"

"Errrr."

"Well, try not to worry," she told the dog. "Youth is nothing if not resilient. I expect she'll be her old self in a day or two."

Rags's "Erf!" seemed to have a more

positive note.

Samantha ruffled the hair on the back of his neck and hurried to get her purse. "Gotta go. Don't want Janet to have to wait at the hospital."

She snatched up her navy blue purse, put him in his kennel and told her dog, "See you later, Rags."

Great Scott! She really was having conversations with a dog!

***

Jasmine was pitifully glad to see them. Samantha's heart went out to her. Lying on her back day after day had to be getting old. After the introductions, she looked up from her hospital bed and smiled at Janet Wilson.

Janet sat quietly on the smallest chair by the window, the sunlight coming in through the blinds touched highlights of gold in her smooth blonde hair. "So you were Benny's maid, Jasmine?"

Jasmine answered firmly, "I was the Stoddards's housekeeper."

"Oh, of course," Janet smiled disarmingly. "Sorry. Nobody says maid anymore, do they?"

"Not much."

Samantha hoped Janet wasn't offended by Jasmine's mild correction. She also hoped Janet hadn't offended Jasmine by calling her a maid.

Drat it. This was why she never liked introducing people to each other. She was always on pins and needles for fear they might not click. She always felt stuck in the middle and somehow responsible for the outcome. She was relieved when the younger woman didn't seem to notice Jasmine's correction.

"I hear you as good as raised young Benny Stoddard." Janet smiled. "That was nice of you. He must have been a lonely boy." She gestured with one hand. "I mean, having been away so much he probably didn't have many friends here."

"He had a few."

"Oh, who were they? Do they still live around here?"

Jasmine frowned a little, remembering.

"I mean, wouldn't it be nice to get them together for Benny?" Janet turned to Samantha. "Wouldn't it, Mrs. Masters?"

But it was Jasmine who spoke next. "Huh. Don't seem like Benny cares much for his old friends to me."

"Why, what do you mean?" Janet was wide-eyed.

"Well, he hasn't exactly beat a path to my door, and tied up here like this," she indicated her leg, "I'm never out, so he doesn't have to worry about missing me if he comes by. I'm stuck right here."

Oh, dear, Samantha thought, *Jasmine's obviously hurt that young Ben Stoddard hasn't been by to visit with her.* No wonder there was tension in the room. Jasmine was smarting under Benny Stoddard's neglect. Not the best time to bring over a new acquaintance. Samantha wanted to sigh. Life could get so awkward. She felt herself frown. She was doing that a lot lately.

"You must have known Benny well." Janet seemed to be unaware that Jasmine was feeling neglected and Benny Stoddard might not be the best subject to linger on.

"As well as anybody but his folks, I guess."

"I thought Mrs. Talley said he was away at school or camp most of the time."

Jasmine tried to change position a little and gave up, held in place by the paraphernalia cradling her broken leg.

"Yes. He was. The Stoddards didn't think anything was too much to do for Benny. They never guessed he'd rather have just been home. He was too sweet a boy to tell 'em any different."

Janet looked at her blankly. "Why couldn't he just come out and tell them? Weren't they close?"

"He knew how hard they were working to get *Stoddard and Company* off the ground, and none of them thought they wouldn't have time later." Jasmine's eyes grew moist.

"I'm upsetting you. I'm so sorry." Janet rose and handed Jasmine a tissue. "I was too full of the idea of giving a party with all Benny's old friends to think."

"That's all right."

"I guess the party's a bad idea, huh?"

"Well, all of Benny's friends have gone off, now. Nobody's left 'round here. Seems like children don't stay put much anymore, doesn't it?"

Janet smiled at her. "I guess not. I know I couldn't wait to try my wings in the big city."

Samantha laughed. "When I was young, we all had to go to New York. We were sure it was the only place in the world sufficiently challenging to test our mettle."

Janet looked at her, inquiringly.

Samantha responded with, "Well, now there's Atlanta and, now that the gangster image has faded a bit, Chicago, and of course San Francisco. That mecca of the 60s still holds a lot of attraction." She smiled and told them, "But in *my* day there was only New York."

"Oh." Janet looked down at her watch. "Oh! Look at the time. I have to get back to work!" She jumped up and headed for the door. "Nice to have met you, Jasmine," she threw back as she left. "See you later, Samantha!" And she was gone.

Jasmine and Samantha looked at each other.

"You don't think I offended her, do you?" Samantha asked.

Jasmine considered. "No, I think the time just got away from her."

They sat quietly, each lost in her thoughts.

Finally Jasmine broke the silence. "It was nice of her to want to give a get-together for Benny and his friends."

"Yes," Samantha agreed, "It was."

Jasmine sighed. "I jus' wish he'd come to visit me."

Right then and there Samantha solemnly vowed that Benny Stoddard was going to visit Jasmine Johnson before this week was out or she was going to know the reason why he didn't.

And it was already Tuesday.

Chapter Twenty-two

Samantha was on her knees in her garden, her favorite place to be, when she heard the faint pad, pad, pad of running shoes on the asphalt of the street in front of her house. She scowled and wondered what the Colonel was doing running on the short street that passed in front of her house on the way to Laura's gate. She hoped he wasn't coming to see her.

Hope died as the light footsteps crossed then left the cement of her driveway and disappeared altogether. Drat! He was coming to where she knelt. Why did some people have to work so hard at their genius for spoiling the pleasure of others?

She kept her head bent over her flower bed until the shadow of her unwelcome visitor fell across the peonies. Then she reluctantly craned her neck to turn her face to the intruder. "What do *you* want?"

"Don't die of joy at seeing me, Sam, I can't stay long enough to bury you."

She sat back on her heels and looked up at him to fire off the statement he was waiting for. "I prefer not to be called Sam." Her lips tightened as she saw his lips silently form the words in sync with her own. "Honestly, Colonel McLain! Why does a grown man work at making himself unpleasant."

"Just habit." He grinned at her. "Marine, you know."

"I have known several very pleasant Marine Corps officers."

"Huh, they must not have been doing the job right."

"I . . ." Samantha heard the heat in her voice, saw the grin on his face, and stopped before the next word. Rising, she brushed dirt off the knees of her jeans. She didn't need to be at a disadvantage with this man, and kneeling certainly qualified as one. "May I ask to what I owe the honor of this visit, Colonel?" Her voice was gentle— she'd worked at it.

All teasing disappeared from his face.

"Just dashed by to see if you'd gotten any feedback from anyone in the neighborhood about the night that Olivia Charles was knifed."

Samantha joined him in putting aside their mutual animosity. "No. No one has said anything. Not even old Mrs. Carter up near the Yacht Club entrance heard any cars she didn't recognize."

The Colonel quirked a corner of his mouth as he frowned. Correctly interpreting that as a request for an explanation, Samantha explained. "Mrs. Carter is losing her eyesight to macular degeneration, poor dear. As a result, she seems to hear more acutely. She prides herself on being able to identify every resident by the sound of their car engines, and she said no one came into Riverhaven that way except those who belong here. Right on up until the ambulance arrived.

"Hmmm." The Colonel accepted Mrs. Carter's ability to differentiate between the sounds of car engines without question. "Could have come in the other way. From the side toward the naval base."

"Yes," Samantha was glad that he was as eager as they all were to believe that the person who had murdered poor Olivia was not one of them.

He began running in place. "Any chance of hot chocolate this evening?"

"I suppose I can."

He turned like a leaf in the wind, beginning to run off. "Geeze, Sam, don't be so damn eager to have my company. You'll make me blush." And with that he was gone, running lightly down her drive and back up the street.

Samantha settled back down on her knees. She sat there a second, feeling the sun on her shoulders, and tried to recapture the peace she always found in her garden. After a while, she began to scratch lightly in the dirt at the base of the nearest peony plant.

Peace did come again. She was smiling as she fed the voracious plant and its neighbors the necessary bone and blood meal that would guarantee the profusion of glorious blooms for which peonies were prized.

Peonies were her favorites. Until she looked at the Iris bed. Or the roses. She loved them all. Even the more humble Shastas and Coreopsis. They were like children to her—responding to care, giving delight.

Samantha heard the phone ring, but decided to ignore it. The portable was only inches from her, but her gardening gloves were so dirty she hated to touch the instrument. It stopped ringing, and she settle back on her heels with a sigh.

"Laurie was right," she told the plants just in front of her. "You peonies really are pigs, you know." She reached for the bag of bone meal on her left, and spilled out some of the gray, sand-like substance into her gloved left hand.

The phone started ringing again.

"Oh, darn!" She spilled the bone meal back into its bag, grabbed the fingers of her right hand glove and pulled it off. Now she could touch the 'talk' button without filling it with soil supplements at any rate. She poked it and tried to sound pleasant as she said, "Hello?"

"Would you like to go to lunch today?" Janet Wilson's voice was eager.

Samantha's annoyance faded a little. The girl must be lonely, indeed, to seek out the company of someone almost twice her age like this. In contrast, Alison had to be either past desperate or feeling really charitable before she'd volunteer to go to lunch with her aunt or her honorary Aunt Samantha.

While Samantha hesitated, Janet said, "After all, we didn't get to go to lunch yesterday, just to visit Jasmine."

"I'd love to." It was a blatant exaggeration. She'd really rather finish all the spring fertilizing she'd had planned, but Janet needed her, and it was always good to get out.

"I thought we could try that new Mexican restaurant that just opened in Chesapeake. I know it's kind of far, but Herb—I mean Mr. Talley—said I could take two hours for lunch because he's all caught up on letters, so we could make it."

"Sounds lovely."

"Okay, I'll pick you up."

"But, I . . ." Samantha was talking to a dead line. "Drat! I wish she wouldn't do that!"

Rags came over from where he'd been sitting on the sun warmed rock that she and Andrew had brought back from a vacation in New Mexico. Flat and rectangular, it had still taken both of them a super effort to get it into the trunk of the car. Worth the effort, though. It was the only rock in her garden. "Huh," she said aloud at that thought, "It's the only rock anywhere around."

Tidewater was all sandy loam except for the heavy clay soil down nearer Dismal Swamp. There were no rocks in Tidewater. The early settlers of Norfolk had used the cobblestones brought over as ballast in ships from their native England to build the first streets.

When Samantha had been a little girl, her grandfather had lived on Marshall Avenue in the once elegant section called Brambleton. She could still remember, vividly, how difficult it had been to ride her bicycle on the cobblestone surface of the street between his corner house with its tall Victorian tower and the school yard of John B. Goode Elementary.

The remembrance of her Grandfather's tower sent her gaze toward John McLain's. "At least my Granddaddy didn't use *his* to snoop," she muttered. Rising, she slapped her gloves together to get the dirt off and used them to brush off her knees.

Rags turned and led the way to the garage for all the world as if that were the mission for which he'd left the warm surface of his rock. Trotting over to the side of the large double garage where Samantha stored her garden tools, he stood waiting while she hung her kneeling pad and replaced the bag of bone meal in the cabinet over the potting bench. He was used to her routine, obviously.

"I'm going to lunch with Janet Wilson, Rags."

"Errf."

Sealing her gloves in an old coffee can so that no spiders could get into them, she thrust her stainless steel trowel into the bucket of oiled sand that she kept for the purpose of cleaning and protectively coating her tools and worked it up and down a few times. "You don't seem enthused, Rags."

Rags just stared at her. Unblinking.

"You wouldn't want to come. Dogs don't eat Mexican food. If you did, you'd disgrace yourself."

Rags turned his head away with slow deliberation and stared out at the birds on the driveway.

"Don't be insulted, Rags. Any dog would have problems. The hot spices are difficult for dogs." Samantha was flabbergasted. Was she really placating her six pound tyrant? She was very much afraid that she was. This had to stop. Who was in charge here anyway? "Rags!" she said, attempting to treat him like a dog. "Get in the house." Then she had to rush to get to the door and have it open so that she could be obeyed.

She needn't have bothered. With his usual measured tread and newly injured dignity, Rags paraded to the door like a king walking up the aisle at Westminster and entered the house. He never looked back.

"Oh, Dammit." Samantha slammed the door behind her. First she couldn't finish fertilizing her flowers, and now her dog was mad at her.

***

"Here we are!" Janet swooped her car into the parking spot closest to the door of the restaurant and slammed it into park even as she stomped on the parking brake. The little red sports car rocked hard against the parking pin, and Samantha made a solemn vow to drive in the future.

Samantha knew she was a fast driver

herself—Laurie called her 'zippy but safe,' but she'd always thought of her car as a helpful extension of herself. Janet Wilson treated her vehicle like something to be subdued by force! It had been . . . Samantha searched for something charitable to think about their wild drive . . . an exhilarating experience to ride with the younger woman.

Samantha levered herself out of her side of the tiny car and stood tentatively. Good, her legs still worked. She must be getting old to have wondered if they would, but they had been really cramped in the little sports car. She glanced across the roof of the car at the lithe young girl smiling at her and knew that, compared to Janet, she already *was* considered old.

Boy. That thought could spoil the day if she let it, so she didn't. She'd just remember that she had it all over youth in experience and accumulated knowledge. Not to mention social graces, she added, as Janet turned and entered the restaurant's vestibule without waiting for her.

By the time Samantha caught up to her, Janet was sliding into a booth at the front windows.

"I hope you like a booth."

"Yes, I prefer them."

"I know it's silly, but I always feel I can talk more freely when I'm in a booth."

Janet's bright smile drew an answering one from Samantha.

They ordered from a waiter who knew only enough English to help them get what they wanted. Samantha refrained from using her Spanish, as she'd found it just threw the young waiters into confusion, except for telling him, 'solamente queso, no carne' in her chili relleno.

Confused waiter or no, she wasn't taking any chances. She hated the way stuffed chili peppers had been ruined in so many Mexican restaurants by the addition of the ground meat used to make tacos. A friend had told her they'd done this in order to please the American palette, but it certainly did *not* please hers!

The orders placed, and the cola she always drank with Mexican food tall and frosty in front of her, Samantha stripped the last bit of paper from her straw and watched as Janet carefully poured her beer into the glass she'd asked for.

Janet looked up from her task. "I like it

without the head," she offered.

"I've never had a taste for beer. My husband drank it with Mexican food, too, though."

"Have you been without him long?"

"Four years."

"I'm sorry."

Samantha smiled. "Yes, so am I. He was a wonderful man. Thank you."

"I enjoyed meeting Jasmine."

"Oh," Samantha accepted the shift gratefully, "I'm so glad. I'm afraid she's getting tired of inactivity. She wasn't quite her usual self."

"I think she's just pissed, if you'll excuse my French, that Benny Stoddard hasn't been to see her." Janet watched her intently.

Samantha was a little slow in admitting, "Yes, I think you have that right." She sat up even straighter. "However, you may rest assured that I have every intention of getting him to go see her soon. Very soon." She gave a decisive little nod. "Even if I have to drag him by the hair of his head."

Janet's eyes went a little wide at that. Obviously she wasn't used to women like Samantha being ready to get physical.

After a little silence, she asked, "Were Benny and Jasmine really close, then?"

Samantha considered a moment. "I think that Jasmine stood in a place very close to that of a parent with Benny. Certainly they were together almost all the time the boy was at home. As I understand it, Benny Stoddard wasn't what you would call an outgoing child. 'Pleasant but not sociable', is how Jasmine describes him. He liked his greenhouse and always read a lot, according to her. Summers when he was home, he sailed his Moth every good day. And you know there's no room to take anyone else in a Moth."

Janet's lovely brow was furrowed. "Is a Moth some sort of sailboat?"

"Yes." Samantha smiled. "My husband and I had a Hampton. That's larger."

"Such funny names for boats." Janet laughed. Men lunching in the table opposite them turned and smiled appreciatively at the sound. Samantha thought again how lovely the girl was, and how sad it was that she had lost the last member of her family so tragically.

Their meal arrived, with the usual warning about the plates being hot.

Janet asked, "Why do you think Benny hasn't gone to see Jasmine?"

"I wish I knew. He seems rather shy. I don't know if that's the way he's always been, but he's almost . . ." she sought hard for the right word. ". . . tentative. He was constantly looking to Brenda for reassurance. At least he was when I crashed in on them the other morning and as good as demanded that he go to the hospital."

"Perhaps that's it."

"What's it?"

"The fact that you pressured him a bit. A lot of us really hate to feel as if someone else is making our decisions for us." Her face grew solemn. "I know I do."

"Do you suppose that's it? It never occurred to me that he might take it that way." She thought a minute, cutting vents into her stuffed chili pepper to help it cool. "It never occurred to me that he'd be slow to visit Jasmine either." She added, "No matter. I'm *taking* him to see Jasmine, and that's that."

They ate a while in silence. Then Janet looked as if she'd just thought of something. Something that caused her to freeze with her fork halfway to her mouth. In hushed tones she asked, "You don't suppose . . . ?" Then her voice brightened. "No. That's too unbelievable!"

"What?" Samantha's interest was aroused.

"Oh, it was just a silly . . . No, a totally ridiculous thought. I've obviously been watching too much TV."

"What was it, Janet. Even if it is ridiculous, it just might get us thinking."

"Well." Janet was blushing a little. "If you promise you won't laugh."

"Of course, I won't."

"Well, just suppose that perhaps Benny doesn't want to go see Jasmine because . . . Oh, this is too silly!" She stabbed her fork into the mound of Spanish rice on her plate and ducked her head so that Samantha couldn't witness her embarrassment.

"Janet!" Samantha had to work to keep her voice from being sharp. "Even if it is the most far-fetched idea in the world, you've begun it, and you've got to finish it or I'll die of curiosity."

"All right. But it really *is* asinine."

"Tell." Samantha didn't even try to keep the menace out of the word.

"I just thought that . . . Well, I thought what if . . ."

Samantha gripped the edge of the table to keep from shaking the girl opposite her and demanded, "What!"

"What if Benny Stoddard . . . isn't really Benny Stoddard?"

Chapter Twenty-three

Samantha called Laura the minute Janet dropped her off. "Just wait, Rags," she told the impatient dog at her feet. "I'll take you out as soon as I make this call."

Laura Fulton's breathless "Hello," was all Samantha needed to hear.

"Laurie. I've got to talk with you. The most amazing idea has just been expressed—"

"By Janet Wilson?"

"Yes. How did you know?"

"Saw her pick you up. Saw her drop you off. If this keeps up, we'll have to plant a tall hedge between us. I'm beginning to feel like a snoop."

"Oh, never mind that. You'd be a friendly snoop. Can I come over?"

"Is this about Olivia?"

"No." Then Samantha hesitated. *Could* Janet's suggestion that someone might be impersonating Benny Stoddard have anything to do with Olivia Charles's murder? A chill passed over her.

Sensing her change in mood, Rags gave a low growl and came to stand close beside her.

When Samantha spoke again her voice was strained. "Well, maybe. Yes. It very well could be."

"I'm calling the Colonel."

"No! Wait. Let's talk it over first. I don't want . . ." But she was talking to an empty line. She slammed the phone into its cradle, exasperated. "Not you, too!"

"Yerrrrap!" Rags was staring at her wide-eyed.

"I can't help it Rags. I'm getting sick of people hanging up on me without saying goodbye. Especially people who know better."

"Erf?"

"Oh, all right. So there *is* more to it than that. I hate having Colonel McLain called into everything, too."

She shot a final glare at the telephone. She supposed she should be glad she hadn't had time to change into her gardening clothes—no need to feel at a disadvantage when the lofty new neighbor was on his way. How that man had weaseled his way into the heart of their group when it took most people months and months and months to be accepted was beyond her!

Oh, he'd have been given the traditional dose of Southern Hospitality—which some newcomers mistook for instant friendship only to be disappointed later when they were all settled in and folks stopped helping—but this was more than that. He'd been really accepted almost immediately. Now she had a problem with it. Why did that irritate her?

She whistled Rags to heel, took him to the part of her yard reserved for his necessity and headed for Laura's as soon as he'd done his business. As she and Rags reached the house, the Colonel was loping across the lawn from the high wall that separated his place from Laura's. *Having leaped it in a single bound, no doubt,* Samantha thought uncharitably.

Without preamble he asked, "Miz Fulton lets you bring that mutt, does she?"

"Only on special occasions until now,"

Laura said pleasantly from the open door before a more caustic comment could be made by Samantha. Then she turned her attention to the dog. Leaning down toward him she said, "But you'd better be on your best behavior, Rags."

Laura's attitude toward the terrier had softened considerably since he'd saved her best friend from the water moccasin.

"Ruff," her diminutive guest promised, and she held the screen door open for him.

"Let's sit in the kitchen, shall we?"

Since Laura's kitchen boasted a comfortable breakfast nook with a bay window that looked out across her fabulous lawn and gardens to the river, no one would have minded even if half the conversations in the South didn't take place around kitchen tables anyway.

They settled, Rags at Samantha's feet, and Laura brought cups and the coffee pot.

Steam rose in a straight line from the Kona coffee in their cups as Samantha told them what Janet had said at lunch. They sat motionless, each thinking of the ramifications of Janet Wilson's hesitant question.

When the Colonel finally hunched

forward to put his elbows on the table, the steam from their coffee cups wavered with the currents in the air. It was as if some sort of a signal to begin to talk had been given.

Laura blew across the surface of the coffee in her cup and sipped. "Hmmm. Too hot."

McLain took a gulp of his and grinned. "Coffee's no good unless it's hot enough to crack the enamel on your teeth, Laurie."

Laura smiled back at him.

Samantha frowned. When did he get to calling Laura *Laurie*? And why did she resent it? It seemed she was the only one he rubbed the wrong way. Well, maybe her and Arthur Chamberlain. When in heaven's name was she going to admit to herself that this man *belonged* in Riverhaven now she wondered? She didn't usually behave so churlishly.

Taking a sip of her coffee, Samantha burned her tongue. Scowling at him, she blamed that on the fact that McLain was drinking his down as if his mouth were lined with asbestos, and decided she didn't care if she ever accepted his presence here in her neighborhood!

"Stop glaring at me, Sam, and put your mind on remembering what Janet told you. Start as far back in the conversation as you can recall. The very beginning if you can, and tell us the whole thing."

"You don't want much."

"Samantha," Laura chided gently, "we're only trying to help."

Well, if that didn't just cap the whole thing off! Now she was 'Samantha' for her, and Laurie and the Colonel were 'we'! Oh, well, it served her right for being so sour when it came to the new neighbor. She promised herself to try to behave. She didn't have much hope she would, though.

"We ordered our food, talked about Benny and his sailboat." She frowned in concentration. "I said I intended to get . . ."

The phone rang.

Laura didn't make a move to answer it.

"Laurie. The phone."

"The answering machine will get it."

Samantha was surprised. "I thought you said you'd never have one."

"That was before every telemarketer in the United States got my number and decided that it was easiest to catch me at dinner time." She smirked at her friend. "Now I can screen my calls with the best of 'em."

Samantha said, "And give Alison all her messages."

"Oh, stop. I do remember most of them."

"Uhhmmm."

"Ladies. We're recalling the conversation over the tacos, please." McLain brought them back to the subject at hand as the caller hung up rather than leave a message.

"Yes. Well, it was shortly after the sailboat discussion that Janet suggested that maybe I had made Benny feel pressured the day I'd met him at Brenda's, and that maybe that was why he hadn't gone to see Jasmine. Then we agreed that Jasmine was upset that he hadn't, and I said I'd get him to go or know the reason why. Then Janet sort of froze and got all wide-eyed. When I asked her what she was thinking, she kind of dithered around and finally she said," Samantha hesitated for drama, then told them, "'What if Benny isn't Benny?'"

The Colonel let his breath out in a whoosh. "Damn."

Laura managed to get her mouth

closed, then opened it again to say, "Oh, dear. That's an awful thought. Why would anyone come and pretend to be Benny?"

The question was purely rhetorical. The answer was obvious to both Laurie and Samantha.

McLain looked at each of them in turn. "I take it the Stoddards left a pile of money."

"Yes," they both told him.

"But how would he . . . ?"

"He'd have to have help."

"Oh, no." Laurie was firm. "No one we know would ever do such a thing."

"What 'such a thing'?" The Colonel's voice was dry.

"Why, help someone deceive us all into accepting a stranger as Ben Stoddard Jr., of course." Samantha was looking at him as if he were retarded.

"Yeah. Right. But *you* just thought of it. You just said it. The only difference is that someone else may have done a great deal more than just think about it."

Samantha and Laura just stared at him.

"Okay, ladies. Time to take off the pretty little white gloves and get down to business. Forget that all your neighbors are certified saints and that you'll be condemned to hellfire forever if you express an uncomplimentary thought about a single one of them and tell me who knows enough about the Stoddards, their son and the rest of the neighborhood to be able to pull off a scam like this one."

Chapter Twenty-four

Samantha and Laura stared at each other as if something dreadful had just entered the sunny breakfast nook. And it had. The idea that one of their friends might have brought an imposter into their midst *was* dreadful. It outraged every finer feeling.

McLain, however, had no qualms about finer feelings. Samantha doubted that he had any of his own. "Come on, ladies. I'm new around here. I don't know what makes everybody tick. But you do. You've played Bridge with 'the girls' for years. By now you're bound to know what somebody might or might not do."

Samantha and Laura looked at each other again. It was true. One discovered a great deal about friends over a card table. Concentration on the hand that was being played often led to letting slip tiny bits of personal information that might not have been shared under other circumstances.

"Never mind the guilt, gals. Just put your minds to weighing what you've heard and dredge me up a list of reasons people you know might bring in a ringer for Benjamin Stoddard Jr."

After exchanging rueful glances with Laura, Samantha told him, "Money, of course. Mimi and Ben Stoddard left three or four million."

"Is there anybody else but Benny to inherit it?" McLain's eyes had narrowed.

"No. Ben used to say they were a pitifully small family to be a Southern one. Just the three of them and one sister of Mimi's who died of cancer just before they left for Florida."

"So if somebody had the guts to go out and find somebody who was a Benny look-alike . . ."

Laura interrupted him. "That wouldn't be as difficult as you'd think. None of us really knew him very well."

McLain went on as if she hadn't cut in, ". . . and bring him here with the story that Benny had been in some foreign prison all these years . . ." McLain deliberately left his sentence hanging.

Laura gasped. "Brenda Talley."

Samantha stared at her a moment before slowly adding, "Yes. Maybe. Brenda found him. He's staying at her house." Her reluctance was clear in her face. It disappeared slowly as she added, "And he was always looking to her as if for approval or guidance when I went over to the Talleys's to try to get him to come with me to the hospital to visit Jasmine."

"And, even so, he hasn't yet been to see Jasmine, either," Laura put in. "In spite of the fact that they were so close when he was growing up."

Samantha and Laura were regarding each other with eyes that were as round as saucers. Finally Samantha said, "Maybe *because* Jasmine and he were so close! So if we want to be suspicious, we could say that it looks like Brenda just might have gone and found a look-alike and brought him home to inherit the Stoddard fortune. And, of course, split it with her."

"Yes. She could have. She was clearly triumphant about having him come to stay at her house." Laura was thoroughly upset by the thought that someone she knew could be perpetrating such a ruse.

"But why?" Samantha still didn't want to believe it of someone she called her friend.

"Do Mrs. Talley or her husband have any money problems?" McLain's was the voice of reason. "Money problems can make the best of people do some pretty unacceptable things."

Samantha shot Laura a glance. Both were clearly hesitant to speak.

"Oh, come off it, ladies. This is no time for coy glances. Spit it out."

While Samantha glared at the Colonel, Laura told him, "Well, as everybody knows, Herb Talley took on a big financial obligation when he built the condominiums that Alison is one of the salespersons for. Alison says that constructing them cost a lot, and that it must have been quite a strain on Herb Talley's resources." She twisted a strand of hair next to her face nervously. "And Brenda is always lamenting the fact that she's had to curtail her shopping trips to the D.C. area because of it."

"That's true." Samantha corroborated a little reluctantly.

"Okay.   Then there's a motive for bringing in a false Benny. The Talleys are in a financial pinch, and they've thought of a painless way out of it."

"Oh, surely not Herb!" Laura was upset at the thought of pleasant Herb Talley being embroiled in such a scheme.

"Not Herb?" McLain's tone was caustic. "You had no problem suggesting Mrs. Talley for the role of villainess."

Samantha turned an unattractive shade of red. Ashamed, she admitted, "We don't like her as well."

"Oh, for G—Pete's sake." The colonel shook his head. They could both imagine hearing him mutter *Women!* He didn't, but out loud he went on, "No doubt there's an agreement that they'll get half the loot, maybe more, for their sponsorship of the bogus boy." He sat looking at them, his expression dead serious. "And if he is possibly a substitute for the real Benjamin Stoddard Jr., then . . ." He stopped himself from finishing the sentence.

"Then what?" Laura wanted to know.

"Yes," Samantha pushed. "In your own inimitable words, Colonel, 'Spit it out.'"

"If the boy is a ringer, and if there is a

great deal of money at stake, then someone might be willing to go to great lengths to ensure that nobody rocks the boat."

"What do you mean?" Samantha wanted to know.

"I mean that the people who set all this up might have had to be willing to do bodily harm to anyone who could upset the apple cart."

Laura looked puzzled.

"I'm saying, Miz Fulton, that they would stop at nothing to guarantee that this imposter inherits."

Samantha looked horrified. "Do you mean . . . ?" She couldn't bring herself to say what she had finally understood.

The Colonel nodded. "Yes. That's exactly what I mean."

Samantha gave a strangled sound and lunged to her feet. Her cup sloshed coffee across the table. "No!"

Laura cried out, "What are you two hinting at?"

Samantha sat again and took Laura's hands, oblivious of the spilled coffee. "John means that whoever is behind bringing an imposter here would have to make sure that no one could say he wasn't really

Benny Stoddard."

Laura burst out, "But no one knew him very well except Jasmine and . . ." Her eyes grew wide as the full horror of it hit her. Her voice sank to a bare whisper. ". . . and Olivia."

No one said anything for a full minute. Then Samantha said to McLain, "Remember the day you drove me back from the hospital where they'd taken Jasmine?"

"Of course."

"You told me about the accident then. You hinted that it hadn't been an accident at all. That it had been someone's deliberate attempt on Jasmine's life."

"True."

"In light of this new thought, your suspicion that the person who hit Jasmine was coming back to run over her a second time makes sense."

"I usually do make sense."

It was a measure of her agitation that Samantha wasn't even annoyed. "And what you are *not* saying is that the same person—" She stopped abruptly, halted by the enormity of what she was about to say. Her voice dropped to a whisper just as her best friend's had. "You're saying that it was the same person who stabbed Olivia. Stabbed her to stop her from unmasking their Benny."

"Oh, no. Brenda couldn't possibly stab anyone. Neither could Herb." Laura was positive. "Never."

There was a long moment of silence.

McLain broke it. "Someone told me that Herb Talley served in the Rangers during our last 'police action'?" McLain spat the last two words out as if they were a bad taste in his mouth. Sending men to die in anything less than a war went against his grain.

There was silence again as Samantha and Laura understood that their favorite real estate broker had probably stabbed enemies in the performance of his duty. The realization stunned them.

Finally, Colonel McLain broke the ugly spell. "So, ladies, whada we do?"

"Should we go to the police?"

"No." Samantha had a quick answer. "We have no proof. And besides, I'm sure we're all hoping that we're wrong about the Talleys."

"You've got that right. All of us want

it to be somebody outside our sphere of friends. People always do."

Samantha shook her head. "I hate this."

"Me, too." Laura turned pain-filled brown eyes to the Colonel. "But we do have to do something, don't we?"

"Unless you want to let 'em get away with it."

Samantha straightened and took a deep breath. "So what do we do? We can't go to the authorities because it would be a dreadful scandal for the Talleys."

"Yeah. Especially if we've got it wrong."

"But as Laura said, we have to do something."

"Yeah."

"Well, I propose that we try to get proof, ourselves."

Laura was relieved. "Oh, yes. That way we won't embarrass anyone unnecessarily."

McLain groaned. "God deliver me from women."

Samantha said automatically, "And us women from men like you."

Seeing her heart wasn't really in it, McLain decided to ignore the dig. "Okay. So we're making this a DIY Project."

Laura whispered, "Do it Yourself?"

Samantha nodded.

"Very well," McLain clinched their decision. "I can handle that. Let's let the murder go for now. If we're gonna find the answer, we've gotta get to work. We need to establish some priorities. And the first thing we gotta do is find some way to decide if this guy is the real McCoy."

"How can we do that?" Laura was eager to think of anything, anything at all, to turn her mind safely away from the murder that had taken place in her driveway.

"Pictures. Do any of you know where there are any pictures of young Stoddard.

"He'll have changed."

"Yeah, but there are some things that never change. Eye color, the set of the ears, the shape of his eyes. We just need to compare this new Stoddard with some pictures of the old one."

Samantha shook her head. "I imagine all the pictures will have been moved to Florida with the rest of the Stoddards's personal property."

"What about Jasmine? Wouldn't she have had one of the boy?"

"I can ask," Samantha responded. "I'm

going to the hospital tomorrow. I'll find out."

"Okay. That's a start. I'll trundle my Lear out and fly down to the retirement town the Stoddards were headed for. I'll see if I can get into the house or storage or whatever. I'll leave first thing in the morning."

Laura was blinking at him like an owl. "You have a Learjet?" She wanted desperately to think about anything but the burden of proving that one of her friends had murdered another in cold blood.

McLain reached over and squeezed her hand. "It's okay, Laurie." He sought to reassure her that they'd get through this awful time. He waited until he saw in her eyes that the comfort he offered had taken hold, then he grinned at her and turned it into a joke about his plane to lighten the atmosphere, "It's last year's model."

Chapter Twenty-five

Samantha pushed rags away from her face and peered at her bedside alarm clock. "All right, boy, I guess I *was* oversleeping." She scratched him behind the ears, and he jumped down off the bed, happy to be forgiven for staring his owner awake. Samantha stretched like a cat and yawned mightily.

Then everything came crashing back into her mind, and she bolted upright. Proof. They had to find proof of the scam that they suspected was being perpetrated so that they could go to the police and let them take over.

She agreed with Art Chamberlain, who insisted that murder was a matter best left to the proper authorities, but those authorities had to be given a reason to investigate their suspicions of Olivia's death. They were unlikely to be impressed by the opinions of a bunch of civilians, as the police called those not on the force.

They—Laurie, John and she—must each get busy trying to locate someone with pictures of Benjamin Stoddard Jr., and it was high time she got cracking on her part. Comparing photographs of the real Benny to the boy at Brenda and Herb Talley's house would, she had no doubt, prove that Benny Stoddard wasn't really Benny Stoddard.

She tossed back the covers and swung her legs over the side of the bed. Things were getting serious. Very serious indeed. Janet Wilson's hesitant suggestion had taken on a significance the poor girl could never have foreseen.

Purposefully, she headed for the shower, slipped out of her satin pajamas, and stepped into the brisk spray. After she'd gotten the shampoo out of her hair, she twisted the control and the cool rinse with which she always finished her morning ablutions pelted down bracingly. The lower temperature of the water chased the last of the cobwebs from her mind, and as she reached for her towel, an idea presented itself.

"Janet!" she said aloud.

"Grrowff?" Rags looked up from his post on the far edge of the fluffy bath mat, curious.

Toweling briskly, Samantha told him, "I must call Janet." Pulling on her terry cloth robe as she padded out to the bedside table, she picked up the telephone and punched in the number for Greater Tidewater Realty. It was early yet, not even nine, but just maybe . . ."

"Good morning. Greater Tidewater Realty. How may we help you?"

"Janet, is that you?"

"Yes, it is. Samantha?"

"Yes. And I have a question I must ask you."

"Of course, what is it?"

"Yesterday after you dropped me off, Laura Fulton, the Colonel and I got together for coffee, and I told them about the suggestion you made at lunch."

"Oh, Samantha. You didn't! That was such a silly, irresponsible thing that I said. I'd hoped you'd forget it. You weren't supposed to tell anyone."

"I do apologize for not asking if you'd mind me repeating it, but the more I thought about what you'd proposed, the more important it seemed to me. I truly hate to say it, but we think maybe the Talleys might have brought a false Benny here."

"Oh, Samantha. Now Laura and the Colonel will think I'm awful." Her voice took on an edge. "Not only paranoid, but also ungrateful. Mr. Talley was very kind to give me this job. I hate it that I've caused you to suspect him and his wife of—of anything underhanded."

Samantha brushed Janet's worry aside. "I'm sorry, Janet, really I am." She hesitated.

Janet sensed it. "What is it? What were you about to say?"

Samantha experienced a pang of guilt at saying what she knew would hurt the girl, but Janet had asked to be kept appraised of their plans, and this was certainly a major development in their investigation of her Cousin Olivia's death.

Samantha's voice showed her sympathy as she said, "And I am even sorrier to tell you the suspicions that arose from our impromptu meeting, but Colonel McLain thinks there is a very good possibility that your cousin really might have been murdered to keep her from exposing a bogus Benny Stoddard."

When Janet didn't speak, Samantha told her the rest of it.

"Furthermore, he thinks that Jasmine's accident may have been an attempt on her life, as well. She and Olivia were the only ones left of us here in Riverhaven who knew Ben Junior well enough to identify him, you know."

"Oh." Janet went quiet, and Samantha didn't speak while she let the girl come to grips with the dreadful news.

After a moment, Samantha spoke again, "We determined that we have to find pictures of Benny Stoddard to compare with the young man at the Talleys's. Colonel McLain says that there are many things about a face that age wouldn't change, and that by comparing, we can at least discover whether or not this is really the Stoddards's son and heir."

"Oh, dear. I should never have voiced my far-fetched thought."

"Don't regret it, dear. You wouldn't want someone to get away with such a dreadful thing if it is indeed an imposter."

"Yes. That's true. And you think that comparing Benny to old pictures of him might answer the question?"

"We certainly hope so."

Janet cleared her throat, and Samantha was sorry she had reopened the wound of the young woman's grief. Her voice sounded forced. "So, how can I help?"

"I'm going to the hospital today and while I'm there, I'm to ask Jasmine if she has any pictures of her and Benny. If she does have, I'll whip right over to her place and dig them out."

"She just might have some. I know they were close."

"There's something else. Just a few minutes ago in the shower, I thought of Olivia's pictures. You know, she was always taking snapshots of her Sunday school class when they went on outings or did anything special, and I hoped you would know where those pictures are."

Janet took a deep breath and said. "Oh-oh. Here comes a client. I'll have to get back to you, Samantha. I'm the only one here."

"Call me back as soon as you can!

Goodbye."

"Yes. Yes, I will." Janet hung up.

"Oh, blast, Rags. Why is it that something always happens to interrupt important conversations."

"Errf." His eyes brightened, and his lips lifted in a doggy grin. "Yap."

"Right. Nothing ever happens to rescue you when you're being bored to tears, only when something is interesting. There must be an evil principle at work here."

"Yap, yap, yap." Rags ran in small circles that got closer and closer to the hall door.

"All right, all right. I'll get dressed. I know you want your breakfast." She walked to the closet, and Rags sat down with a satisfied sigh. Samantha whispered, "Tyrant," into the sweater she was pulling on over her head.

***

The phone rang when she had half finished her breakfast.

"Hello?"

"Samantha? I've gotten the afternoon off. We can go look at Olivia's photo albums if you'd like."

"Oh. Wonderful. I'd planned to go

out to Jasmine's if she says she has any pictures of Benny at home, but I can do that tomorrow morning."

"Are you still going to the hospital, then?"

"Yes. I'd hate to disappoint her. This is her last day in traction, and I'd like to make it pass as quickly as I can."

"Okay. Why don't I pick you up at the hospital, then? It's a bit of a drive to where I've stored Olivia's things, so it's silly to take two cars."

"Fine." Samantha glanced out the window. The day had turned gray and sullen clouds were drifting in over the river. "Better bring a raincoat. It looks as if the weather's turning ugly."

"Will do. I'm finally getting used to all these sudden changes in the weather here in Virginia."

"Just wait till summer. Then the changes are even quicker."

"I'll see you in the hospital parking lot at . . . one, shall we say?"

"You're condemning me to a lunch there?"

"I have a few things to take care of before we go. I hope you don't mind."

"Of course not. I'm just eager."

"Yes. I can understand that." She hung up.

For once, Samantha wasn't annoyed. "Poor child." She looked down at her dog. "This must be very difficult for her, Rags."

Rags cocked his head, but didn't say a thing.

"Oh, Rags. You're such a good little dog. You can even understand Janet's grief."

Chapter Twenty-six

At the hospital, Jasmine fished in her purse as soon as Samantha had bent down and reached it up for her from inside the bedside cabinet. Keys jangled and papers rustled. Finally Jasmine handed her employer and friend her door key.

"I keep meaning to pin those keys to the lining of my purse so's they stay put, but I do keep on forgetting. What do you want pictures of Benny Stoddard for, Samantha Masters?" Jasmine frowned, suspecting something.

"Janet Wilson—the young lady I brought to see you—has expressed a shocking theory, Jasmine, and I want to prove or disprove it before I tell you what it is."

"And it has to do with Benny."

Samantha couldn't deny it.

"With pictures of Benny."

"Yes."

Jasmine lay and looked at Samantha a long minute. Then she said very carefully, feeling her way, "Yes. I suppose that would explain things, all right. Benny, if he really was home, would have come to see me by now." She sighed. "So I can guess what's happening. You want to compare the pictures of my Benny with this boy who won't come to see me, don't you?"

"Yes, Jasmine. We do."

"Who's 'we'?"

"Mrs. Fulton, the Colonel and I."

"Not the Wilson child? How come?"

"No, Janet put forth the question, but she was at work when Laurie and Colonel McLain and I got together. After discussing it, we decided we had to go looking for pictures we knew were Benny."

"She's poor Miss Charles's cousin, isn't she?"

"Yes. Though it seems they were more like sisters. If I remember right, Olivia said that Janet had lived with them from the time she was about twelve because her—Janet's—parents were killed in a fire. Anyway she's most eager to . . ." Samantha left their attempting to solve Olivia's murder hanging. There was no benefit in upsetting Jasmine while she was trapped in a hospital bed.

Jasmine wasn't having any. "She wants to know who killed Olivia Charles, is that right?"

"Of course. We all do."

"That's surely a fact. That was a dreadful thing, somebody stabbing that lovely Miss Olivia that way."

She shook her head and ordered Samantha, "Well, you have my door key, so you'd better go be about it. Go to the house to the right of mine—to Ms. Smithers—and take her with you into my house.

"She's always home, and she's a regular old nosy. She never misses a thing, that woman, so she'll come over to be checking on you if you don't go get her first. *I* know you're honest, but my neighbors don't." Jasmine smiled a crooked little smile. "Besides, it'll just look better. That way nobody'll take you for a burglar."

"Jasmine!" Samantha laughed with the woman in the bed. Then she said, "I'll go first thing in the morning. This afternoon

I'm going with Janet Wilson to look at Olivia's photo albums. She knows where Olivia's things are stored, of course."

Jasmine looked out the window at the gray skies. "I hope you brought your raincoat."

"You know I keep one in the car. But thanks for reminding me. Janet's driving from here, so I'd be soaked if I forgot to take it with me from the looks of the weather."

"Yeah. Good old Norfolk weather. No wonder most of us carry an umbrella in our cars." She sighed. "And now I have my very own built-in weather predictor." She tapped her cast.

"That's so, unfortunately. My left arm still aches when the weather takes a turn for the worst, and I broke that when I was a teenager."

"Well," Jasmine said in a dry voice, "I do thank you much for that cheery bit of comfort."

Samantha chuckled, gave Jasmine a hug and pecked her on the cheek. "I love you, you silly thing." She hugged her again. "I've got to go. Janet will be in the parking lot at one, and I want to get something to eat first."

"Be careful."

After Samantha had gone, Jasmine wondered what in the world had prompted her to say 'be careful' instead of 'goodbye.' She looked out the window again. Rain was coming. That must be it. Everybody needed to be more careful driving in the rain.

*****

While she took the elevator down to the cafeteria level, Samantha mulled over the fact that Janet seemed to think the Talleys were behind the bogus—if he *was* bogus—Benny, too. Grabbing a grilled cheese sandwich and a coffee she gulped them down. Not only did she want to hurry out of the large, echoing room with its capacity crowd of people in varying stages of grief or worry, but she also wanted to have time to phone Laura Fulton.

She wanted to tell Laurie where she was going. Not that she knew, come to think of it, but she wanted to tell her that they were about to get hold of Olivia's photos of Benny Stoddard.

"Yes," she told her best friend. "Janet is picking me up here at the hospital and taking me to wherever Olivia's things are stored. She says there are several albums of pictures among Olivia's belongings. Which certainly makes sense. You remember how Olivia always took pictures of everything we did in Garden Club or Bridge. I'm assuming she did the same for all the Sunday school projects and outings. Don't you think?"

"Yes. That's probably true. But where will you be? I went to your house to borrow your Bundt cake pan, and Rags is howling."

"Howling? How odd. Must be this storm coming in. Tell him it's all right and to be quiet. I'll call you the minute I get home, okay?"

"Samantha . . ."

"Gotta go." Samantha hung up before Laura could tell her she had no intention of going out in the rain again just to tell Rags to be quiet. Hmmmm. Maybe the hanging-up habit was contagious—and just maybe it had its uses.

She was a little worried about Rags. He never howled. Heaven knew he growled, barked, yapped or yipped, but he never howled. She hoped Janet would get her back home in time for her to take Rags to the vet to be checked out.

In the parking lot, Samantha could see no sign of Janet's little red sports car. So she was startled when Brenda Talley's black Lexus slid up beside her while she was retrieving her raincoat from her own car and Janet called, "Here I am."

"Oh. I was looking for your little red car." Samantha slipped into the passenger seat and threw back the hood of her raincoat.

Janet grinned at her. "I noticed how uncomfortable you were in it when I took you for our Mexican lunch so I borrowed Brenda's car. It's bigger."

Yes, thank heavens. But if you manhandle it the way you do your own car, Brenda will kill you. "How very nice of Brenda. I know this car is her pride and joy." She hoped that last statement would cause Janet to drive the Lexus more considerately than she did her own vehicle.

It didn't.

Samantha settled into the luxurious leather seat and set her mind to keeping the younger woman from learning that it was her driving, not the size of her car that made her uncomfortable.

"Yes, it was nice of Brenda to lend me her car, wasn't it? She leant me her raincoat, as well." Janet gestured toward the back seat.

Samantha glanced at the coat there and saw that it was, indeed, Brenda Talley's distinctive red raincoat. "So today *you'll* be Little Red Riding Hood." She chuckled. "We all tease Brenda that that's who she looks like in that coat."

"It is sort of one of a kind, isn't it?"

"Oh, yes." Samantha told her. "Brenda sent away to some out of state shop so that she could avoid looking like one of the," she formed little quotation marks in the air toward Janet with the first two fingers of each hand, "'usual flock of khaki-clad pouter pigeons' that she calls the rest of us."

Janet laughed, but the sound had a brittle sharpness to it. Samantha could easily understand that because of the rain. What had been a gentle mist when she'd gotten into the car had become a driving downpour. Being responsible for somebody else's expensive car had to be causing Janet anxiety. Samantha saw that her knuckles were white as she clutched the steering wheel.

Windshield wipers flailing, they passed the Norfolk Yacht and Country Club and headed toward Naval Station Norfolk. How annoying. Samantha felt a moment's irritation. They were quite close to home here. She could very well have left her car in her own driveway instead of at the Hospital downtown.

Hampton Boulevard was so puddled and shining wet that the rain pelting its surface made it impossible to tell where the lines marking the lanes were. She wished Janet would slow down.

In no time they'd passed the Destroyer Piers and Naval Station Norfolk and were whizzing down I-64, throwing plumes of rain water to either side like the bow wave from under a ship's prow. A driver blew his horn angrily as the Lexus inundated his Honda.

They whizzed past Forest Lawn, where Samantha's Grandmother and Grandfather Swann were buried. The cemetery's well-kept monuments and wide green lawns were all but invisible behind the sheets of rain blowing across Granby Street. Samantha was thankful Janet slowed a bit as she swept into the curve that took the highway on over Willoughby Spit.

Janet had slowed, however, to take the first exit. She shot onto the ramp like a bullet. With no more than a slight hesitation, she zipped through the stop sign at the end of it and sent the big car racing down the road away from what had once been Ocean View Amusement Park.

Samantha couldn't help herself. She said, "Its fortunate there was no traffic coming then."

"I'd checked. I can't see any reason to stop if there's nobody coming, can you?"

"Well," Samantha said dryly, "there is the law."

Janet laughed. "Nobody sane is out in this storm. And no policeman would want to stand out there in the rain just to give me a ticket for a boulevard stop."

"A boulevard stop?" Samantha had never heard the expression.

"That's Californian for a rolling stop. Everybody runs stop signs out there."

Samantha thought that that was a rather extreme statement. She'd certainly not run any stop signs when Andrew had been stationed at San Diego and she'd lived in

California three years. Neither, as well as she could remember, had anybody else there—always excepting the irresponsible few.

She glanced at Janet. The girl's profile was calm, if a little tense. Was that what was bothering her? Was she sitting here finding Janet Wilson one of those irresponsible few?

At that instant, the car jolted as it hit a pothole hidden in a puddle. Janet seemed unaffected by it. Samantha, in her place, would have cringed to have done that to a friend's car.

They'd reached an area where the old beach houses were spaced further apart. Many had been bought by people who had turned them into lovely year-round homes, Samantha remembered rather than saw. The rain was still obscuring everything, falling in heavy sheets that washed across them in undulating patterns like vertical waves, giving only a glimpse now and then of the scene outside.

Suddenly, Janet slowed, peered across Samantha and slewed into a driveway. Ahead loomed a large, square, four story house set seven or eight feet above the sand on pilings. Broad wooden steps led up to the porch that surrounded the house. Gracious in its heyday, it still maintained a forlorn air of dignity in neglect.

Lights glowed from the first floor windows in an obvious attempt to combat the gloom of the day. There were two cars parked near the stairway, and a third just around the side of the house. Janet pulled in between the two in front, nosing the Lexus to the foot of the stairs.

"Here we are. Olivia's apartment's upstairs. The two downstairs ones were already rented when she started buying the place. She let the tenants stay." Janet reached into the back seat for Brenda Talley's raincoat and struggled into it. Pulling the hood well forward to shield her face from the rain, she opened the car door and rushed for the steps, slamming the car door behind her.

Samantha closed the passenger door carefully and hurried after the slender girl in the red coat. She was full of questions.

Janet sensed it and smiled. Her voice was low as she slipped a key into the door's lock. "Olivia was buying this place. She thought she—we—could live in part of it and rent the rest out. Or, if she could get the zoning, she really wanted to turn part of it into a youth center. You know how she always worried about keeping kids off the street."

"Yes." Samantha smiled too, pleased at the way Janet kept her voice down in consideration of the people occupying the ground floor apartments. "Olivia was not only wonderful with children, she had an honest desire to make the world a better place for them. She had a real burden for them."

"That's a Christian phrase, isn't it?"

"Yes, I think it is. I can't imagine why I used it instead of just saying she was concerned for children. I suppose I just wanted to express the fact that her concern went deeper than most people's. I've rarely used that phrase."

Janet laughed as she swung the door open for them. "Well, I certainly heard it enough." Her voice was a husky whisper. "You probably picked it up by some sort of mental osmosis. My father was a preacher. Did you know that?"

"No I didn't." Tactfully, Samantha didn't ask anything about the girl's parents. She remembered that Olivia had mentioned at Bridge that they had died in a house fire when Janet was only twelve and that Janet had been raised as Olivia's own little sister from then on. Now Janet was alone, and the least they could do was to find the person responsible for making her so.

Samantha pushed her hood off the back of her head and wondered why Janet didn't do the same. The damp on it was going to ruin her hairdo.

Janet led the way upstairs as someone opened and peered briefly out of one of the doors on either side of the huge foyer from which the stairway rose. On the second floor, Janet used a key to unlock a paneled door. Inside, there was a spacious room with windows all along the wall that overlooked Chesapeake Bay. Looking around, Janet finally threw back the hood of Brenda's raincoat.

The room they were in was obviously the living room. There was a sofa sitting on a lovely Oriental rug with an expensive floor lamp beside it. The sofa was situated so that anyone sitting there could enjoy the view of the bay. A small bookcase stood nearby, the books arranged neatly by size. Olivia's reading glasses were on the forward edge of its top shelf. There were no other furnishings.

"Olivia was just beginning to move in when . . ." Janet left her sentence unfinished.

Samantha was all quick sympathy. "Oh, my dear. I know how difficult this is for you, and I'm so sorry to have to ask it of you."

Janet didn't answer. Instead she walked across the room to a hall that must lead to the bedrooms. In the dull gray of the stormy afternoon the hall was dark. Samantha, who had never been particularly afraid of the dark, suddenly felt somehow threatened.

Suppose whoever had brought the false Benny Stoddard to Norfolk was here, waiting to make sure nobody found proof of their perfidy? Suppose the impersonator himself had heard that she was looking for Olivia's pictures of the real Benny? Suppose. . . Her dreadful musings were cut short.

"I've stored all of Olivia's belongings here," Janet told her. "It seemed the easiest thing to do."

"Yes," Samantha shook off her

bothersome fancies and answered the bereaved girl. "Of course. Renting a storage shed would have been foolish when you have all this space."

"Yes." Janet's answer was almost inaudible. "I guess it is *my* space now."

The lump in Samantha's throat kept her from saying anything to comfort the girl.

Janet led the way to a door, pushed it open and felt for the light switch. "This is Olivia's bedroom." After the dark of the hall, the bedroom leaped into light.

And Samantha gasped.

***

Laura had had all she could stand of Rags's howling. Pretty soon now, Agnes Chamberlain would be calling the police or the animal control people! Under that abrasive facade she showed the world, Agnes might be only faintly tolerant of people but she had no patience at all with the idea that an animal might be suffering or in trouble while she stood around doing nothing.

Laura pulled her khaki raincoat off its hanger, and kicked off her loafers to slip into her rainproof Duck shoes. Glaring out the window, she wondered if she preferred the gentler rain she saw there to the pelting downpour of only a few minutes ago.

At least she hadn't been able to hear Samantha's Rags when the heavier rain had been stomping the starch out of her flower beds. Now she could. The dog was attempting to wake the dead! She grabbed her copy of Samantha's door key off the key rack. "At least I won't drown in this," she muttered as she went to Rags's rescue.

The phone rang the minute she was gone. "Hey, Laura. McLain here. Good thing you got this damn answering machine, after all. Just got back from Florida and need to talk to you and Sam. Couldn't get her. What's up? Call me."

At Samantha's, Laura let herself in and went straight to the indoor kennel Samantha always put her terrier in when she intended to be out for any length of time. "All right, Rags. It's all right. I'm here."

Rags had made a wreck of his kennel. His pad was scrunched untidily in one corner, and his food bowl was tipped up on edge and leaning against a side of the cage. The newspapers Samantha always left for him in case of necessity were shredded and soaked because the little dog had turned his water bowl upside down too.

Rags himself was in a state. He'd stopped howling and started barking the minute Laura had put the key in the lock. He was barking still, and Laura covered her ears. "Enough! I can't hear myself think!"

Rags increased the tempo of his barks.

"Shut up or I won't let you out."

The instant silence was a shock. "Oh, dear. You really do understand some things, don't you?" Laura was surprised.

"Yap!" Rags's bright shoe button eyes avidly watched her fingers as they worked the latch. The instant she had it undone, he lunged out, flinging the cage door wide. He headed for the back door in the kitchen like a shot.

"Oh, no. I'm not just letting you out to run around," Laura told him. "I need to find your leash."

The little dog stopped leaping at the door and turned in mid-air. Now he was looking at the door to the pantry.

Laura felt as helpless as she did around

babies. "What do you want? Are you hungry? No, you couldn't be. There's food all over your kennel." She opened the door to the pantry. "What do you want?"

Rags flew into the pantry and looked up. There on its hook was his leash.

Laura took it down muttering, "Lord, this dog makes me feel retarded."

Rags refrained from comment.

Laura snapped the leash to his collar, and the two of them left the house.

She was feeling more than a little disheveled after having been dragged around Samantha's house, up and down her driveway twice and all over her own yard before the little tyrant at the other end of the leash let her pick him up—getting muddy paw prints all over her new London Fog—and dash into her house carrying him.

She had the dog toweled half dry when she noticed the red light blinking on her kitchen desk. "Oh!" she told him, "I have a message."

Pushing the play button, she heard the Colonel's gravelly voice. When he said he hadn't been able to reach Samantha, Rags whined.

Laura picked up the phone to call McLain's number. Before she could, the answering machine beeped again and a second message came through.

The recording lost none of the anger in the speaker's voice. It was Brenda Talley and she was clearly upset. "Listen to me Laura Fulton! Benny is gone. I can't find him anywhere. If that friend of yours, Samantha Masters, has taken him to visit her precious Jasmine without so much as even leaving me a note so that I wouldn't worry, then you'd better tell me! I want you to know that . . ."

But the machine cut her off before Laura could hear what Brenda wanted her to know. She stood staring at the machine as it beeped the series of beeps that signaled the termination of the recorded calls.

Outside, lightning flashed. An instant later, thunder shook the panes of the windows around her. Laura picked up the phone with fingers that trembled and pressed in the Colonel's number.

Chapter Twenty-seven

Samantha stood transfixed with horror. Everything she was looking at had been violated. Olivia's bed clothes were slashed, baring the mattress, and that was slashed, too. All four creamy beige walls bore blots of crimson paint that seemed to have been hurled at it with great force, splattering then running down in rivulets, the splotches bleeding like wounded hearts.

Scrawled across the mirror above the triple dresser were the words, "Leave me alone!"

Madness had run rampant in this room and the chilling residue of its malice reached out even now.

Samantha shuddered. He'd been here. The murderer had been here and had destroyed Olivia's lovely room. Her mind refused to analyze or accept the depths of hatred he must have felt for poor Olivia. Or the bounds of his madness.

She took a backward step, distancing herself from the obscene destruction. With a tremendous effort, she pulled herself together. "Oh, my dear," she managed at last. "This must be so awful for you." She turned to Janet. The girl was statue-still. "Let's go back into the living room."

"Don't worry, Samantha dear. I've seen this room before." Her face was stony.

Samantha's heart went out to the poor child. She'd no doubt discovered this dreadful destruction of her beloved cousin's room when she'd come to make certain that Olivia's picture albums were here. How brave she was to have opened this particular door now. Obviously she sought comfort from her, but Samantha had none to offer.

How could she comfort Janet when the girl had lost the mainstay of her life? She could, however, offer her an escape from this brooding house. "Are you certain you want to go on looking for those pictures, Janet? We could come back another day." She couldn't help adding, "A sunny day."

"No," Janet said, her voice tense, "It's best to get this over with now."

***

Laura let go a sigh of relief when John McLain answered his phone. "I'm so glad you're back, John. How did you make the trip so quickly?"

"I left at two in the morning, so I was in position to investigate by the time offices opened down there in Florida." He sounded disgusted. "A fat lot of good it did. Everyone was courteous and curious, but nobody'd gimme the time of day when it came to where I might find the Stoddards's belongings, much less a chance to look through them for photo albums. Seems they're all locked away until the heir to the estate is found." The sound he made Laura could only interpret as a snort. "When I couldn't even bribe 'em, I gave up and flew out of there."

"Oh, John. How disappointing." Then, "Hush, Rags. I can't hear."

"Is that racket Sam's mutt?"

"Yes, it's Rags. Nothing I do seems to reassure him. He's been carrying on for hours now. Samantha's not back from going to look for Olivia's photo albums, and he's pitching a fit. That's why I have him here. If I'd left him at Samantha's he'd have raised the dead by now."

"Where'd Sam go to look?"

"I don't know. She didn't say. Just that Janet Wilson was picking her up."

McLain was silent for a long minute. "Look, Laura, I'm coming over. I have something to tell you, and I think I'd better do it there."

***

In Ocean View, the rain renewed its attack on the tall windows of the beach house. Sheet after sheet of it dashed, wind-driven, against the glass, setting the panes to vibrating in their frames.

Janet reached into the vandalized room and switched off the lights. Dark mercifully covered the pitiful wreckage of what had been Olivia's elegant bedroom. The abrupt darkness caused the two tall windows opposite the doorway where the women stood to glow with the deepening gray-blue of the rain-washed twilight outside.

Samantha turned away to Janet. The eerie light emphasized the strain on the girl's face, and quick pity rose in Samantha. She wanted to get Janet away from here as soon as possible. "It's getting late. Do you know exactly where the pictures are?" Try as she would to sound less grim than she felt, her voice was still flat with the depression she felt.

Questions flooded her mind. Why would anyone do this to Olivia's lovely things? Wasn't it enough that they'd taken her life? And what did the scrawl on the mirror mean? "Leave me alone!" The red-painted words were forever emblazoned on her mind. Leave who alone? The answer was obvious. The young man at Brenda Talley's, of course. Certainly he wanted Olivia to leave him alone. It was *his* plans Olivia might have interfered with.

Certainly neither Herb nor Brenda would have had any reason to write those words. Nor, she was certain, would they have been guilty of the wanton destruction of the room she'd just seen. Not even if they were driven to the brink of desperation. She closed her eyes for a moment, thinking on that.

Somehow the assertion made her feel better. Relief flooded her. No, her neighbors were most certainly not capable of that.

Thanking God for small favors, she wondered if the perpetrator of the destruction could still be here, hiding somewhere. There *had* been that third car parked around the corner of the house as if it were trying not to be seen, she remembered.

She shoved aside the thought that a murderer might lurk here, and grasped at the memory of the utter stillness she'd felt when Janet had opened the door to the apartment. That feeling that a house was empty or occupied had never failed her. Whenever she'd opened a neighbor's kitchen door for a visit she'd always sensed whether or not anyone was home. She wasn't going to ignore that feeling now. She'd known this apartment was empty before she stepped into it. She wasn't going to deny that just because she'd had an awful shock. If Olivia's poor young cousin could be brave, so could she!

But, oh, how she wished she could shake off this feeling of dread that had come over her when Janet opened that door!

Squaring her shoulders she said, "Janet, we must find the pictures that we know

Olivia would have taken of Benny. We must. After the room you've just showed me, I can only conclude that he has to have been the one who did it. Clearly, only a deranged mind could have perpetrated such a horror." Firmly she announced, "I guess that clears Brenda. Say what you will about Brenda's moodiness, she is most certainly not deranged."

Janet turned abruptly and led the way down the hall to another door. Throwing it wide, she switched on its light, and gestured Samantha into the room.

Judging by the rows of neatly stacked boxes, this was a storage space. Turning, Samantha asked the girl behind her, "Where are the photo albums?"

"Through this door. There's another room off this one." She led the way to a narrow door, opened it and stood back.

Samantha took a step into the room, but couldn't see anything. The light from behind her did nothing to illuminate the space in front of her. She took another step and waited for Janet to switch on the light.

Samantha hated dark places, and because of the awful room she'd seen down the hall, this one seemed full of menace. She could feel the hairs at the back of her neck rise.

***

Laura was at the door before John even appeared over the tall brick wall that separated their properties. Rags was growling around her ankles, his muzzle pointed unerringly toward the direction from which the Colonel would come.

Laura threw the door wide the instant she saw McLain drop from the top of the wall. It seemed to her that he was taking an inordinately long time crossing the sweep of lawn, and impatience tore at her. "Oh, do hurry," she murmured senselessly. The Colonel was already coming at a dead run.

"Yerapp!" Rags stood on his hind legs and pushed at the screen door. He jumped back out of the way as the Marine tore it open and charged into the house.

"Have you heard from her yet?" he demanded.

"No. And it's getting late. Past time for feeding Rags. This isn't like Samantha."

"Yeah, I know."

"Brenda Talley left me a message that Benny is missing. She thinks Samantha took him to visit Jasmine. But Samantha didn't."

"Damn. I wish I knew what the hell's going on." He scowled. It was a measure of his degree of distress that he neglected to apologize for his profanity. He always did with her, while letting it stand to irritate Samantha. "This is getting complicated, Laura."

"You said you had something you wanted to tell me. Something that you had to come here to tell." Her brown eyes were solemn, anxiety at the back of them.

"Yeah." He was looking at her as if assessing her.

"Oh, do tell me," she burst out. "I can handle whatever it is."

He wondered if that was true. Somehow he considered Samantha the stalwart and Laura Fulton the dreamer of the group that he'd come to know over the last few weeks. He wondered just how much he could tell her without sending her into a fit of hysterics. Laura was no Samantha Masters, and Sam was bad enough.

Rags leapt against his leg, whining.

"Okay." He pushed his hand through the short hair on the top of his head. "Look,

I could do with some coffee."

"Oh, dear. You're stalling." Nevertheless, Laura went to the coffee maker and poured steaming brew into the mug she'd had waiting for him since his call. She turned with the mug in her hand and asked, "Is it so dreadful, then?"

He threw himself into a chair at the kitchen table and told her, "It's not good."

"But what could you have learned in Florida that would be so upsetting? You said they wouldn't give you the time of day." Laura eased into the chair opposite him and clasped her own mug with hands that suddenly needed the warmth it offered.

"It wasn't in Florida. It was in South Carolina."

Laura frowned, bewildered. "What were you doing in South Carolina?"

He took a swallow of coffee, regarding her levelly, marshaling his thoughts.

Laura frowned. "Will you please *tell* me!"

Rags jumped into her lap and stared at the man across the table. Laura was so distressed she didn't even notice the dog.

"I stopped off in Charleston because I remembered that Olivia Charles had lived there. I had plenty of time, thanks to the guys that wouldn't give me diddly in Florida. In Charleston, I looked up an old Marine buddy. The guy's a private investigator now, and I wanted to ask him to dig up any info he could find on Olivia Charles. And boy, did I hit pay dirt. Seems he was actually born and raised in Charleston, and his sister and mother had known Olivia's family. He knew all about 'em. Seems you Southerners take an inordinate interest in the lives of your friends and neighbors."

Laura didn't think anyone who cared could take less than an interest in their friends, but she didn't think this was the time to argue him into understanding. She nodded her head at him, urging him to go on.

"Olivia and her folks were thought of as saints, but get this. My buddy Josh McClaren's mother and sister thought that they were a little nuts, too, to take in a twelve year old girl who . . ." He paused as if measuring her possible response before he finished. ". . . who was suspected of burning the house down around her own parents to get rid of them."

Laura stiffened. Her eyes got as big as

saucers. McLain watched her carefully. Her nerve held.

The sound of a powerful engine approaching the house interrupted them. It circled the drive and returned across the front of the house to stop at the point in the drive nearest the side door.

"Get your coat." McLain gulped the rest of his coffee, jumped up and put his mug in the sink.

"My coat?" Laura stood.

Rags was dumped unceremoniously when she stood. Unruffled, he ran to where Laura's raincoat was hanging to dry and waited for her.

She shrugged into it, scooped him up and followed the Colonel out to the driveway. He helped her into the passenger side of the huge vehicle that brooded there, engine throbbing, and asked the man inside, "All gassed up?"

"All ready to go," Frank Takamoto answered from where he'd moved to the middle seat of the big SUV.

"Good." McLain put it into gear and exited Laura's property carefully. A nearly four-ton vehicle could do a lot of damage to a dry gravel drive, let alone a wet one.

Once he hit the asphalt that ran along in front of Samantha's house, he shoved his foot through the fire wall.

"Yap! Yap! Yap!" Rags vibrated with approval.

For such a behemoth of a vehicle, it took the corner on two wheels very nicely.

"You had to bring the mutt."

"Yes," Laura was staring straight ahead, rigid, but she could still speak. McLain decided that was good. He took the next corner a little more slowly, and Laura added, "I hadn't the heart to leave him all by himself."

Nobody was coming either way when he got to the stop sign after the Yacht Club, so McLain ran it and screeched left toward the naval base.

Laura clutched the grab bar with one hand and Rags with the other.

The terrier had most of the breath squeezed out of him, but decided to be generous and refrain from complaining.

"That mutt'd probably die of apoplexy if you'd left him." McLain grinned, striving to make her relax. "Or tear up all your furniture."

Laura did relax a little at that. "Believe

me, if I'd been thinking clearly, my furniture would have been a very valid consideration. I just couldn't bear to leave him all alone. Where are we going?"

"To Greater Tidewater Realty. They're the ones who should know where their receptionist is."

"Of course. Janet. Samantha's with her."

"Yes."

***

Samantha gazed around her at the tiny, windowless room. There was nothing in it but a trunk in one corner. It was a small affair with bright brass hinges and colorful designs painted on it. It was strangely out of place, somehow, in this otherwise empty room.

Samantha turned back to face Janet, frowning slightly. Were the albums in this brightly painted trunk?

"That's my trunk. My daddy made it for me. It used to hold my dolls and their clothes. My mother made them lots of clothes."

The size of the room gave Janet's voice a strange, childlike quality.

Samantha didn't know if she was lulled

by the steady rhythm of the rain or by the eerie twilight, but she felt almost as if she *were* talking to a child. "It's very pretty. It looks as if your father took a great deal of time making it."

"Oh, yes, he did. I've always loved it. It was the only thing he ever made me. I was careful to get it out of the house before the fire."

Samantha's whole mind was focused on the chest. She answered automatically, "How fortunate that you could. So few things are ever saved when there's a fire." She moved toward the trunk with the care of someone almost afraid to find themselves finally standing on the brink of discovery.

Suppose there were no photos of young Benny Stoddard after all? Or suppose the photos proved that the young man at Brenda Talley's was indeed the long lost son of Mimi and Ben Stoddard, and indeed their legal heir? Then what would they do? They'd be no closer to the identity of the murderer.

She shook off the myriad doubts and questions plaguing her. Smiling a tight little smile over her shoulder at its owner, Samantha opened the trunk. There, in the carefully crafted tray at the top of its interior, were several photo albums.

Samantha breathed, "Oh, Janet. Here they are! The albums we were searching for."

Janet came to stand close behind her. "Yes." Her voice was as calm as Samantha felt excited. "Those on the top are Olivia's old ones. Then there are a few more recent ones under them."

Samantha sat down on the clean-swept floor and pulled the first of the books out of the trunk and into her lap. The light from the unshaded bulb hanging from the center of the tiny room's ceiling was more than bright enough for them to see the pictures Olivia had taken. There were pictures of a large home in a lovely garden.

"That's Olivia's home in Charleston." Janet reached over Samantha's shoulder and turned the next page. "Those are her parents."

The picture was of a kind-faced couple past their prime, smiling into the camera and squinting a little in the sun. Olivia stood between them, a teenager in bobby socks. "They look very nice. It's easy to see why Olivia was so gentle. Growing up with them as your parents must have been a happy experience."

"Yes. They were very nice. Very kind." Janet turned several pages at once, and they were looking at an older Olivia. Other pictures on the same page showed groups of children with whom she must have worked. Another bunch of pages flipped past, and Samantha was looking at a picture of Mimi and Ben Stoddard. This time the child between the parents was Ben Stoddard Jr, and Jasmine, a younger edition of her very own Jasmine, stood close by. "Ah. Good. Here's Benny."

Abruptly, Janet dropped a second album in Samantha's lap. She crushed it down on the first, covering the page to which Samantha had opened it. A quick sensation of danger shot through her. Samantha tried to dismiss it as overburdened nerves, but alarm bells were beginning to go off in the back of her mind.

Janet commanded, "Look here."

There were two people in the picture to which she pointed. One was a young man who bore a startling resemblance to the youth in the picture with Mimi and Ben Stoddard, the other was a girl.

Behind the two people in the picture, Samantha could see a wall with words on it. Words carved in granite. The first was hidden by the boy's head, but over his shoulder she could read part of them. It said —*hiatric Insti*—. Then the remainder of the last word was cut off by the photographed face of a pretty, smiling girl. And the girl was Janet Wilson.

Chapter Twenty-eight

McLain gunned the SUV into the neatly landscaped parking lot of the Greater Tidewater Realty building, slammed it to a rocking halt and stepped out into the downpour. Opening the passenger door, he grabbed Rags from Laura and tossed him to Frank Takamoto. "Here, keep the mutt happy, Frank. We'll be right back."

Laura and he ran for the building. Inside they shook off the raindrops and Laura told McLain, "I thought that was Janet's little red car I saw parked on the side street, but we were past it before I could be certain. Did you see it?"

"I . . ."

Brenda Talley burst into the room from one of the private offices. "So that's who took my car! I thought it was Benny. She took my raincoat, too. The little bitch! I'll kill her!" Fury radiated from her.

"Hey! Take it easy. What's going on?"

Brenda turned on him like an angry cat. "My Lexus is gone! Benny left me a stupid goodbye note that I almost didn't find and has run away, so I thought he'd taken it. I wondered what in hell he wanted with my raincoat, the stupid bas . . ."

"Hey! Watch it. There's a lady present."

Brenda ignored him, her eyes on Laura. "But you say you saw her—Janet's—car parked down on the side street, so it must be Janet. Damn that girl! I wondered why she watched me like a hawk when I put the spare keys in my desk. Now, I know! How dare she? If she puts one scratch on that Lexus I'll . . ."

"Yeah, yeah. We know. You'll kill her. Later. Right now we have something more important to worry about than your blasted over-priced wheels."

Brenda sputtered through the first part of his explanation, but by the end of it McLain had her complete attention.

"So," he concluded, "where are Olivia's things—that's where they're headed."

Brenda was immediately all efficiency.

Samantha was more important to her even than her Lexus. If anything happened to dear, stuffy Samantha she wouldn't have a single true friend left in Tidewater.

Wimps always found Brenda Talley of Greater Tidewater Realty too hard to take, and she knew it. And she considered so many of her well-bred 'Vah-gin-Yah' friends, thanks to their soooo good manners, wimps. Her habit of getting right to the point and saying exactly what she thought had disconcerted more than a few lovely Southern Belles, but Samantha Masters could take it. Or at least understand it, and Brenda cherished her for that.

She walked back into the broad hall from which she'd come and studied the key board. Neatly labeled keys hung there on numbered pegs that were matched to files of their listings with Greater Tidewater Realty. Studying the board for a moment, she put her finger out and touched the blank spot under a peg. "Laura, you know where Olivia's apartment is, of course."

"Yes, over on Stockley Gardens."

"Right. But see this. Unless I'm mistaken, this was the peg for her newly acquired beach house. We still had copies for the workmen Olivia commissioned us to send out there. And the keys are missing."

"Where is the place, woman?" McLain had to hold himself back from shaking it out of her. "Where!"

***

Samantha woke up with an awful pain in her head. Without opening her eyes, she tried to raise her hand to the knot she felt certain must be at the center of the pain, and found that she couldn't move. Her eyes flew open!

She was on the cold, bare floor of the tiny room she last remembered, and she was bound hand and foot. Who could have done this? Where was Janet? Was she all right?

Her eyes refused to focus. She blinked them into obedience and looked up. The bare bulb hanging from the ceiling fused into a single glare after a moment, and Samantha thanked the Lord that she didn't have a concussion. "Janet!" she gasped. "Janet, are you all right?"

Turning her head to look for her young friend, she saw Janet sitting quietly on the glossily painted trunk.

Janet smiled brightly. "Ah, you're back.

Good. Now I can talk to you."

Samantha's mind rioted. She wanted to demand answers. What had happened? Who'd hit her on the head? What was the matter with Janet? Untie-me! Why aren't *you* tied? All of it ricocheted around in her mind, one question colliding with another.

Then the spinning stopped, and she knew the reason that she was lying on the floor with her wrists and ankles bound and Janet was sitting calmly on the trunk watching her. The trunk Janet had been able to get out *before* the fire that killed her parents!

Oh, how could she have been so stupid? How could she have been so focused on finding the photo albums that she hadn't picked up on what was said? It had been Janet who'd attacked her and trussed her up like a Christmas turkey!

As the last of the fog dissipated and an infinite sadness filled her heart, she concluded Janet was indeed all right in the sense of being unharmed physically. But Samantha now realized that the lovely young girl sitting there so calmly was far from all right in quite another way.

Samantha didn't say any of what was

running through her mind. Somehow, she sensed that saying nothing at this point was the wisest choice she could make. So she lay and looked up at Janet, letting the questions she had on the tip of her tongue speak from her eyes.

"You want to know what's going on, don't you Samantha dear?"

Samantha nodded carefully. Surely that was the safest way. She very desperately wanted to play it safe. She was more than deeply troubled by the odd expression in Janet's glittering eyes. Much more than that—she was terrified.

"It's quite simple. As you've probably guessed by the picture of 'Benny'"—she used the gesture in the air for quotation marks that Samantha had used in the car and giggled. "I like that, that's cute."

She stroked the quotation marks in the air again, then grew serious. "The picture of Benny and me that I showed you just a while ago, I'm the one who brought Freddie—that's really his name—here to pretend to be Benny Stoddard. I knew the story of the lost Stoddard boy from Olivia, of course. I can't tell you how often she whined about him. Wherever we went,

Olivia tried to fill me in on everything and everybody so that I'd feel at home and part of things.

"She hated moving around, but since she was my keeper, she had to when I . . . made someone upset, but she always hoped I'd settle in.

"I hated her for that. For being my keeper, I mean." She shifted a little. "The courts awarded me to her after her sanctimonious parents died. I was still in the mental institute at the time, but meddling old Olivia got me out and promised that she'd keep me with her always and that we would live a happy life together in the real world."

Janet laughed scornfully, the sound sharp and brittle in the small room. "The real world. And they thought *I* was crazy! Olivia really believed I'd settle down into the tiresome grind that she considered 'a good life.'" Her eyes narrowed, and she spat venom into the two words, "The fool."

She sat, quiet for a few minutes, then spoke again more calmly. "As I said, I hated her for always being there, always looking after me, always caring what I did. Always having her nose in my business. She was my jailer!"

The girl took a deep breath to steady herself. "When she found out that I'd brought Freddie here to pretend to be Benny Stoddard, she had a fit." She laughed again, and Samantha could clearly hear madness at the base of it. She tried to squirm away from the slender girl on the trunk.

Janet was beside her in an instant. "Here, let me help you sit up." To Samantha's utter surprise, the girl grasped her under the arms and pulled her over to lean back against the wall. Again Janet smiled brightly, "There. Isn't that better?"

"Y-yes," Samantha's voice sounded as if she hadn't used it for a month. Long habit forced the words, "Thank you."

"Oh, you're welcome. I don't want you to be uncomfortable just because I have to kill you, after all. Now where was I?"

Samantha didn't hear the neat repetition of what Janet had already said as she led up to what she wanted to say next. Her own mind was too occupied with trying to grasp that she was going to die! Janet intended to kill her! As difficult as it was, Samantha understood that. She was going to die here in this bare little room, and she didn't even know why. Before Janet had begun to explain to her, she hadn't known that the girl was in any way implicated in . . .

"Are you listening to me?" Janet stamped her foot and spoke sharply. "You'd better be listening to me, Samantha Masters!"

Samantha didn't want to listen. Samantha wanted to ask. "Why? Why do you think you have to kill me?"

"I was getting to that if you would just *listen!*" Janet looked as if she wanted to slap the older woman.

Samantha closed her eyes for an instant, then opened them and looked Janet straight in the eye. "I'm listening!" she told her captor testily. After all, what did she have to lose at this point? Nobody even knew where she was.

"Oh." The girl looked momentarily taken aback, then the light of purpose returned and burned bright in her eyes. "After Olivia told me I'd have to confess what I'd done, apologize to Brenda and unmask Freddie—Benny to you—I knew I had to act." She smiled winningly. I'd already acted once, and wouldn't Olivia have had a fit if she'd known. I'd already killed Dr.

Tiggs and cleaned his fingerprints off with emery boards so that nobody could find out who he was. The old fool came to warn Olivia that I'd taken Freddie and left the institute. Couldn't have that.

"At Bridge, Alison said that her aunt had the travel brochures Olivia wanted, remember? Then Olivia said when she'd pick them up, and suddenly I saw the way to stop her meddling. All I had to do was wait by the gate at Laura's until Olivia got there, stop her car and kill her."

Samantha shuddered. Janet's casual recounting of how she'd killed her own cousin in cold blood horrified her.

"It was so hard ever to catch Olivia out of the apartment and alone after dark, you know. I knew this might be my only chance. I had the knife ready, and she stopped the car and rolled down the window like a perfect lamb. I think she was surprised to see me." Janet giggled. "I think she was even more surprised to die."

The girl leaned forward earnestly. "Wouldn't you think she'd have guessed? She'd already seen what I wrote on her mirror. She knew I wanted her to *leave me alone!*" She sat back. "But, oh, no. Not

'Miss perfect-everybody-loves-me, I-love-everybody Olivia'! She couldn't see me living without her. Without her meddling care and guidance—not for one minute. Well, I showed her!"

Samantha's eyes misted. Poor Olivia. Poor, dear Olivia.

"Are you crying?" Janet demanded, obviously annoyed.

Samantha shook her head vehemently. She wasn't going to let this woman think she'd made her cry. Though she supposed she *was* someone to weep for. It didn't seem that she was going to have time to come around to weeping for Janet, however.

"You know, Samantha. This is all your own fault. You'd have been all right if you'd just left well enough alone. The only reason I have to kill *you* is because you vowed to get 'Benny' to go to the hospital if you had to drag him. I couldn't let you do that. Jasmine seeing Freddie would have ruined everything."

She sighed. "She should have just died when I hit her with the car I stole. Then it wouldn't have mattered. After I killed Olivia, there was no one else left who really remembered Benny Stoddard except Jasmine." She stirred restlessly. "But oh, no. You had to promise yourself you'd get Benny over to visit Jasmine. And you told me so at lunch, remember?"

Yes, Samantha did remember. Oh. *Why* did she have to talk so much!

Janet glanced at her watch. "Well, it's still a while until the girls in the downstairs apartments leave for work. They're young sailors's wives, you know, and they work as waitresses in the evenings while their husbands are out at sea. One of them has a cat. Do you like cats?"

"I have a dog, but I like cats, too." I have a dog. Rags. I'm never going to see Rags again. What will he feel when I never come home? Who'll take care of him?

"I have to wait to burn the house down until the girls are gone and I can let Tom out. That's Lucille's cat. Tom. I couldn't bear to kill Tom."

Samantha wanted to shout at her, *Well you don't seem to be having any trouble with the thought of killing me!* but she said instead, "Janet. One of the women downstairs opened her door as we started upstairs here. If you know her well enough to know what she does for her job and that she has a cat named Tom, don't you realize that she might have recognized you?"

"Of course. That's why I took Brenda's car and raincoat. That's why I didn't put my hood back until she had seen us and closed her door. I knew she'd look. She's a terrible snoop. She feels it's her responsibility to look out for the girl across the hall from her. Mary's even younger, you see, and it's her first time away from home. So Lucille—that's the snoop— promised she'd keep her eyes open. Now she'll think I was Brenda because Brenda has shown the house in the rain before Olivia bought it and she'll remember the red raincoat, and Brenda will be blamed for killing you." She smiled brightly. "Aren't I clever?"

Samantha didn't answer. There seemed to be no end to the lives this woman was willing to ruin—or to take.

When Samantha refused to answer, Janet lost her patience. "You want to be quiet instead of answering me? Then be quiet!" With that, she slapped piece of duck tape over Samantha's mouth.

She stood a moment regaining her

composure, then glanced at her watch. "Since I have a little while before I can set the fire. I think I'll go get a cup of coffee somewhere and come back around five-thirty. The girls leave about five-fifteen." She rose quickly, and the hem of Brenda's red raincoat caught on the brass trim of the trunk. With a rip, it bent the brass away from the corner of the trunk.

Janet turned on Samantha savagely. "Now look what you've done! As if it isn't bad enough I have to leave it in here to be destroyed this time, now it's hurt! You've made me hurt the trunk my daddy made me! For that you can just sit here in the dark until you burn!" She flicked off the light and slammed the door behind her.

Samantha was left in total darkness.

Chapter Twenty-nine

With McLain driving, they reached Stockley Gardens in less time than Laura had thought possible. He dived out of the car and ran into the handsome old brick building that housed Olivia's spacious apartment before she could even frame a protest, much less voice one.

The rain slacked off as he disappeared into the doorway. It remained light enough for those waiting for him to make out his form as he ran back toward them a few minutes later.

Then, just as he reached the vehicle where Laura, Frank and Rags waited, lightning forked from the sky. Thunder rolled in its wake as McLain ducked into the Suburban and the heavens reopened.

With renewed vigor, the rain drummed

down on the metal roof of the SUV. McLain raised his voice to be heard over it. "Not here. They're not here, and the neighbor on that floor says nobody's been here for a coupla days."

"You had to check. We'll have to go on down to Ocean View." Laura's voice was as tense as the hands she clasped in her lap. She jumped when Rags yapped agreement from the seat in back of her.

McLain glanced at the dash clock. "Damn. It's almost five. We'll be lucky to get out of town, much less get to Ocean View."

Laura thought hard. "Let's try to go the slow way. If we're lucky, we can cut out a lot of the traffic."

"The slow way, huh? Well, you'll have to guide me. I'm not that familiar with the area yet."

"Turn left here," Laura peered out at the broad meridian-like park of Stockley Gardens. The boxwoods could hardly be seen through the sweeping curtains of rain. "Left again here." They passed the corner on which the private girls' school she'd attended had stood. Even the rhododendrons that had been the head mistress's pride and joy were gone, she'd been told, but in this rain today she couldn't see well enough to verify it. "Go left on Colonial. And . . ."

"And what?"

"Nothing." Laura had been going to say 'hurry', but there wasn't any need. McLain was flying down the street. In the big Suburban, and with cars parked on both sides, what had originally been thought a broad thoroughfare seemed more narrow than a lane.

When Laura braced her feet so hard that her bottom came up out of the seat, he told her, "Relax, Laurie. I'm not gonna hit anybody."

"That's nice," Laura gasped and took a firmer hold on the grab bar over her door for an instant. Then she realized that her arm would block his view of any cars coming from her side. She transferred her grip to the arm rest, trying not to puncture the leather with her fingernails.

"God, Laura, don't go all white-knuckled on me."

"I'm not!" she lied. She was thinking hard, trying to decide if she should take him over to Monticello where there was an underpass. If there wasn't a train in the way, that detour would waste two minutes, and she was driven by a terrible sense of urgency. If there were a train, Colonial, as well as Llewellyn, would be blocked.

She opted for the safest course. "Go right here." She had almost taken too long to decide. They were on top of the intersection. The big vehicle took the corner on two wheels, slewing out of its lane as it did. A car approaching in the oncoming lane swerved. Its horn blared wildly.

McLain cursed under his breath as he wrestled the behemoth back where it belonged, slamming the rear right wheel on the curb as he did. "Damn thing corners like a baseball bat," he muttered. Aloud he said, "Thanks a lot for the lead time, Laurie."

"I'm sorry!" she yelled at him as he shot through two more traffic lights, one of them still mercifully green. They had used up almost all of Twenty-first Street before she could shout, "Left! Left next!"

They shot past Doumar's. Its canopied parking spaces were nearly deserted in the drenching downpour. On their right, the Coca-Cola bottling plant went past in a blur. They were in and out of the overpass in one rain-spewing plunge, hit the merge point of Monticello and Granby at sixty-five and streaked down past the old Jewish cemetery and the City Park.

Over the Granby Street Bridge they flew with Laura breathing a prayer of thanks that the light at its foot was green and there was nobody trying to get out of Willowwood for them to kill!

On past Cromwell Place, Thole Street and Granby High School, where Samantha's cousins had gone, they sped. As they passed Pamlico, they could see the cars bumper to bumper parked on the elevated freeway over to their right, and she could finally sigh with relief. She'd been right to take them the slow way.

McLain shot her a grin. "Looks like you done good, Laurie. Ya' done good."

The clock on the dashboard said five-nineteen.

***

Awake, Samantha lay and hated the dark! Though she might love it for sleeping, any time she was awake, she craved light. That was why she had so many windows in her house, and why the first thing she did every morning when fully clothed and in her right mind was to pull open every drapery and let in the sunlight.

But there was no way she could let in the light here in this cramped, windowless little room and never had she craved it more. The darkness was impenetrable. It had weight, a weight that was almost suffocating. It made her skin crawl.

Suddenly, downstairs, she heard a murmur of light feminine voices. Then the outer door to the house closed. Frantically, she rubbed her cheek against her shoulder, trying to dislodge the duct tape Janet had put over her mouth. Then a car engine started, and she knew it was too late to scream for help.

Tears trickled down her cheeks. For a long moment, she slumped against the wall where Janet had left her. Then she reared up and scrubbed the duct tape against the shoulder of her raincoat with greater determination.

She had no intention of dying quietly here just to please Janet Wilson! She was going to get free and get out of here if it was the last thing she ever did!

She refused to give any consideration to the way she had phrased *that* thought.

But, oh, how she wished she could see.

Finally the tape came off and she told herself aloud, "Well lying here complaining that you can't flick the light switch isn't going to get you anywhere, Samantha Eugenie Swann Masters!"

Ignoring the slight tremor in her voice that threatened to defeat her, she said with more firmness, "Think. Prioritize. You're supposed to be so blasted good at prioritizing. Do it!"

She lay still for a moment, hoping for inspiration. A picture of Rags's dear little face was all that came to mind. Who would take care of him if she died here in this tiny, dark room? Who would put up with him? Maybe . . .

"Stop that!" she said so loudly that it bounced back at her. She gave herself a shake, literally. Her bonds pulled at her wrists and ankles. The ropes were certainly tight.

"Well, at least you learned something useful. They don't feel like ropes. I think they're drapery cords. Drapery cords should be easier to get out of than real ropes. Heaven knows Rags chewed through them quickly enough when he was a puppy."

But even if she'd had his sharp little teeth, she couldn't chew cords that bound her hands behind her back. How to cut through them? She thought a minute. "Of, course! That piece of brass that Janet caught Brenda's raincoat on!"

She slithered and squirmed over to the doll trunk. With a little manipulation, she got the cords that bound her wrists up against the piece of twisted brass trim. Triumphantly, she began sawing them back and forth across the sharp edge of the displaced ornamental brass piece.

***

"There! I think it's there! Didn't Brenda say it was a great big square building on a large lot?"

"Yeah. She did. Is it the right number?"

"Oh, John. I can't see any number in this rain!"

"Well, let's hope your woman's intuition is operating full swing, then, Laurie. Damned if I can see, either."

Frank Takamoto spoke quietly from behind them. "This is it."

"Howdaya know?" McLain growled the question even as he sent the Suburban skidding into the narrow driveway.

"Because Rags is at attention like a pointer. He says Mrs. Masters is in that house."

They all flinched as Rags's agonized howl assailed their ears.

That's when they saw the flames.

***

Inside, in the dark little room, Samantha had freed her wrists and was working on the knots that held her ankles. Bent double and fumbling in the dark, she finally worked the cords free. Leaping to her feet, she threw herself at the door. Grasping the knob, she paused. Somewhere below, she thought she heard the crackle of flames.

She had to get out! This old wooden beach house would burn quickly. Out of the first room, she threw herself at the door of the storage room beyond it. Frantically she twisted the knob.

The door was locked!

***

McLain hurtled out of the SUV and rushed toward the house, Rags at his heels. Over his shoulder he yelled, "Call the fire department!"

Frank Takamoto gestured with the cell phone to signify compliance even as he sucked at the wounded finger Rags had bitten in his determined bid for freedom.

Laura shot out of the vehicle to scoop up a cat that was about to run back into the house. As she caught up the cat, the rain whirled away in the wind, and she saw Janet Wilson running toward Brenda Talley's Lexus hidden in a stand of live oaks.

"Frank," she shrieked, pointing.

Takamoto was out of the car in a flash, dashing to cut off Janet's escape.

***

Samantha slammed her shoulder into the door with all her might. She hoped to splinter one of the old panels and somehow reach through and unlock the door. She knew she wasn't strong or heavy enough to burst the lock or thrust through the whole door, especially since she remembered it opened inward. Hopelessness began to take hold of her as she admitted the door was too sturdy.

And now she could smell smoke.

Praying frantically, she renewed her

assault on the door.

***

Storming across the broad porch, McLain wrenched at the knob and threw open the door to the building in which fire burned. "Sam! Sam! Where are you?" This damned house was so big. What if he didn't find her in time?

Then he felt the tiny teeth savaging his ankle. Rags! The mutt had known she was here! The mutt was trying to get him to follow him!

God bless the little fellow, Rags *knew* where Samantha was. "Thank God!" He turned and raced after the dog.

Smoke was worse as he climbed the stairs three at a time. Rags still remained ahead of him, his little claws beating a frantic tattoo on the old pine floor boards of the hall. The dog threw himself at a door, and McLain kicked it in. No time to try the knob to see if it was locked. Smoke was billowing up the stairwell, and he could hear the flames roaring now.

Rags tore across a spacious living room and darted down a hall. McLain was right behind the terrier as he slewed into a room, claws scrabbling on bare wood.

McLain had no time to wonder if he was right. He grabbed the knob of the door at which Rags jumped and jumped again. "Sam! Sam!" He shouted at the top of his lungs. "Are you in there?"

"Oh, yes! Yes! Get me out! Please!"

"Stand away from the door." McLain rammed his shoulder into it. The door splintered and what was left of it slammed back against the wall inside the room.

Samantha dashed out. "We've got to get out! The house is on fire!"

McLain was all but struck dumb. "No shit, Sherlock," he muttered, and rushed after her.

Rags lost the rhythm of the run as they plunged down the stairs and tumbled to the bottom in a heap. He didn't even yip. Samantha turned back to go to his tiny motionless body.

McLain shoved her unceremoniously out the door into the scream of fire engine sirens. Doubling back, he scooped up the little dog. Carrying him like a football, he surged out of the burning house.

Samantha met him as he reached the distance the firemen had insisted she retreat to. "Oh, John. Is he all right?"

McLain cradled the tiny animal in his arms and felt over his limp form carefully. "No broken bones. I think he just knocked himself cold in that fall down the stairs."

Samantha reached out for him, and McLain placed Rags in her arms. "Oh, Rags, please be all right. Please wake up."

"Merff."

Samantha smiled radiantly. "Oh, see, John. He's talking to us."

"God, Sam. Don't go all goofy on me. It's bad enough you give that dust mop house room without letting him make you sappy."

Rags raised his head and glared at McLain.

Samantha said, "So I won't get sappy. But what do you think your chances of finding me in time would have been without him?"

McLain surrendered. "Okay, mutt. You're a hero. Again. Good dog. Let's leave it at that."

A moment later, out of the chaos of idling fire engines, shouting firemen and webs of hoses snaking across the sand, Frank Takamoto appeared with a struggling Janet

Wilson held firmly by the arm.

Caught red handed and incapable of fighting loose, Janet then stood calmly and watched as men risked life and limb to stop the flaming damage she had set in motion from progressing any further.

McLain looked from the slender girl in the red raincoat to his disheveled neighbor. "Now, how the hell did you let her sandbag you, Sam?"

Samantha let the 'Sam' go again. She didn't feel she had the right to carp just now. "I know. I was stupid. I had it so fixed in my mind that Janet loved Olivia as much as Olivia loved her that I didn't see it coming. And I should have.

"When Janet told me she had made sure the doll trunk her father had made for her was safely out of it before the fire destroyed her parents' house in Charleston, I should have wondered how she knew there was going to be a fire. I knew her parents perished in it. I should have wondered why she didn't get *them out as well!* Then, I'd have registered that she deliberately hadn't. That she was every kind of a monster! And I most certainly wouldn't have sat there feeling sorry for her with my back to her!"

"Yeah." He bit back the great comment about hind sight that rose to his lips. Sam had had a bad time, he could be generous just this once.

Chapter Thirty

Except for Janet Wilson's tuneless humming, they were all silent as McLain drove them to Norfolk to the police station.

By the time they arrived the rain had let up, and there was only a light mist in the air. Street lamps wore hazy halos, and the streets themselves still gleamed like black mirrors in the twin beams of the Suburban's headlights. The punishing rain that had made getting to Ocean View to rescue Samantha such a harrowing trip was a thing of the past.

At the station, the men walked on either side of Janet, an arm grasped firmly by each. Samantha and Laura walked behind them, Rags in Samantha's arms.

"She looks so small," Laura whispered almost to herself.

"Yes," Samantha answered. "It's hard to believe that she's capable of the things she's done."

Lieutenant Nichols met them on the steps. "Thanks for the heads-up, McLain. I'd gone off duty at five." His gaze touched Janet speculatively then went on to assess the rest of them. "Come on in, we'll talk inside."

The Desk Sergeant saw Rags in Samantha's arms. "Sorry, ma'am. No dogs allowed except service dogs."

Samantha tucked Rags into her coat and stared back at the sergeant, her gaze level and challenging.

Lieutenant Nichols saw he wasn't going to get the woman without the dog and told the sergeant, "It's okay this time, Avery." He led the way to an interrogation room.

A patrolman followed. "Coffee? It's pretty bad, but it's hot."

They all accepted gratefully. More than the temperature, the events of the day had left a bone-deep chill in each one of them. Only Janet Wilson seemed completely unaffected, looking around the austere room with casual interest.

As the young officer left, a stenographer

entered the room and set up in a corner. Five minutes later the patrolman came in with the coffee he had offered. There was the usual business of doctoring it to individual tastes, then they settled down.

The patrolman took up a position at the side of the room.

After a long moment, the Lieutenant spoke. "Am I to understand that this young woman is the murderer you told me you were bringing in, Colonel McLain?" There was the faintest hint of disbelief in his tone as he regarded the slender girl.

"Olivia Charles's murderer, and the attempted murderer of Jasmine Johnson and Mrs. Samantha Masters," McLain stated firmly. "Furthermore, Mrs. Masters informs me that she also murdered Dr. Samuel Tiggs, the man you've been unable to identify."

Janet turned to the Lieutenant and said with malicious satisfaction, "You couldn't identify him because after I cut his nails I sanded off his fingerprints with my emery boards!"

Samantha shuddered to remember the casual way Janet had offered those very scissors and an emery board to Tyler for her broken fingernail at Wednesday Bridge. It explained why the police had used the words they had used to report it, too. In her mind's eye, she could see it. Horror shook her.

Janet complained, "He was constantly reminding me to wash my hands. He pushed and harped and couldn't get enough of telling me what to do. 'Let's cut those nails, Janet', 'Keep those nails neat and trimmed, Janet', and 'Wash your hands, Janet.'" The color was rising in her cheeks at the memories. She began to rant. "Well, I showed him, didn't I? I washed and washed his hands after I killed him." She tossed her hair and smiled archly. "Then I trimmed his nails really, really well and filed away every speck of dirt, even the shadows from his fingers." She smiled, pleased with herself.

McLain put a comforting hand on Samantha's.

Nichols watched Janet. "Have you anything more to say?"

"What is there to say?" Janet shrugged. "I did what I had to do. I was given no choice." She arched a scornful eyebrow at the detective. "Surely, even you can see that I didn't have one. My cousin Olivia not only insisted on trying to run my life, she'd lately decided to interfere in a plan that meant a great deal to me. A plan that would have made me rich." She smiled. "Four million dollars rich."

"Two," McLain corrected gruffly. "You'd have had to split with the bogus Stoddard heir."

"Not really." Her voice was as cool as the glance she gave him. "Freddie would have been as easy to dispose of as Olivia was. And murder makes it mine. All of it. Right?"

"Miss Wilson," Lieutenant Nichols cleared his throat and suggested to her, "perhaps you'd like to have your lawyer present before you say any more."

Janet turned on him, fury in her eyes. "Why! Why would I want another *meddler* in my life? Haven't I tried hard enough to get rid of them?" She stabbed a finger at him. "None of this would have happened if it weren't for all the people who keep trying to run my life."

Quietly, the Lieutenant read Janet her rights.

Janet waved a dismissive hand. Then

dropped it and gripped the arms of her chair. "I thought I was free when I got rid of my parents, but, oh no, Cousin Olivia's saintly pair had to step in and snatch away my new-won freedom."

She glared at the homicide detective through narrowed eyes. "It was all I could do to refrain from getting rid of them, too. But they were old and I decided it was wiser to wait. I was only twelve, after all, and the world would have thought I still needed the protective cover of a family. So I waited."

She shot out of her chair, suddenly agitated. "Then when they finally *did* die, and I thought I was free at last, what happens but that dear, saintly Olivia sweetly promised to take up just where they left off!"

The patrolman shoved away from the wall he'd been leaning against. Nichols gestured him back.

Janet began to pace the room.

The patrolman moved to stand in front of the glass-topped door.

Janet went on. "Boy, did she *ever* take over! Dragging me to psychiatrists. Visiting the asylum when I had to be sent back there. Yammering about how she would always be there for me. Always take care of me. Huh! She even gave her fiancé, Yancey Devlin, back his ring." She shot her gaze around at each of them. "Can you imagine anything more stupid than that?"

No, I can't imagine anything more noble, Samantha thought, fighting back tears of sympathy and admiration for her murdered friend. *But then, I'm not a psychopath.* She didn't speak. The ranting girl was hanging herself nicely, Samantha thought with malice. Olivia Charles had been noble. She, Samantha Masters didn't share that quality just now. She had no inclination to save Janet Wilson from herself.

"Cousin Olivia moved here to Virginia while I was still at the institute. She liked Norfolk and settled in as if she'd always been here. She thought all of you were soooo nice that even *I* would like being here.

"She used to write me long, long boring letters telling me everything about all of you there in Riverhaven. I had plenty of time to read them. I was stuck there at the institute for years." She plopped back down in her chair. "When she finally found out that I'd used all the things she'd told me about the Stoddards to brief Freddie, she went ballistic." She laughed. "Oh, that was so funny, seeing Saint Olivia blow her cool."

She turned to the Lieutenant and explained politely, "You see, Freddie was in the institute at the same time that I was. He had a terrible crush on me, so when I saw that he looked just like the Benny Stoddard in my cousin's photo album, I simply went back and got him to *be* Benny so he could inherit the four million for me." She smiled when she saw that the man did understand.

She received no answering smile from the homicide detective. Lieutenant Nichols understood all right. Too well.

Spreading her hands wide, Janet asked, "So you see why I had to kill her, don't you? She wanted me to unmask Freddie and even apologize to Brenda Talley for deceiving her. Can you believe how utterly stupid *that* would have been after all the trouble I'd been to?" She cocked her head inquiringly. "Embarrassing, as well, don't you imagine?"

Receiving no answer from those around

her she shrugged and stated simply, "Well, surely you can see that Olivia was getting in my way."

She spun to face Samantha. "I slipped up when I tried to kill off Jasmine Johnson. I ran her down with the car I stole, all right, but I was too slow turning the car around to come back and finish her. That interfering man had already run out to see what happened, and his wife was on their porch so I couldn't finish the job. I could hardly kill them all, could I?

"It would still have been all right since she had to spend so long in the hospital. That would have kept her from seeing Freddie was an imposter until the game was over."

She spun toward Samantha. "But no. *You* had to get stuck on the idea of dragging Freddie up to the hospital to see her, Samantha. I could see you really meant it." She threw her hands up then slapped them down to her hips. "That would have given the game away for sure, and I couldn't let you do it.

"Except for Olivia, Jasmine was the only one who would have recognized that Freddie wasn't the real Benny. So then I had to take care of you, Samantha Masters. After all, you were determined to get 'Benny'!" she made the little air quotation marks as she spoke the name and giggled, "and Jasmine together."

Samantha was too busy thanking God that the man who lived at the site of the attack on her housekeeper had come out of his house in time to keep this madwoman from driving over Jasmine again that she didn't even register that it was her own turn to be explained away.

Janet smiled sweetly at the patrolman guarding the door. "You can see why I had to take Mrs. Masters out of the picture, can't you, officer?"

From her corner, the girl at the stenographic machine looked up, horrified, to meet the young officer's incredulous gaze. She went back to her stenotyping when Janet turned from him and continued. "That was simple, of course, because all of you let me in on your plans to catch Olivia's killer." She laughed. "You were all so very, very sorry for poor little me."

She grinned cheerfully at Samantha. "I knew I had you, Samantha, when you fell for my bait. And you were all so dumb!

It scared me a little that you told Laura and Colonel McLain about my saying that Benny might not be Benny, but I had to give you that clue. After all, every one of you missed the one I gave you about Olivia and that maid maybe having some dangerous common knowledge." She shook her head. "I thought you were really dense when you didn't pick up on that. Things were getting dull, though, and I gave it to you because I needed the challenge." Looking around at them she explained, "I can't stand being bored."

She tossed her hair back and smoothed it with both hands. "I knew I was home free, though, when you wanted to go paw through Olivia's precious photo albums alone. Just the two of us. At that point, I could really begin to feel the excitement.

"I couldn't wait to show you the picture Olivia had taken of Freddie and me at the institute to see what you'd do." She cocked her head to one side and frowned a little. "Did you know, Olivia even commented on how much Freddie looked like a dear, lost friend of hers, but I didn't put two and two together until later." She frowned mightily. "I guess I was the slow one then.

"Oh, well. I needed the time to become a trusted member of the community anyway, so it didn't matter." Janet was glowing at holding center stage, basking in their undivided attention.

"After I killed Olivia, I had to figure out how to put suspicion on somebody. Brenda was perfect. She'd jumped at the chance to have 'Benny Jr.' stay at her house." She made a little moué of distaste. "She even bragged about it. Since it was obvious that nobody liked her much, I chose her.

"Then I needed to add you, Samantha, to my list. To make that work, I needed to bury Brenda deeper. So I stole her car—that was easy, I just had to watch until I saw where she put her spare keys—took her raincoat, which was one of a kind remember, and picked you up in the hospital parking lot. Anyone seeing us would have figured I was Brenda. Which, of course, was the whole idea.

"When we got to Olivia's old beach house on Willoughby Spit, I let the snoop in the first floor apartment see me in Brenda's raincoat with the hood up to hide my face. And that was all it took."

She stared at Samantha in triumph.

"All I had left to do then was knock you out, tie you up, and set the house on fire." She ticked each task off on three fingers. "Then nobody would ever figure out who Freddie really was.

"Everything would have been fine, too." Her nostrils flared and her voice took on a hysterical quality. Her hands clenched and unclenched spasmodically. She turned and glared at McLain, her control beginning to slip. "Samantha would have burned to a crisp except for your damned *meddling!*"

At that, shrieking "Meddler!", Janet Wilson lost control completely. "Meddler! Meddler!" She flung herself at McLain, her fingers extended like claws.

Rags barked a warning.

At the last second, McLain caught her wrists and fought to hold her. In her madness, she was as strong as a large man.

The patrolman sprang forward to help. Janet fought like a wild animal, teeth bared. When at last they had the panting girl subdued, Lieutenant Nichols ordered, "Book her. And you'd better get some help."

"Yessir!"

***

And it was all over. They were simply told to go home, the police would handle the rest.

It seemed so anticlimactic.

Frank was driving Brenda's Lexus, taking Laura to her house to get her own car. Sensing that none of them wanted contact just now with anyone who 'hadn't been there,' Laura had volunteered to follow Frank to Greater Tidewater Realty and bring him home after he'd dropped the Lexus off for Brenda.

That left Samantha and Rags being driven home by the Colonel in the big black Suburban. As the miles passed, silence stretched out between the Colonel and Samantha.

Even Rags was quiet. Occasionally he'd lift his head and look at the Colonel. Snuggled as he was in Samantha's arms it would have been easy for her to tell if he was growling. There was no vibration, no hint of his 'percolating.' Samantha wondered if her little darling could have had a change of heart toward their neighbor.

She seemed to have had one herself.

She wasn't finding him as insufferably annoying as usual. Maybe both changes, hers and Rags's, were based on the fact that the 'Dratted Colonel' had saved both their lives.

Looking down at him, she gave the little Yorkshire a loving squeeze. He settled more firmly against her.

At last, Samantha spoke. "Janet won't really pay for killing Olivia, will she?"

"Ah, Sam," the Colonel's voice was a soft rumble, "don't tear yourself to pieces. The girl's nuts. She'll spend the rest of her life in an asylum for the criminally insane."

"And nothing will bring Olivia back." Samantha wanted to weep. Finally she sighed. "A wonderful woman is dead, and a truly pitiful one will never really even realize what she's done."

She tried for a firmer tone, one that would seem to give them some small victory. "I suppose that justice has been done as well as it can be."

"Janet *has* been stopped."

"Yes. We did that. We all did that." Samantha sighed again.

There was another long silence in the car. Samantha put her head back against the headrest. Slowly, bit by bit the tension of the past few days drained out of her. Her muscles relaxed, and she settled more comfortably into the luxuriously padded leather seat.

Finally she turned to face McLain. She could stand the silence no longer. "So, what now?"

"Now I take you and the mutt home, and you promise to stay out of trouble," McLain told her.

Samantha tried a tentative smile. He *had* saved her life, after all. Immediately, she felt a little better. Looking over at him she said, "Only if you'll promise to do the same." Her smile became real. "What do you think the odds on that would be?"

McLain steered the big car into her driveway and stopped it. "Living here with *you* for a neighbor?" He turned and looked her straight in the eye. He was chuckling. "Zero to none, Sam. Zero to none."

If you enjoyed this book, please help us grow by spreading the word.

- Be on the look out for the next Masters & McLain book by Christina Strong!

- "Like" and "Share" our Facebook page (Steeplechase Publishing) to enter for a chance to win one of five copies of the next release (in any format we release it in: print, large print, e-book and audiobook when it comes out.)

- Spread the word to friends and family.

- Ask libraries to carry our books.

- Let us know what you think!

- Visit the Masters & McClain website at www.MastersandMcLain.com

Thank you for reading!